The Templar's Daughter

THE AGENCY OF THE ANCIENT LOST & FOUND

JANE THORNLEY

D1522198

RIVERFLOW PRESS

Disclaimer

This is a work of fiction. Names, characters, businesses, organizations, places and events other than those clearly in the public domain, are either the product of the author's imagination or are used fictiously.

Foreword

One of the key drivers in this series is to tell the stories of the women missing from history, either by design or happenstance. Little has been written about what role women may have played in and around the lives of the Templars, but they had to have existed...somewhere. Is it possible to eliminate fifty percent of the world's population so cavalierly? So, here is an imaginary herstory to explore the possibilities with plenty of true historical detail woven in along the way.

But in the end, I aim to entertain.

Chapter One

I don't usually prowl the London streets alone after 11:00 p.m. these days and yet there I was, doing it for a second time that week. I would have preferred being at home reading or, better still, snuggled up in bed, the perfect place for a chilly November evening. But not on that November evening. Instead, I was wrapped in a scarf and wearing my darkest coat, stalking a man down Fleet Street.

I have more experience being the one being stalked so playing the opposite role was proving a challenge. I could dash into doorways, keep to the shadowy edges of any sidewalk, dodge behind postboxes or trash bins as necessary, but none of it was coming easily that night. No matter what I did, I felt both exposed and out of my element.

A sharp wind was gusting down the concrete canyons of Fleet Street, the city's business district, swirling the papery leaves in tiny vortexes at my feet while enhancing the stern demeanor of the offices' inscrutable fronts. Nothing is lonelier than a busy road gone silent at day's end. All the pubs and coffee shops had closed and, other than the occasional car, I may as well have been the only living person around.

Because the man I had been following had disappeared. One minute, I had him in my sights—a portly man in a long dark coat apparently marching down the sidewalk with his hands in his pockets—and the next, he was gone. He couldn't have been more than fifty feet ahead of me.

I reached the last place where I had spotted him and looked around. At this point, Fleet Street meets the Strand, putting on a show of monumental buildings such as the old Bank of England building and other hallowed structures that had been converted into a slew of businesses designed to sustain the busy worker bee—all closed, of course.

So where could he have gone?

I studied the landscape. Across the street, a timber-framed Jacobean town house hunkered next to a little bookshop specializing in law books. A number of doors from different periods stretched down the sidewalk, with not a single pedestrian in sight.

Sudden movement sent my gaze back to an almost undetectable little stone archway next to the building where one side of a set of black doors was just easing shut. Damn. Oh, he was wily, this one. He'd probably pulled some kind of directional bait-and-switch since I hadn't noticed him crossing the street. I pulled up my coat collar, clutched the phone in my pocket, and bolted across the road.

The doors could have come straight out of Middle Earth—coal-black, hobnailed, and nearly completely round like a hobbit hole, yet I knew exactly where they led: into Temple Lane, the leafy enclave of the city's legal district. Of course, the doors would be locked at this time of night but I knew that my quarry would have no more trouble disengaging the lock than I would. I tested the latch, found it secure, and quickly unlocked the mechanism using the app on my very smart phone. I was safely through to the other side in seconds.

Now, I had plunged into a hidden world of Gothic and Victorian buildings where stately trees stood watch over tiny courtyards, and miniature gardens and wrought-iron fencing lined the winding paths. Lit as it was by old-fashioned replica carriage lamps and lampposts, I may as well have been dropped into another age. I could feel time tugging at my senses and I ruthlessly shoved it back.

Where did he go? He must have known that he was being followed. Though not particularly quick-footed, he had tricks for shielding his every move. Like me, he probably anticipated stalkers as a matter of course and had developed a multitude of dodging skills, the least of which was to wear foam-soled shoes to avoid echoing footsteps. But he wasn't getting away from me this time.

He had to be somewhere up front. Keeping my head down and my senses alert, I slipped down Temple Lane, one of the many little pathways weaving through the back streets of London that linked the modern with the ancient by corridors of stone and brick. A few windows were illuminated above—probably some barrister burning the midnight oil. Surely my quarry didn't have a mysterious assignation with a lawyer?

I had just reached the shadows under a huge tree when I realized that he had disappeared again. I stared. The lane ahead was empty—nothing but the intersection of two buildings with no place to hide en route and no time to get that far in front, anyway. To my right, the tall side of a brick building loomed into darkness and to my left, on the other side of a low wrought-iron fence, sat the round building I knew as the Temple Church.

The Temple Church—of course! That had to be his destination. Consecrated in 1185, the ancient site that had once been the British seat of the Knights Templar was tucked away in the midst of Britain's legal establishment, where most of its London property had ended up after the Order's dissolution. A faint glow illuminated the stained-glass windows. He was there, I was sure of it, but why?

My phone began vibrating in my hand. I pulled it out. The perimeter alert was flashing. Somebody was stalking me? Oh, come on! Can't a woman take a late-night stroll without becoming the target of some random annoyance? I could chase him down and zap him, of course—that might be fun and good practice, too, since I was a little rusty—but I had better things to do just then. I'd ignore the bastard unless he made a move.

Turning back to the church, I studied the entrance behind its wrought-iron gate. I knew from previous visits that this wasn't a big church, that the circular "tower" that formed the nave was based on the Temple Mount in Jerusalem and that a rectangular chancel attached to it had been built approximately a century later. There had once been a large monastic complex in the surrounding area, too, including residences and military training areas, but that property had all since been consumed by the courts.

The church had been badly damaged in World War II so this building had been extensively rebuilt. That didn't mean that it couldn't trigger some kind of timewalking reaction in me, but I had become much better at controlling those episodes. Now, I could stand among ancient stones rich in history and human endeavor, safe behind a mental wall that kept me grounded in the present century.

The bigger issue was to get inside undetected. There would be security cameras at key points and, if my quarry knew that somebody was tracking him, which I suspected he did by now, he might take precautions. Obviously, I couldn't simply follow him through the gate and through the door.

Or could I? Maybe it was time for a confrontation. The gate opened easily in my hand. If he hadn't locked it behind him, it probably meant that I was expected. I'd simply abort the cloak-and-dagger stuff and confront him head-on. Whether that approach was ballsy or simply foolish, it didn't matter since I didn't fear bodily harm from this man.

After checking my perimeter alert screen one last time and determining that my stalker was lurking back down the lane somewhere, I turned and strolled through the gates, letting them clang shut behind me. May as well announce my arrival.

But once I had slipped under the arched vestibule and through the impressive church doors—also unlocked—nobody waited. I stood gazing around the circular nave, noting how the lights glowed in sconces at the tops of the Purbeck marble pillars, uplighting the graceful Gothic arches into the dome.

Resting for all eternity on the floor before me lay the church's key attractions—effigies over the tombs of what were believed to be some of the original Templar knights, including the most famous British knight of all time, William Marshal. Not a single living person was in sight. The chancel and main church remained in shadows.

So much of the building had been rebuilt after the war that it looked and felt almost new and yet not, in that strange way of old reconstructed buildings. Nothing moved or breathed that my senses could detect and yet I knew I was not alone. Maybe I had heard the faintest sound of whispering somewhere but it was difficult to tell.

Overhead, a row of pillars rimmed the upper dome circumference with periodic arched openings leading into what I knew to be a triforium gallery. The whole domed area was fully lit. Maybe he was up there? I'd check in a moment but first it made sense to briefly survey the lower level, since the main body of the church had pews with plenty of seating and the gallery did not. Besides, the main church lights weren't on. If you want privacy, hang out in the shadows.

I was halfway down the chancel heading toward the altar with my phone held in front of me when I heard a door click open somewhere at the same time that my perimeter alarm beeped. Swinging around, I caught the flash of something dark streaking across the nave. In an instant, I was bolting in pursuit, my blood thundering in my ears.

The figure darted through a little doorway behind which a steep circular staircase twisted up into the shadows. Damn, I hated those things. This one was so narrow I could grab both the rope guide and the iron railing opposite to help heave myself along, but whoever was ahead of me still had too great a lead. By the time I burst panting through the door at the top, the circular corridor in front of me was empty. And then a gunshot ripped the air.

It took only seconds and maybe half the distance around the gallery before I saw two men sprawled facedown on the tiles, one lying still with his arms thrown over his head. A figure in black leaned over the second man, trying to turn him onto his back, but he held his arms beneath his body as if protecting something. Blood was oozing from his shoulder. The assailant viciously kicked the wounded man before casting a quick glance in my direction and aiming a gun straight for the man's head.

I skidded to a stop.

"You move, I'll shoot again, and this time I'll shoot to kill," the assailant said.

"Don't be stupid. If you shoot, I'll taser you so hard you'll be toast. Drop the gun and back away before this gets uglier." I glanced at the other man, stifling my panic. He didn't look hurt but he was lying far too still. "What did you do to him? I heard only one shot."

I sensed the perp smiling behind the black stocking mask. "He clutched his chest and fell to his knees. Probably a heart attack, but no matter as this is the one I want."

Relieved, my gaze returned to the wounded man—lean, gray-haired, strands of his scant comb-over racing away from a high bony forehead. He turned his head toward me, pale blue eyes pleading for something I couldn't decipher.

"If he gives me what I want," said the assailant, "I'll let him go and you all go unharmed."

"Wow, so generous," I remarked.

The man was trying to say something. "No!" he gasped.

The assailant went to kick him again. I pressed the stun app on my phone, jolting the gun from her hand, at which point the second man swiped it up from the floor, and scrambled to his feet. He had been playing possum—his specialty.

The assailant leaped over the fallen man and raced past me down the corridor, shoving me aside in passing. She was out of sight around the corner in seconds.

I swore and took after the fleeing figure, knowing as I did that circular corridors and circuitous stairways make catching a quarry challenging once they had a head start.

"Phoebe, stop!" Sir Rupert Fox called. "Let her go."

Chapter Two

"Why?" I demanded, striding back. I was furious at him, even more so now that I knew beyond a doubt that he had gotten himself into something deadly, which I had suspected all along.

"Because we must get Mr. Hogarth home at once and you'll never catch up to her, in any event. If she has any sense at all, she'll disappear. At least she did not get what she sought," said Rupert.

"Which was?" I demanded.

But he had pulled out his own phone, proceeding to speed-dial someone. Immediately, he was speaking in a low voice into his phone.

Mr. Hogarth, on the other hand, was struggling to his feet, looking amazingly unperturbed considering the dark stain seeping into his tan cashmere coat, and the fact that his complexion had taken on a ghostly pall. His attention remained fixed on the green-plastic-wrapped item that he clutched with his good arm. I swear I had seen him muttering to it seconds before.

I steadied him by the elbow, catching Rupert's eye as he pocketed his phone and returned to stand before us.

"Mr. Hogarth needs to go to the hospital," I said, "and we need to call the police, whom I hope you just phoned." I studied the surrounding corridor. "There must be cameras everywhere, so possibly they can find some identifying features of the assailant. On the other hand," said I, fixing on Rupert, "that

6

might bring up a whole pile of difficult questions, wouldn't it, like the bullet that must be embedded somewhere around here?"

"I disengaged all interior systems, including surveillance on Temple Lane and environs," Rupert said, holding up his phone. "There will be no police interference for obvious reasons."

Obvious reasons being that he had no right to be here in the first place.

"Police are absolutely out of the question," Hogarth managed to say, his pale gaze turning to me at last. "I...appreciate your assistance, ah, miss, but I really...must insist—no police. Please go away and say nothing...of what you have seen."

"Not happening," I replied.

"Hogarth, allow me to introduce my obstinate daughter-in-law, Phoebe Barrows," Rupert said, pocketing the gun. "Phoebe, meet Clive Hogarth, an old friend of mine. We went to Eton together."

"How nice for you both," I remarked, "and I'm Phoebe *McCabe*, as I have retained my maiden name. Nice to meet you, Mr. Hogarth, even if it is under extreme circumstances. You need urgent medical care, by the way. You've been shot and I—"

But before I could say anything further, Hogarth began sinking to his knees.

Rupert rushed to help me ease the man into a sitting position against the wall. "Steady there, my good fellow. We shall take you to my house and call for the assistance of a discreet medical professional to attend to your injury. I believe that you have suffered a mere surface wound."

Clive leaned his head against the wall and closed his eyes. "I'm not as young as I once was."

"True for us all, my good fellow," Rupert remarked.

I glared at my father-in-law over Mr. Hogarth's head. "How do you expect to get him anywhere? He can hardly walk," I whispered.

"I have called Sloane to pick us up on Fleet Street and requested that a couple of dependable lads help us get Mr. Hogarth to the car. Do not be such an alarmist, Phoebe. I have it all under control."

I resisted the urge to roll my eyes or to make a snarky remark—so tempting. I should be used to this by now, and needed to go along with Rupert's directions, at least until I could get him alone and demand an explanation. However, I couldn't resist asking a few questions in the meantime.

"Why the Temple Church? And who let you in?" I asked.

"The circumstances of the task Mr. Hogarth had requested of me necessitated a rendezvous on this particular site, Phoebe, the reasons for which I will provide at a more opportune time. As for who let me in, may I say that I find that a somewhat ludicrous question, considering."

Okay, so he was as annoyed with me as I was with him, but I was the one who had the right to the attitude, in my opinion. "So, using your agency smartphone, you broke into a church—which happens to be a Grade I listed site, as well as a national historical treasure—disengaged the security system, encountered a possible thief and would-be murderer, and now accuse me of asking a ludicrous question?"

"Yes, well, would you mind terribly forgoing the interrogation until after we are safely back at home. And may I ask of you a small favor, while I am at it? Please go back to the entry to Fleet Street and let in the two lads who will be assisting us. I must remain with Mr. Hogarth, as I am certain you understand. Thank you very much and do be careful, Phoebe—the assailant may still be lurking about. Do keep your phone on stun and your eyes peeled."

Insult added to injury: on top of everything, I was to be provided with a to-do list accompanied by handy-dandy safety tips? I left without a word, ensuring that this time the doors to the Temple Church were secured behind me before marching down the lane, fuming. No perimeter alerts flashed this time and I sensed that the assailant—that vicious mysterious woman in black—was not hanging around. No doubt she'd made the reasonable assumption that the police would be called, given that she had shot somebody.

By the time I eased open the hobbit doors, two young men were leaning against the wall, one dressed like a trendy young leather-clad dude who had just exited some chic uptown nightclub, and the other wearing a spiffy suit, as if he had just escaped from a Fleet Street office. They both wafted men's cologne and wore their hair short with plenty of product, slicked in to form a spiky feature over the forehead.

Dex and Jason knew one another, as it turned out, and had often done jobs for Rupert. They were on "The List," the compilation of agency resources on which members could call on, if needed—all properly vetted by Rupert himself, of course. Was I surprised? They seemed nice enough, didn't bat an eye at my very smart phone, and knew enough to keep their eyes open for sudden movements or odd sounds. They acted as if they were there to watch my back, which I appreciated, but I was uncomfortable by how much they seemed to know about agency technology.

"You know about our smartphones?" I whispered.

"Everybody knows about the smartphones," Jason told me, "at least, all of us on Sir Rupert's call list. We know that you can disengage the CCTV cameras around here, too."

Because they knew that the security systems had been deactivated, they felt free to talk. Thus, I discovered that Jason worked for the London Underground, happened to be on strike that day, and had been at a club when Rupert called, while Dexter worked part-time as a barista and had a room nearby. Curiouser and curiouser. They also knew my husband, Evan, and had apparently done odd jobs for him, too.

By the time we reached the Temple Church, we were on friendly terms. Rupert ensured that everything was returned to its original state and locked up the church behind us, while Jason and Dexter helped Mr. Hogarth down the lane to Fleet Street, making out that the older man had had too much to drink. Rupert's butler, Sloane, was waiting in the Rolls as we climbed in—Hogarth in the back seat between Dexter and Jason, Rupert and I up front with Sloane.

"Any signs of trouble, Sloane?" Rupert inquired while tapping something into his phone. As best as I could tell, he was remotely reengaging the security systems.

"No, sir. Some kind of disturbance in Hyde Park has diverted most of the police activity. Would you like me to tap into the Metropolitan Police communication channel and check, just in case?"

"No need, my good man. I have every reason to believe that all is clear."

I sat back in my seat, gazing straight ahead. What was Foxy up to now, and why in hell was he using technology that had been assigned solely to agency business? There's no way Rupert was authorized to use those tools for his own purposes. I was so angry and alarmed just then that I was ready to scream.

I had promised Evan that I'd keep an eye out for his father but neither of us expected it to be such an endeavor. We'd been married for less than two months, with a honeymoon providing a blissful five-week respite, only to return home to live with his dad. While the agency headquarters were being rebuilt following the bombing months ago—with the lovely pied-à-terre we designed as part of that reconstruction—it made sense to take up temporary residence with Rupert. Cramming theory into reality wasn't an easy fit.

I'd only been with Evan for two days under Rupert's roof. No sooner had we returned from our honeymoon than he'd been unexpectedly called away on Interpol business—very hush-hush—thinking that he'd be able to get home in a few days. A few days had grown into weeks and here I was living in captivity with an irascible, secretive man who I adored but couldn't live with.

Nobody in the car said another word. The guys tended Hogarth in the back seat, passing him bottled water from Sloane's built-in mini-refrigerator while Rupert fixed his gaze on his phone. The moment that we drove through the gate of Rupert's Belgravia mansion and into the garage, everybody sprang into action: Sloane and Rupert ushered Hogarth and the lads into the house and up the stairs to a second-floor guest room, me tagging along behind like a lost puppy.

I waited in the second-floor hall lounge beside Cicero, one of Rupert's mounted Roman acquisitions. Rupert's abode had ten bedrooms across three floors and, yes, each floor had a landing lounge complete with a small library and at least one Roman bust. I had to wait apart because, of course, a woman couldn't possibly be admitted into the room where a man's bony chest might be exposed.

The doctor arrived fifteen minutes later, a small balding man with a ready smile. He nodded to me briefly before Sloane showed him into the bedroom down the hall, at which point the two guys exited to stand watch outside the door. I left my perch to join them.

"So, is Mr. Hogarth doing all right?" I asked, sidling up to them.

"Wound wasn't deep," Dex told me. "We cut off his shirt to prepare for the doc. There was plenty of blood but looks like the bullet passed right through the upper arm—not life-threatening."

"In which case there may be a bullet lodged somewhere in the Temple Church gallery," I pointed out.

"Yes," Jason said, running one hand through his near-nonexistent hair. "Sir Rupert considered that and will send someone around to do a clean."

"Do a clean" was a term for eradicating signs of a crime using a professional and ultra-discreet scrubbing service. Managing that in a historic property was no small feat and very expensive. "When you were in the room with Hogarth, did you happen to see the package he was clutching?" I asked.

"We certainly did—wrapped in a trash bag like it was something ready for a jumble sale. Very heavy. Hogarth kept a grip on it until we forced him to set it aside—couldn't get his coat off with that in his hand, could we? Sir Rupert will put it in a safe place, he assured him. Says he won't let it out of his sight," Jason told me.

I just bet. Whatever was going on here, that package was behind it. I needed to find out what that item was, and where Rupert fit into this mess.

It was nearly 1:00 a.m. before Rupert and the doctor emerged from the bedroom, the latter almost immediately taking off down the back stairs, accompanied by Sloane.

"The gentleman is sleeping and we expect him to make a full recovery after several days' rest," Rupert announced, the package held in the crook of his arm. "Thank you all for your help, gentlemen."

"Would you like for Jason and me to stick around and help with anything else?" Dex asked. "Be happy to help any way we can."

"An excellent idea but just one would do. Dex, would you do the honors? Take the bedroom next to Hogarth, if you don't mind, and, Jason, shall I have Sloane call a cab to take you home?" he asked.

"That's not necessary but thanks just the same." Jason held up his phone. "I'll call an Uber."

Rupert nodded and I watched while he passed them several large denominations of pound notes before Jason descended the stairs to the main hall. I estimated that each man received at least 1000 pounds that night. No wonder they were more than happy to do other odd jobs. Minutes later, Dex took off to his guest room, Jason waved goodbye while leaving the house through a side door, and Rupert and I were alone at last.

"Rupert, let's talk," I said.

"Phoebe, let us not. It is a great deal past my bedtime and I am quite exhausted, as I am certain are you. We can reconvene over breakfast tomorrow."

He was heading back upstairs to his rooms, which lay on the far end of the second floor. He had graciously assigned most of the third floor to Evan and me in the hopes that we would extend our stay.

"What's the package, Rupert?" I asked, following him up.

"Nothing which I am at liberty to disclose," he replied.

"Why?"

"Because, dear Phoebe, this is Hogarth's business and I have been sworn to secrecy, which I shall uphold on a manner of principle. Had you not followed me tonight, you would have been none the wiser."

"And had I not followed you tonight, one of you might have been shot a second time and had your booty stolen."

"What nonsense. Had I not known that you were stalking me, I would not have left the church door unlocked, thus permitting the assailant to enter. As it was, I figured you may as well discover what you came for, seeing as you have been tailing me for days. Why the devil didn't you lock that door behind you?"

He had reached the door to his quarters, which consisted of a suite much like Evan's and mine, and turned to fix me with an accusatory gaze. It was an expression that he had mastered over the years, especially when enacting the "best defense is a good offense" strategy.

"That's not going to work on me, Rupert, so don't even try." And yet I felt compelled to explain myself. "I didn't lock the door behind me because I figured that you had left it unlocked for a reason. And I followed you because I promised Evan that I'd keep an eye on you, something that I shall uphold on a matter of principle. I will also find out what you're up to so you may as well tell me everything."

"Evan asked you to keep an eye on me? How preposterous! That boy knows better than to keep tabs on me."

"You turned off your tracking device, which is bound to give him the heads-up, as it did me, considering that you usually leave it on permanently, and there is no way that you should be using agency technology when not on agency business!"

"Speaking of Evan, I presume that you will not bother him with this minor incident, considering that he is on a significant case and should not be distracted with such palaver. Good night to you, Phoebe."

The door closed in my face, causing me to swear silently all the way down the hall and up the stairs to my rooms.

Chapter Three

The fact that I had been unable to reach Evan for days didn't help. When on special assignment, he was often offline or constrained in some way that kept him from making contact. We'd been attempting to sort through the boxes of stuff salvaged after the agency headquarters, my flat, and the carpet gallery had been bombed, when he had to leave. Just like that, I found myself standing alone in a suite of rooms trying to start my new life with only scraps of my old life for company.

Standing in the hallway of what had become my suite, I checked my phone for messages—again. Admittedly, I did so compulsively lately, but once again, no messages.

Of course I missed Evan, but I wasn't feeling sorry for myself so much as disorientated and furious at Rupert. Only Evan could curb his father's actions and force him to stop using agency technology for his own ends, something that we all strived so hard to protect. On the other hand, informing him of what was going on back home would only take his mind off his case.

Meanwhile, I mourned my cozy flat with all the things I'd collected over the years, the loss of which I really hadn't processed properly with the wedding (very small in Italy), followed by the honeymoon (very luxurious in the South Pacific), taking place just months after Evan had proposed in Zimbabwe. We pressed fast-forward on our marriage plans as a distraction and, trust me, Evan can be very distracting. Yet, at some point, one has to drop back to reality. Mine hadn't been a soft landing. Living with my father-in-law had been challenging enough.

Despite the lack of contact, I tried to send my husband little messages every day—just snippets in case he had time to read anything. That same night before going to bed and using the agency's secure line, I emailed him saying that I was keeping an eye on his dad, as planned. I didn't mention anything about following him to the Temple Church or that he was definitely up to his neck in something. Why worry the man until I had more details? After hitting Send, the lack of response was deafening. That part was killing me.

The next morning, I dragged myself out of bed early, determined to confront Rupert over breakfast. Usually I avoided these habitual 8:00-a.m.- on-the-dot endeavors. I preferred to down a cup of coffee and nibble on toast while slowly rousing myself into a fully functioning human state. Rupert, on the other hand, insisted on a full egg and kipper extravaganza. He encouraged me to join him at first but I begged off, assuring him that I'd dine with him every night instead.

Tossing on a sweater and a pair of jeans, I was down the stairs and in the breakfast room overlooking the garden promptly at 7:50, expecting to see Rupert behind his morning paper enjoying a pot of tea, his plate graced by his favorite foods.

I stared at his empty place at the head of the table and then at the cold chafing dishes lining the buffet against one wall—empty, all signs of breakfast cleared. He'd been and gone?

I headed into the kitchen looking for Sloane. No Sloane in sight, either. Mrs. Kravets, the cook, smiled when I asked where everyone was but clearly had no answer, at least not in English. Seconds later, I had tracked down the latest housekeeper, Irina Polishchuk, who was arranging a flower display in the main hall. Both women hailed from Ukraine but Irina could speak multiple languages and informed me with her unflappable efficient friendliness that Sloane, Dex, and Sir Rupert had left very early and would not return until later. Dinner was 7:00 p.m. sharp, she reminded me. I smiled and thanked her before bolting up the stairs to the second floor.

If I expected to easily nab an unrestricted moment to speak with the recu-perating Mr. Hogarth, I was wrong there, too. Really, I should have known better: a guard now stood at the door—an Indian Sikh, no less, a departure for Rupert, who usually went for the English bulldog type. The man shook his head resolutely when I requested to see the patient. Not allowed, he told me. He was under strict instructions that no one was to enter the room without Sir Rupert's permission, no exceptions. I could tell that there'd be no talking him out of that position.

Which meant that I had to take another approach. Returning to my rooms,

I opened up my very smart phone and studied the apps. Before leaving on holiday, Evan had performed another upgrade on all our devices, and I knew that he had particularly focused on the stun feature, which we referred to as the "Sleeping Beauty" app. All the other tweaks could wait for me to learn them. I was definitely a proponent of learning on the need-to-know concept, rather than cluttering my brain with vast amounts of extraneous information in advance.

Sleeping Beauty was my favorite app as it allowed me to incapacitate people without harming them. At my insistence, Evan had broadened the sliding bar to include a setting so mild that the stunned individual briefly blanked out, rousing momentarily later confused but convinced that they had been awake the whole time. Evan, who had experimented with the app on himself, remained convinced that it caused no damage on its mildest setting.

With the Sleeping Beauty app set on mild, I returned to the guard and relaunched my case for speaking to the patient. This one was younger than the others among Rupert's hired guns that I'd seen so far, and I sensed that he was generally a friendly guy. Trying to be straight-faced and stern didn't come naturally to him, but his training forced him into stiff-eyed-straight-ahead mode. His name, he told me, was Devaj.

"Devaj, I am, as I said, Rupert's daughter-in-law and I was there when Mr. Hogarth arrived last night. All I need is a few minutes to check on his status and then I'll let him rest."

"No, Mrs. Barrows, this is not possible. I am most sorry. Sir Rupert said no visitors, no exceptions."

He knew what I was up to, of course. I touched his arm, my phone hidden in my hand. "Oh, all right, Devaj, but I'll be back."

In an instant, Devaj's head fell back against the wall. I lowered him carefully into the nearby chair, jimmied the locked door with my de-locking app, and slipped inside the bedroom. I only had moments before Devaj would awake.

The room was dark, the curtains pulled across the windows. I slipped up to the bed and switched on the light. Clive Hogarth was lying on his back, his hands folded on his chest on top of the covers, and appeared to be sleeping peacefully. Three pill bottles sat on the bedside table along with a water glass and a still-warm cup of tea. On the other side table, a breakfast tray sat with half-eaten toast sitting beside an eggcup.

"Mr. Hogarth?" I lightly touched the man's one good arm.

The pale blue eyes fluttered open. "You," he whispered.

I was about to reintroduce myself but stopped. He thought he recognized me? "What do I need to know?" I whispered.

"You must not interfere!" he whispered, trying to sit. "Your role has been completed and I thank you—the Order thanks you—but I, as master of the Temple Church, will carry forth the task so ordained!"

"What do I do next?" I asked, playing on instinct.

"Hide!" He peered at me intensely for a second before falling back on the pillow. "Go!"

Damn! I only had a few seconds left at most. "Hide where, go where?"

"Stay away!" he gasped. "I forgive you." He closed his eyes, as if falling back into some half-conscious state. I touched him lightly but he did not rouse a second time.

Gathering up the breakfast tray, I made to leave. Just as I reached the door, Devaj opened it and stared at me blankly.

"Just collecting the breakfast things. Bye." I bolted upstairs, sliding the tray beside Socrates on the nearby table and scampering to my rooms.

He told her to hide? He would carry on from there? And why had he referred to himself as a master of the Temple Church?

Then my phone pinged in my pocket. Pulling it out, I read the text.

Peaches: *Got in last night. Slept all the way from Harare. Are u still on board to meet me for lunch today or is Ev keeping you too blissed-out? Bring him, too.*

I responded immediately. *I'll be there. Can't wait! Evan is off on a case. See you at Côte at 12:30.*

Pocketing the phone, I practically ran for the shower, suddenly feeling so much lighter. My bestie was back! All was right with the world, or at least had the potential for getting so much better. After dressing, fluffing my hair and generally making myself presentable, I actually planned to tackle some of the boxes I'd been avoiding. I couldn't keep tripping over them indefinitely.

There wasn't much left after the explosion—a few items had managed to escape Semenov's blast, including a handful of trinkets from my past that Max had boxed up while Evan and I were honeymooning. The carpets and ethnographic artifacts Max had accumulated during his years presiding over the Baker and Mermaid gallery on the main level had been lost forever, a source of pain for us both. I couldn't even bear to look at the scorched and blackened remains of those beautiful old textiles, though Max had taken some pieces home in a box as if they were the ashes of a loved one. Even that was heartbreaking.

What I wanted to find above all else was the tapestry my mother and brother had made long ago, Tide Weaver, which had hung over my mantel in pride of place. As long as there was a faint hope that it had miraculously survived, I'd keep looking. Losing that was like losing my family all over again.

Even my brother, Toby, had shed a tear when I told him over the phone what had happened.

Looking for lost items was one thing but at least the people I cared about were safe. Following the explosion, Max had decided to take the insurance money—once the claim cleared the courts, that is—and retire, which had not been something he had ever seriously contemplated before. After our wedding in Italy, he and Serena, the gallery manager, had taken off for weeks of travel in order to test the retirement lifestyle. At least that kept him occupied while the insurance claim navigated the courts. Meanwhile, I focused on my own adjustment.

The agency lab, at least, could be rebuilt. Being underground and secured, that facility suffered the least damage. Now, all that was needed was for the construction to be completed on the top-level pied-à-terre that Evan and I had designed to be our London home. Then, presumably, our new life would begin and the Agency of the Ancient Lost and Found, London division, would get back on track.

But first, there was now and I was temporarily way off-track—no work and no husband (in the immediate sense) as well as no home. Perhaps "stuck" was a better term.

Back to the unpacking. I opened one of the cartons and pulled out what looked to be a smoke-smeared photo of my parents, Toby, and I, taken in front of our old cottage in Nova Scotia. Wiping it off, I placed it on one of Rupert's bookshelves, closed the box back up, and called it a day. I'd just stroll past the construction site to see how things were getting along before meeting Peaches. The unpacking and sorting could wait. I sent messages to a few contacts, downloaded some research material, and left the house.

November is one of my favorite times of year in London. The oppressive heat and the tourist crowds had dissipated and there's something fresh and new in the air, even if, in reality, it's only pending winter. The holidays were just around the corner and everybody couldn't seem to wait to get into the spirit. The more political tensions increased and world news worsened, the more festive the city seemed to become.

That day, the sun shone, glinting off the roofs of the cabs and red buses and putting a lift in the steps of passing pedestrians. Maybe I was just imagining it, but everything seemed ready to move on.

By the time I'd caught the tube and exited at the Sloane Square station, apparently moving on applied to the sun, too. Turning up my coat collar, I lowered my head and dashed through the rain, glimpsing the holiday decorations twinkling in every shop window, most of which I had never entered. This was the land of designer stores and high-end names like Tiffany's, which exceeded both my budget and, mostly, my inclination. On the other hand, I left no art gallery unvisited, often on a weekly basis.

When I finally darted down the lane to the street off of King's Road where our gallery once stood, I tried to prepare myself. Every time I saw the ruins, it hit me like a blow. Gone was our glorious storefront with the Baker and Mermaid sign and the luminous carpets spotlit in the window, along with my cozy little flat on the top floor. I longed for both in different ways. Though I knew that looking behind created a logjam for moving ahead, I couldn't help myself.

I gazed through the drizzle at what used to be my home, relieved to see that at least steel girders had been erected, which presumably meant that work was progressing on our future abode and workplace. Soon, there'd be walls, windows, and, perhaps shortly afterward, maybe even a roof. I could actually hear the sounds of pounding behind the barricade. So, why wasn't I delighted or encouraged or something? Why did I still feel as though a piece of me had been wrenched from my chest with a pair of pliers? Damn, I had to stop this moping.

Turning on my heel, I marched back the way I had come. I'd just go to La Côte early and have myself a pot of tea while waiting for Peaches. Maybe being surrounded by socializing people would help my mood. Minutes later, I was dodging buses as I scampered across Sloane Square toward the café, surprised as always to see the outside seating area under the awning crowded, even in the rain. The smokers and those accompanied by their dogs claimed those prized seats no matter what the weather—got to love the English.

I aimed for a favorite inside back booth and ordered a pot of tea. While I was pouring my first cup, I caught a glimpse of Peaches striding into the restaurant and was temporarily transfixed. She had changed: leaner, in jeans and a winter jacket, hair shorn short, which suited her, a glow about her that wasn't just from the chill. She seemed vividly alive yet simultaneously exhausted. In seconds, she was embracing the stuffing out of me until we fell back laughing into our seats.

"I missed you, Phoeb!"

"Same here," I said. "You're positively blooming! I love that short hair. Is Africa giving you that glow or is a certain African responsible?"

"Kaggy is the man, *the one*," she said with a dreamy smile totally uncharacteristic for her, "and yes, the months I spent exploring the continent with him was the stuff of dreams: wild vistas, equally wild nights, explorations and discoveries—did I mention the wild nights? I loved every moment I spent with him—well, almost every moment—and he's absolutely what I want in a man—well, almost everything." She fell silent and lowered her gaze to the tablecloth before suddenly lifting her eyes to mine and adding: "Forget about me. What about you and Ev?"

"Whoa," I said, holding up my hand. "Kagiso's the one, you say, and yet I hear an unspoken 'but.' But what?"

Peaches sighed and picked up the menu, making a show of reading every line while clearly not seeing a thing. For the first time, I noticed that she wore an intricately beaded, multicolored bracelet on her right wrist, probably Zulu. "Have you had the French onion soup? I'm such in the mood for soup. For weeks, all I've eaten is yams and goat curry—really big in the bush and almost everybody's homes, I can tell you, and there's no form of corn that I haven't eaten. Don't speak to me about corn—maize, as they call it."

"Peach, there is no French onion soup on the menu and no corn anything, either. Speak."

She lowered the menu. "Yeah, okay, so here's the issue: Kagiso wants to live in Africa, and I don't."

"All right, simple enough," I said slowly, assuming the voice of reason. "So, one of you has to move."

"Ah, but that's the thing," she said, meeting my eyes. "I don't want that someone to be me and he doesn't want that someone to be him."

"Okay, but is that a deal-breaker?" I said, studying her. She looked more than a little sad, despite the outward changes. "Are you going to let geography break up a relationship and threaten your chance for happiness?"

"Maybe, if it means that our being together makes one of us unhappy. Kagiso is committed to Africa, as in slit-his-wrists-and-bleed-into-the-soil kind of committed, while I realize that I'm more of an urban, high adrenaline type. I like my creature comforts in between my thrills, you know? And while living simply or camping out under the stars is definitely thrilling, as a sustained life-style it's not for me. Besides, I miss the agency, my work. Anyway, enough about that. We'll either figure it out or we won't, right? I suggested we take some time apart and, really, I wanted to get back to London, so here I am." She shrugged.

The waiter appeared and we ordered. After he left, I leaned across the table and grabbed her hand. "And you have no idea how delighted I am to have you back but I want you to be happy. Give this relationship snag some serious thought."

"I will. So, tell me what's up with you and Ev? You say he's on a case?"

"You being off-grid most of the time has made it hard to keep you up-to-date but, yes, a very mysterious case came up at the last minute and, no, I have no idea what it is, in case you planned on asking."

She grinned. "Back up, then: the last I heard, you were on your honeymoon. Begin there," she said. "Was it fantastically wonderful?"

"It was, absolutely, but when we returned to London, there was still no reconstructed agency headquarters and no home to go to, which, as you know, Evan and I designed to be one and the same—"

"Perfect work/life balance."

I smiled and brushed away the comment. "I was living above the office before, remember? Anyway, construction has been delayed—like everything else, it seems—so once we arrived in London and found ourselves still homeless, the most expedient thing was to move in with Rupert. He had been campaigning for that arrangement from the beginning."

"I just bet," Peaches said dryly.

"It might have been bearable, at least for the short term, had Evan been able to stay around but with him leaving suddenly—"

"That left you rattling around under your father-in-law's enormous roof with the staff and the *butler*—I mean, who even does butlers these days? —and your father-in-law. Did I mention the father-in-law part?"

"We have been on excellent terms until recently, and I can't forget the days when we were actually friends. He treated me like family and fawned all over me right up until suddenly he didn't. The last thing Evan said to me before he left —besides things too intimate to mention—was to keep an eye on his father. He had reason to believe that Rupert was getting involved in something and he was right."

I filled her in on recent events, watching expressions of amazement, annoyance, and irritation cross her face. "It sounds like the moment that Ev vacated, Rupe turned up the trouble dial," she said.

"My thoughts exactly. In fact, Evan's exit probably gave him the opportunity he wanted. There's no way that Rupe should illicitly use agency technology when not on a case and he knows it."

"Then why did he?"

"Boredom. Evan knew that he was growing bored since his retirement from Interpol. With the Agency of the Ancient Lost and Found temporarily on ice, he thought that Rupert might be looking for a little excitement. I kept checking the agency app to keep track of his movements but then Rupert went dark."

"I thought we had agreed not to use the tracker app when not on a job, anyway?"

"Rupert never paid attention to that guideline. He'd always leave his on until recently. I check the location app as a matter of habit now, hoping that Evan's dot might appear—which it doesn't when he's on an Interpol case, of course. Anyway, Evan was concerned that his dad seemed distracted, and even the night after we had arrived home, Rupert claimed he had an 'engagement' and took off."

"You mean, he didn't stay home to continue welcoming his son and new daughter-in-law?"

"Nope, and right after that, Evan hopped on a plane. From that point, Rupert began disappearing at dinner time almost every night while claiming to be dining out, at which point I knew he was up to something. So, I followed him. The first time, he had Sloane drop him off near a restaurant across from Hyde Park, went in, and must have exited through the rear door because I lost him. The second time was last night when I tracked the wily fox right to the Temple Church."

"But, seriously, the Temple Church?" she exclaimed, her usual enthusiasm returning.

"Keep your voice down, woman. You're back in the wilds of London, remember? There are snakes and beasts here, too," I admonished.

"Right you are," she whispered, making a show of looking around. "Big sneaky ones—my kind of wild—and you're living under the roof of the worst. I missed them, all of them, by the way. Wild animals are boring, by comparison," she added. "So, what do you think is in that package this Clive character was willing to risk his neck for and this woman in black tried to snatch?"

"That's what I need to find out," I said, leaning over my plate of eggs and smoked salmon.

"*We* need to find out."

I grinned. God, I was glad that she was home. "I managed to sneak into Hogarth's room this morning. He's disorientated, maybe even feverish, and definitely confused. The doctor has given him at least three sets of pills but I only recognized one—a sedative. Anyway, he thought he knew me and said that my task was done and to hide. Peaches, it seemed as though he thought that I was that mysterious woman who shot him last night, and that he was still a master of the Temple Church."

"Seriously, you think he knew his assailant?"

"He said that he forgave me—her. I think that's who he meant. Anyway, we have research to do. I've already put feelers out among my contacts to glean information. Luckily, though the agency might be temporarily on hiatus, personal networks still function. As for Clive Hogarth's treasure, Rupert has a safe in his rooms that I'm sure is as impenetrable as possible—probably designed by Evan, come to think of it. That's where he's probably secured this mysterious object."

"Are you thinking of breaking in?"

"Absolutely not. The familial relationship has taken enough of a hit since he caught me stalking him last night and might soon discover that I've spoken to his guest. Imagine how it would go if I were to break into his vault, too?"

Peaches propped her chin in her hand and leaned over the table. "So, it's an actual vault, is it? I could crack that with my phone—Ev's given me lessons—and you wouldn't be involved. I wouldn't even tell you what I was up to."

"Don't be nuts," I hissed. "You and Rupert are just beginning to warm up to one another. Breaking into his safe would implode that relationship pretty quickly."

"Only if he found out, and there isn't a lock that Ev's designed that he hasn't worked out a corresponding app for breaking into. He just updated the de-locking app before you two tied the knot, you know—oh, wait, you wouldn't know, would you? You don't keep up with those piddly details."

"Peaches, *think*. Rupert has surveillance everywhere for his most priceless objects. Even with Evan's super apps, he'd find out who did it. He spent decades in Interpol, after all. No, there has to be another way."

She sat back. "Like what?"

"I'm thinking," I said, "but let's begin with researching the Templars in London first. The British branch was based at the Temple Church and environs. That has to be significant. We'll start there."

"Sure," she said, "let's research away, but never underestimate the power of a direct approach."

"Anyway, if all else fails, the direct approach is on the list."

"Do we have a list?"

"We do. A long one," I assured her.

Chapter Four

"Okay, so give me the elevator view of the Knights Templar," Peaches requested as we strode to Sloane Square station, heading for Fleet Street. "I'm a bit lacking in the British history department. I've seen all the movies, if that helps."

"It doesn't in this case," I said.

By then it had stopped raining, and the sun was gilding everything with the glow of good cheer. While I plotted out our route in my head, Peaches kept talking. "I know that they were medieval holy knights—monks, weren't they? —who were established to protect the pilgrims heading for Jerusalem, and later led the Crusades. Oh, and they wore white tunics with big red crosses on them. Right so far?"

"Correct," I said. "They originally named themselves 'The Poor Fellow-Soldiers of Christ and of the Temple of Solomon,' which in Latin is 'Pauperes Commilitones Christi Templic Salomonici.'"

She sighed noisily. "I hate it when you do that."

"I only just learned the Latin equivalent this week so I'm showing off," I said, laughing. "All right, here goes: the Knights Templar were a holy monastic order of knights formed to protect pilgrims going to the Holy Land and later to fight in the Crusades—you're right there. They gained a reputation for being fearless even in the face of certain death. The king of Jerusalem was so impressed that he gave them headquarters on the Temple Mount, hence their name. As the Order grew in numbers and spread across Europe, they became incredibly wealthy. Rumors of their treasures including everything from the Holy Grail to the Ark of the Covenant, as well as huge amounts of gold and property, but far as historians can tell, only the last two were true."

"So much for the vow of poverty," Peaches remarked as we each inserted our Oyster card into the turnstile at the tube station and headed for the trains. "Go on," she prompted once we had nabbed a seat on the Central line minutes later.

"Like you said, so much for poverty. Many wealthy landowners would parcel out part of their holdings to the Templars, and any man who chose to join the Order had to take monastic vows and give over their wealth and property. They had so much money and real estate that they started history's first bank and lent funds to countless people, including kings. In fact, they became even wealthier than the monarchs, which ultimately led to their downfall and dissolution in 1312. By that time, King Philip IV of France needed money to fund his wars, and so possibly wanted to get his hands on their wealth. He badgered Pope Clement V to denounce the Templars and to dissolve the Order, since the Crusades were over by this time. Most of the Templars, at least those in France, were tortured and burned as heretics. There it is in a nutshell."

"I never did get the torture thing. I mean, was that really necessary? Dissolve the Order and be done already."

"They tortured them, at least in France, in order to force them to confess that they were devil-worshippers and performed perverted ceremonies in secret, which had King Philip of France's stamp all over it. That was the only way the general populace would ever accept the brutal way in which the Templars' possessions were confiscated and the Order dissolved. They were highly respected as holy knights and had fought in the Crusades. One minute they were hallowed and the next vilified, persecuted, and stripped of their titles and possessions. That took a mammoth PR campaign to mechanize."

"So, what happened to all their assets?"

"Most of it went to the Knights Hospitaller, who had established hospitals during the Crusades to tend to the sick and wounded. Their full name was—is —the Order of Knights of the Hospital of Saint John of Jerusalem, which is where the St. John Ambulance stems from, by the way. They are a branch of the original Knights Hospitaller."

"Well, wow," Peaches whistled. "I never knew that."

"It's not well known, nor is the fact that the Order still exists, but I suspect that there are many knightly organizations still at work worldwide. Some are secret and shrouded in history and others are honorary knighthoods. Remember that the British monarchy still knights individuals every year. Here's our stop."

Though I enjoy summarizing history for anyone who asks, I knew that I hadn't done this subject justice. Everything I told Peaches was true in terms of known facts but, at the same time, the currents of little-known facts, possibilities, and myths below the surface made the Templar tale even more fascinating. I had already downloaded a few key books on the Templars that very morning, and tingled with anticipation as I contemplated digging in. Research was one of my biggest thrills.

"What do you think our favorite snake-in-the-grass has in that package he's presumably keeping for Hogarth?" my friend asked as we crossed the street toward Temple Lane, the doors of which stood open as if welcoming us into some secret garden.

"It looked like a small shoebox wrapped in a garbage bag," I told her.

"A garbage bag? Points lost for lack of reverence, then. Probably not a reliquary or the Holy Grail."

"Definitely not. Reliquaries of the day would be small chests but still too big to fit into whatever Hogarth was gripping, and the Holy Grail is most probably a myth, at least in the literal sense."

"What then?"

"I have no idea and it's driving me crazy. Using the container as a guide, I estimate that the item is smallish, like maybe twelve centimeters by ten centimeters and approximately this thick." I held up my thumb and index fingers. "And it couldn't have been all that fragile since Hogarth kept his full weight on it when the woman attacked. It has to be enormously valuable, though, since he was willing to die rather than to relinquish it."

"Where was Rupert when this woman in black was coming after Hogarth?" Peaches asked.

I turned toward her, making a face. "Playing possum—his specialty. He feigned a heart attack."

"The sneaky bugger." Peaches grinned.

"Nobody does it better. So," I said, stopping, "the Temple Church is farther up the path that way but we're not heading there just yet—too obvious. Rupert is having us followed—at least, that's what I would do if I were him. Instead, we're going to visit an old friend of mine."

Peaches raised her brows at me. "A mysterious assignation?"

"Not really. Margaret and I were classmates back in law school decades ago, only she passed her bar exams and I didn't. She didn't want to go into law, though, and went on to library school to become an archivist. We hit it off because we both shared a passion for history as well as for a certain graduate student. Neither of us ended up with either the guy or the profession—luckily, since neither suited us—but we both ended up in London. Anyway, I wanted to talk to her about this because her name is totally off Rupert's radar and therefore not on his Agency Screened Resources List. I'm almost certain that Rupert will follow up with anyone I contact from that list, so I need my own resources."

"So why is Margaret such a resource?"

"Because she's an archivist at the British Museum with a specialty in medieval history, which makes her perfect. She wrote a paper that was recently published in one of the history abstracts. She only just got the job at the museum, by the way—her dream position. Margaret is a phenomenal source of British history on her own, and even writes historical novels."

"She writes historical novels, too? Really?"

"Really. It turns out that she'll meet us on her lunch break for a few minutes today. Usually she's very busy. Here, this way."

"Does she write romances about sexy Scottish Highlanders, by any chance?"

"No, she does serious historical fiction, not romance, but there's lots of sex in her books. Bet you'd enjoy them. Come, we'd better up our pace or we're going to be late."

Other pathways branched off from Temple Lane, deep into the expansive environs of the British legal system—Inner and Middle Temple, and beyond that, Lincoln's Inn and Gray's Inn, most of which had been built on what had once been Templar land. Later the property went to the Knights Hospitaller and finally ended up in possession of the courts. Today, the paths were filled with legal students scurrying along with arms laden with books, men and women in sharp suits, and even a few wigged and gowned lawyers dashing from one building to another, dragging little black roller bags behind them.

"I never got that silly white wig business. I mean, are we stuck in the seventeenth century or what?" Peaches whispered as a bewigged woman and an equally coiffed man flashed past, black gowns flapping in the breeze.

"The answer is yes, only add a few centuries to either end. This is Britain, remember, and they wear their traditions proudly. That's Middle Temple over there." I pointed out a stately brick building with a lovely garden tucked into its stone courtyard. "It was constructed on land belonging to the Templars, too, and later Queen Elizabeth I opened up Middle Temple Hall there in 1576, but we're heading this way to Hare Court."

"You sound like a tour guide."

"Been brushing up."

As the red-brick building with distinctive Tudor features rose overhead, nestled around a tiny stone courtyard planted with little evergreens here and there, I asked: "Do you want me to continue with the tour or should I put a lid on it?"

"Keep spouting. I want to learn."

"Okay, so in the early thirteenth century, this was King John of England at Runnymede's famed headquarters. It's been reconstructed since, though. Many buildings were bombed during the war."

Peaches shot me a look. "Runnymede?"

"The Magna Carta—the birth of the parliamentary system and representational government?"

"Oh, right—got you."

"William Marshal, who died as a Knight Templar, helped leverage the deal between King John and the barons. He and his son are buried in the Temple Church. He's thought to be the epitome of the perfect knight, and handsome, too."

"I thought that the Templars had to forfeit their belongings to take holy vows, meaning no fooling around and no kids?" she asked.

"William Marshal did all his fooling around before he took his vows. He wasn't officially ordained until he was on his deathbed because he didn't want to give up his family lands." I paused by a locked side door. "I asked Margaret to meet us someplace private, as in a place not accessible to the common street stalker. She chose here. I just have to text that we've arrived."

"Yeah, it's probably better that we don't just break in."

I stifled a laugh. "Right—not good for relations." I cast a glance back the way we had come.

Peaches followed my gaze. "I've been checking, too. If someone's following us, they are professionals, and there're too many people around for us to use our stalker apps."

We didn't have to wait long before the electronic lock beeped to let us in, the heavily weighted door closing immediately behind us. Margaret was waiting for us at the top of a narrow stairway, a petite woman with short dark hair and startlingly red lipstick slicked across a brilliant smile. Dressed in a trim gray suit with a pencil skirt, she had that buttoned-up-but-bursting-with-restrained-passion look about her. At university, she'd tell the dirtiest jokes and howled the loudest at mine, but she had also been a serious student.

"Phoebe!" she exclaimed, giving me a mighty squeeze. "I haven't heard from you in months! Your message was so mysterious that I'm thoroughly intrigued."

I introduced Peaches as my colleague; the women smiled at one another before Margaret took us up another flight of stairs and ushered us into a small room with space for a table, four chairs, and not much else. A kettle, mug, and box of mixed tea bags sat squeezed on the windowsill.

"Let me crack the window open," Margaret said. "These tiny spaces make me gag—ugh. No ventilation. This is one of the rooms the law students can use for study, only nobody knows it exists but a privileged few so it stays vacant most of the time. You wouldn't believe the number of unused cubbyholes these old buildings have. When you told me that you wanted to meet somewhere very private, this seemed like the perfect place." She began struggling with the antiquated latch until Peaches jumped up and flipped the window free with ease, lifting the frame an inch with one finger to let in a bite of chill air. Margaret cast her an appreciative look. "You're a good one to have around."

"You don't know the half of it." Peaches grinned, sitting back down.

"Which means?" Margaret asked.

"I'm Phoebe's bodyguard," Peaches told her.

"Bodyguard?" Margaret turned her appraising gaze on me. "Do you need a bodyguard, Phoebe? You never mentioned that repatriation requires a personal protection detail but now that I think about it, why not?"

I grinned. "Today I just need information and I'm hoping you can help."

Margaret fixed on my ring finger. "You're married?"

"I am!" I exclaimed. "I should have told you, but it was very whirlwind and is still so new." At that moment, I was distracted by Margaret's ring finger, too, now sparkling with a sizable diamond. "And you're engaged?"

"To a lawyer—surprise, surprise. That's how I got the code to this place— he works upstairs. The wedding's set for December." Margaret beamed.

"Is he hot?" Peaches asked mildly.

Margaret turned to her, straight-faced. "Hotter than an inferno," she said without missing a beat. "Singes me fingers just touchin' 'im," she added with a damn good Cockney accent.

Peaches cocked an eyebrow. "Does he wear one of those curly white wigs?" she asked. "Because, I've got to say, that would nix the sex appeal right on the spot for me."

"I ensure that he's not wearing either his robe or the wig when I get through with him." And the two of them howled with naughty laughter.

This time I did roll my eyes. Several minutes passed before I could restore order. "Margaret, can you help? I know you're short of time."

Margaret was sitting across from us, still chuckling, but instantly sobered. "I'll do anything I can but have you ever piqued my curiosity. What's this about?" She folded her hands on the table and faced us expectantly. "It all sounds so delicious—secrecy, private meeting places, bodyguards—as if straight out of one of my novels. Are you on a repatriation case?'

"Possibly. Actually, it's still too early to tell," I explained. "I'm sorry for not providing more details but this is sensitive. Are you okay with me asking for more information than I provide?"

"Oh, definitely. I'm used to operating confidentially, and if you happen to let something slip, my lips are sealed. I'm very discreet. How can I help you, Phoebe and Peaches?"

I smiled, thinking back to how we used to pass notes at the back of the lectures on corporate law. We were incorrigible. In some ways, she hadn't changed and yet here she was a professional with multiple degrees and a writing gig on the side—my kind of woman. "I know that you specialize in medieval history and I need to pick your brain about the Templars."

"Pick away."

"Have you uncovered even a thread of possibility behind the rumor of lost Templar treasure?" I began. "I know that the hunt for Templar gold has ignited the imaginations of countless treasure hunters over the years, but could there be any truth behind the myth?"

"It's doubtful that much survived the dissolution considering that any items made of gold would have been melted down to fund wars or to plump up either kingly coffers or the Vatican's treasury. Anything of a religious nature that survived probably disappeared into churches, but since the Order was declared heretical, many items were probably destroyed, nevertheless."

"So, you think that nothing has survived?" Peaches asked.

"A treasure hunter claims to have found a Templar stash he calls the Tomar Hoard, which consists of an iron reliquary chest and a white marble chalice, among other items—not many objects, but the artifacts are convincing. It's likely the real thing, in my opinion, but this was in Poland and probably not the only stash. The Templars were widely spread. As for piles of glittering gold, I'd say that that exists only in the realms of the imagination. Long live the imagination." She smiled. "Do you think that you've found something?"

"Not us but maybe somebody we know. What is the possibility of finding Templar artifacts in the Temple Church?" I asked.

"You do know that the church was bombed during World War II, right?"

I nodded. "I do."

"Well, even before that, it was extensively rebuilt by Sir Christopher Wren, and when the Luftwaffe dropped an incendiary bomb on it, the site was engulfed in flames with little left standing. While it was being rebuilt in the fifties, archaeologists had a chance to study the structure for mysteries of any kind. Nothing was found, as far as I've heard, or if anything was discovered, it was pocketed. All too much of that went on during the war, as you know."

"What about something possibly buried in one of the Templar tombs?" Peaches asked.

"Though there are plenty of burials in and around the Temple Church—there are graves all over the Temple area—if you mean the Templars themselves, there were no written records. Burials at the Temple Church weren't recorded until the 1600s. The remains of William Marshal and his son are reportedly not even laid to rest in the church, making the effigies more honorary. And then, if that wasn't bad enough, after the bombing when the church was in shambles, tomb robbers broke into the graves and crypts to steal rings and whatever they could find. They even took skulls away as treasures. After that, the vaults were bricked up and, as far as I know, have remained that way ever since."

I took a deep breath, trying to stifle my disappointment. "All right, but what if somebody *did* find something in the church, what might it be?"

"Hypothetically?"

"Hypothetically."

Margaret studied me appraisingly. "First of all, Christian burials didn't have grave goods so it would have had to be hidden by an individual. It couldn't be jewelry because the Templars didn't wear personal adornment," she said carefully, "and it couldn't be gold for the reasons I mentioned. It might be something that a single Templar hid for himself, especially if he knew that persecution was eminent, but I still don't see how anything would be found in the Temple Church."

"Right, thank you," I said, gazing down at my hands. "I guess we need to come at this from a different angle."

"Come at what from a different angle? If you tell me exactly what you're seeking, maybe I could help you further," Margaret said, leaning forward. "I've accumulated so much research material and interviewed countless people that I'm sure I could help."

I met her eyes. "I'm sure you could, too, but I just don't have enough information to even ask the right questions. Peaches and I will give this whole situation more thought and then circle back to you. At this stage, it's probably still way too early. Thanks for your help." Getting to my feet, I didn't try to hide how deflated I felt.

"I could send you some of the research material I gathered while I was preparing my article on the Temple Church. I've tracked down some interesting items, including a sketch that shows a cross-section of the church circa 1852. Here." She plucked a phone from her pocket. "I have everything digitized and organized into a file, which I'll just share with you right now. Can I use your regular email address?"

"Here, let me give you my secure agency address just in case there are hackers lurking about." I gave her the address verbally.

After two taps of her screen and a moment of typing, a ping announced that I'd received a file from one of the cloud services, with everything down-loaded on the spot.

"Maybe you'll find something useful there," Margaret said.

"I'm sure I will. Thank you."

We were almost to the door when something occurred to me. Turning back to Margaret, I asked: "By the way, does the name Clive Hogarth mean anything to you?"

"Dr. Hogarth? Certainly. He was a Templar historian and briefly the Reverend and Valiant Master of the Temple Church, that is until he disap-peared three years ago."

Chapter Five

"The Valiant Master of the Temple? Seriously?" Peaches burst out the moment we were far enough away from the building.

"It's obviously some kind of honorary title bestowed upon the reverends of the Temple Church. I doubt that they consider themselves as valiant masters of anything these days. Forget about the nomenclature for a moment—Clive Hogarth, Rupert's wounded houseguest, held that title right up until he disappeared three years ago. That's a critical piece of the puzzle."

"Sure, but what does it tell us?"

I turned to face her, the two of us standing like an island in the passing stream of people dashing in both directions. Lowering my voice, I said: "Clive Hogarth disappeared. Why did he reappear in the Temple Church last night, clutching a mysterious package that somebody was willing to shoot him to get?"

Peaches went still and watchful, her gaze fixed on some point over my head. "There's a guy sitting on the bench maybe forty feet down the lane who I saw before we went inside. We're being followed."

"Trench coat, navy blue scarf, kind of a mini-brush-cut thing going on, always looking at his phone?"

"Yeah, that's the one."

"That's Dex, one of Rupert's lads sent to spy on me, no doubt. He's on Rupert's list of vetted assistants and seems deeply involved in Rupert's current affairs and is staying at the house now. It's the man behind us standing by the yew tree in the black barrister's robes apparently studying a newspaper that I'm worried about. I've seen him three times today. Look carefully and you'll notice that his robe looks strangely cheesy."

"All those robes look strangely cheesy to me," Peaches whispered.

"This one looks cheesier—unlined rayon. In textiles, that's a clue, especially here in sartorial law-law land where they take their fabrics seriously." Just in case she didn't get the joke, I spelled out "law-law land." She scowled. "Follow me," I said, and took off toward Dex, who looked up from his phone when we approached with an endearingly startled expression.

"Phoebe, what a coincidence!" he exclaimed, jumping to his feet.

"Hi, Dex," I greeted. "No need to wear your game face with Peaches and me because I know that Rupert's put you on my tail. He must be worried that I might be in danger after last night. What a caring father-in-law, right?" I doubted that Rupert would disclose much detail to his helpers—he never did, being a firm proponent of the need-to-know policy. "Is he trying to ensure my safety?"

"Oh, yes," Dex assured me.

Lowering my voice, I added: "But the real danger is down the lane where a phony barrister in a bad-fitting wig is pretending to read a paper. See him?"

Dex shot a furtive look over my shoulder. "Yeah, got him in my sights."

"I doubt that he's on the 'list,' Dex, yet he's been following us for hours. Track him for me, will you, and keep me informed? Peaches and I are heading home now, anyway. We'll be safe. See you later and give me a report then, okay?"

"Sure thing." Just like that, Dex turned his attention on a new target.

And with that, Peaches and I took off, through the gates and out onto Fleet Street.

"You sly dog, you! That was smooth!" Peaches exclaimed as we dashed down the street.

"I just wanted to get him off our tail but..." I turned around to see if I could see the phony barrister. Though he was nowhere in sight, that didn't mean anything. "Who knows if he really took the bait or is just pretending? One way or the other, it still doesn't bring us any closer to discovering what Clive Hogarth, former Valiant Master of the Temple Church, is protecting with his life."

"He's putting a tail on you, seriously? What's with Rupe, anyway? Weren't you two friends once?" she asked.

"We've had a complicated relationship in the past and now that I've married his son—the one who lived with him, protected him, and acted as his driver and valet at one point, remember—maybe he sees me as taking him away." I turned and began walking down the path, Peaches keeping stride.

"But he's an adult," she said, "and surely adults realize that at some point their children are going to move on and maybe marry. I mean, Evan is hardly a teenager. He's forty years old!"

"It doesn't matter, Peach. I still think Rupert is feeling abandoned at some deep level and, as much as I try to be understanding, that means being compliant and I'm just not that person. Hang on a minute." I stopped dead in my tracks and phoned Rupert's house, connecting with Sloane immediately.

"Sloane," I said breezily. "I'm just checking to see if Sir Rupert is at home and whether he will be joining me for dinner this evening?"

"Most definitely, madam. Sir Rupert is currently resting and wishes not to be disturbed but will be present at dinner."

"Excellent. Please let him know that we will have company tonight. Penelope Williams is home from Africa. Please set another place." Before he could say another word, I clicked off. "You're invited to dinner at Rupert's tonight. Hope you don't mind."

"Are you kidding? That sounds like fun, especially since Rupe is going to think we're ganging up on him."

"We are, just not in the way he expects."

"So, I'm going to have to go home now, try to nap off this jet lag, and change, but that suits me fine because tonight I'll finally get to wear some high-end clothes instead of living in jeans and khakis all the time."

We parted ways at the tube station, Peaches heading for her flat in Notting Hill, me planning on returning home, too. But it occurred to me that maybe I didn't want to return to that house any earlier than necessary. Instead, I darted into a coffee shop and ordered a pot of tea while quickly skimming the file Margaret had sent.

It was, as she promised, a veritable trove of resources, but what caught my attention right away was the pen and ink diagram she had mentioned. The drawing revealed a cross-section of the Temple Church prior to the bombing and clearly showed the oldest nether regions of the building: the crypts. There was a whole other world down there, one that had been inaccessible for decades with in-floor and niche burials—a perfect hiding place for anything.

Suddenly, I had an idea. It was 3:35 p.m., giving me just enough time to pay a quick visit to the Temple Church before it closed at 4:00. Now that Dex was tracking the phony barrister, presumably I could scout around in peace.

I paid my five pound entrance fee and stepped inside, surprised to find the building almost empty. A few people stood around gazing at the effigies while voices echoed from the gallery above, but otherwise the church was relatively peaceful.

After nodding at a guard by the door, I strolled down the chancery as if desiring a moment of quiet contemplation, which in a sense was true. As I walked down the aisle, I asked myself one question: what would keep its value across centuries that wasn't made of gold or precious jewels? It had to be considered hallowed enough not to be burned or destroyed as heretical. A reliquary box, maybe, but the package Hogarth gripped didn't fit the dimensions.

There had to be something that I was missing, something that should be painfully obvious, at least to me. As my eyes scanned the pews, it hit me. It had been hiding in plain sight the whole time and I berated myself for not thinking of it sooner—of course! At that moment, I was certain that I knew what Hogarth guarded.

Turning around, I slipped across the floor toward a stairway I had noted marked on the sketch that Margaret had provided. The crypt lay down those steps and, not surprisingly, the way had been roped off. A sign respectfully stated that the area was out of bounds.

In a flash, I was over the ropes and descending the narrow stone steps, my phone used as a flashlight. At the bottom, where the air was suffused with the strong scent of damp and deepening time, I studied the walled-off entrance to the old crypts. The area had been sealed with bricks, the shape of which stood out against the original stone. I was just scanning it with my X-ray app when I heard footsteps on the stairs. Turning, I saw a man in a black suit wearing a white collar.

"Excuse me, madam, but this area is not open to the public," he said tersely.

"Sorry, sorry, but I was so intrigued when I learned that the crypts had been bricked up that I just had to take a look for myself."

"Whatever for?" he asked

I held up my hands. "Curiosity. I'm very interested in the history of old buildings and that is such a fascinating piece of the tale."

"Nevertheless, I must ask you to vacate this area immediately."

"Yes, of course." Did I feel chastised? No, but I probably should have, especially when I laid the North American accent on a little too thick and went into enthusiastic tourist mode. "Why have they blocked off the crypts, if you don't mind me asking? I can understand not opening the area to the public but blocking it off seems like overkill." If I could dig up any more mildly offensive terminology, I would.

The reverend was ushering me up the stairs as if to imply that he refused to answer questions until I was safely back in the church's public areas. Once in the chancery, the space flooded by washes of stained-glass light across the floor and walls, he introduced himself as Reverend Burton-Jones and, no, he was not the church's current Valiant Master, but would be pleased to answer my questions. Who might he be speaking to?

"I'm Shirley," I said, "but you can call me 'Shirl.'"

A flash of irritation crossed the man's face and was instantly restrained beneath a veneer of courtesy. "The crypt was barricaded following the unfortunate plundering of the tombs by robbers after the bombing of London during the Second World War. The decision was made at that time to allow the dead to rest in peace, something which we adhere to to this day."

"Sure. So, nobody's tried to get in there since, not even archaeologists?"

"No, madam, to my knowledge, they have not, and I cannot understand why you would ever ask such a thing. Now, if you don't mind, only eleven minutes remain of our official visitor's hours. Pardon me, but I shall just see to closing up. Good day to you."

The grumpy reverend didn't like ditzy tourists apparently. In seconds, he was striding down the aisle, his annoyance thinly disguised, leaving me just enough time to revisit the gallery above. My guess was that more than one person had been asking questions about the Temple Church lately, which may have left him a bit on edge. Imagine how disgruntled he'd be had he known that there had been an attempted murder on-site the night before?

By the time I had puffed my way up those stairs, the gallery was empty. Knowing that security cameras would be operational, I strode the circular space admiring the drawings and information posters detailing the Magna Carta, my phone held in front of me as if taking pictures. I leaned over the balcony once to photograph the effigies from overhead—a very touristy thing to do—before walking around a second time.

For this round, I was discreetly checking for signs of structural disturbances. Plaster marks expertly painted to hide a bullet hole wouldn't be noticeable unless one knew what to look for—maybe wet paint, imperfectly matched color —and neither would the odd, slight irregularity of the wall about a quarter of the way around the circumference from the door.

The patched bullet hole in the wall I recognized at once, but it took the X-ray app to detect the recess farther on, about a foot up from the floor. I scanned the surface with my phone in passing, recording the interesting little rectangular cavity that appeared on my screen.

After walking around a few more times, I realized that the cameras mounted near the ceiling to the left and right of the stairway were designed to catch people heading down the corridor in either direction. The fact that there was no line of sight for the cameras where that recess appeared on my phone app told me that the area was in a blind spot. By now, I was gaining a clearer idea of what must have happened with Clive Hogarth and his mysterious package. In fact, the whole day's exercise had been so successful that I was congratulating myself all the way down the steps to the lower level.

Reverend Burton-Jones and two other clergy were waiting by the door to bid the visitors goodbye. I thanked them and exited the church with four others, climbing up the steps into the darkening skies of a late November afternoon.

If I didn't hurry, I'd be caught in the peak hour tube squeeze, something I preferred to avoid. Minutes later, I was seated at the back of the tube car checking my messages for word from Evan—nothing. Three days of nothing. Damn, but at least I had something to keep myself busy.

Chapter Six

When I returned to Belgravia and headed for my rooms, I noted that a different Sikh now stood guarding the guest room. I slipped up the stairs without comment. Meanwhile, Rupert remained in his rooms. Dex was nowhere in sight.

Once inside my own quarters, I remained fixed to my phone and laptop, transferring Margaret's files to my computer so I could study details on the larger screen. Somewhere in the middle of this this process, Peaches texted to say that she planned on making a grand entrance that night, which was Peaches-speak for oversleeping and signaling the possibility of being late.

After going through Margaret's files again, I took a shower and changed into one of my new outfits. Losing my clothes required me to purchase a whole new wardrobe, to which I had yet to grow accustomed. Adding to all these bags and boxes of newness, my friend Nicolina in our Rome office had sent me several packages of couture outfits. She loved to dress me at every opportunity and obviously the bombing incident provided her with the perfect excuse to refresh my image.

Now I had to decide what to wear in the face of almost too many choices. On a whim, I picked out one of Nicolina's gifts—a cream cashmere turtleneck with coordinating loose trousers in a deeper shade of pale, all contributing to what Nicolina considered "understated elegance." I rarely understated anything and elegance really wasn't my thing, but once I added a pair of pearl earrings that Rupert had given me as a wedding present, I looked good even to myself.

Before the appointed hour of seven o'clock, I headed for the lounge to sit by the fire where drinks would be served, prepared to play into Rupert's traditional stye of dining—first drinks, then food. This, Rupert had assured me time and time again, was the "civilized" way to dine, and since Evan had been living with his dad, he had always dressed for the occasion, too.

I probably don't need to mention how devastatingly handsome Evan was in a suit, sitting, legs crossed, listening intently to the conversation. Without getting too mired in detail, let me just say that formal dining with my husband always hit me like an aphrodisiac. My idea of dessert wasn't even on the menu.

The fire crackled in the grate as I sat on the couch near a plate of appetizers, in a room richly decorated in antiques and antiquities. A lighted display case lined one wall, within which Rupert had placed some of his prized acquisitions, at least the ones he'd admit to possessing. This one was graced by an impressive collection of fine china.

Sloane slipped in to ask if I'd like a gin and tonic, my predinner drink of choice. I smiled my agreement and watched as Rupert's longtime personal attendant and butler exited the room to oblige. Sloane was amazing and had long ago accepted me into the family circle, yet he was clearly in Rupert's pocket, as was everyone else on staff. Though I was the daughter-in-law living on-site, it made no difference to the cone of silence with which Rupert had chosen to surround himself in this matter. It was as if the entire house refused to realize that a mysterious wounded guest now occupied a second-floor guest room. When I had asked Irina about him earlier, she had only stared at me blankly.

Rupert appeared shortly before seven o'clock, looking dapper in a maroon velvet jacket and bow tie. "Phoebe, you look quite splendid, and I do adore the way in which you've paired those pearls with the divine creaminess of that outfit. Is that Brunello Cucinelli?"

"I think so." That name sounded familiar, though I had been more entranced by the feel of cashmere than the designer label.

"Was that one of Nicolina's choices, by any chance? She truly has such excellent taste. I have a little gift for you also." He turned toward the door, signaled to a worker bee who stood nearby, and soon a large, extravagantly wrapped package was sitting on the seat beside me. I gazed at the bronze Florentine marbled paper with the huge chocolate-colored silk bow and my stomach sank: I was being what my mother had referred to as "buttered up."

"Well, do open it, Phoebe."

What choice did I have but to be gracious? I plucked at the broad satin ribbon, watching it slide off onto the couch in a stream of fluid color, before painstakingly unwrapping the gift, careful not to mar so much as a smidgin of that gorgeous paper. Soon, I was pulling back tissue paper and gazing into a box of glossy silk yarn in all of my favorite colors—burnished golds, browns, greens —the sight so beautiful that tears pricked my eyes.

"I know that you lost all of your yarn as a result of Semenov's retaliation, so I sought to replenish your stash with silken magnificence."

"Oh, you have!" I fingered the yarn with my emotions so full that I knew they would soon spill over. Rupert could be disarming, thoughtful, caring— and sly.

I leaped from my seat and embraced him. After a few moments, he gently stepped back, his hands on my shoulders. "You know how fond I am of you and so delighted to have you as a daughter-in-law, and therefore, I trust that the misunderstandings of the last few days will do nothing to mar our relationship."

I wiped away a tear. "Misunderstandings?"

At that moment, the doorbell rang and I realized with relief that Peaches had arrived. Saved by the bell. She swept into the room in a column of formfitting black lamé, devoid of ornamentation but for a large pair of gold hoop earrings. In other words, she was dazzling.

"Hello there, Rupe!" she cried, descending on her host, intent on bestowing a full-frontal hug. Rupert attempted to escape the embrace but she was too fast. Soon, the man was crushed against her chest, her bust roughly at his eye level. I almost felt sorry for him.

"Very good to see you, too," Rupert managed to say as he slipped from her grasp at last and attempted to straighten his glasses. "You look truly amazing, Penelope, I must say. Please, ladies, do make yourselves comfortable while I see how matters are progressing in the kitchen. I will return momentarily."

As he scrambled off, I turned to Peaches. "You do look stunning and you are so, so bad."

She beamed. "Thank you on both counts. I couldn't fit into this thing before I left for Africa but now it just slides on. You look pretty amazing yourself, Phoeb. I'm sure if Evan could see you in all that coffee and cream yummi-ness, he'd just lap you up. Have you heard from him yet?"

I knew I looked crestfallen. "No."

"I'm sure you soon will. So, have you managed to squeeze anything out of Rupe?"

"Not a thing. First, he managed to stay out of my way, and then he presented me with that." I indicated the box on the couch.

Peaches leaned over to peek inside. "The bugger. Is that supposed to be some sort of bribe?"

"He implied that it's a peace offering."

She fixed me with a stern look. "Peace be damned. That's a bribe."

"Don't worry, I'm not wavering, but you've got to admit that it's kind of sweet, whatever his motives."

"I'll admit nothing of the kind. Did you know that leopards play with their prey before they make the kill?"

"Perhaps not the best analogy," I said under my breath. "Let me handle this, Peaches. I have it all under control," adding: "Here comes Rupert now."

"Ladies, let us proceed to the dining room," Rupert announced, rubbing his hands together. "Dinner awaits."

"Oh, my God!" Peaches exclaimed. "It's like dining inside a rerun of *Downton Abbey*!"

Rupert appeared a bit put out by the reference but soon rallied, as if determined to make this a memorable dining experience. And a spectacular dinner it was. My favorite dish, sole meunière— served with fingerling potatoes, French beans, and a salad, finished off with the cook's specialty, a custard trifle heaped with fresh fruit for dessert—was simply incredible.

The dinner appeared designed to stifle conversation under an abundance of carbs and sugar, copious amounts of wine, and Rupert in full charm mode. Most of the conversation centered on Peaches's experiences in Africa, and by the time coffee arrived, our host probably thought that he had escaped interrogation. On that point, he was mistaken.

"Everything was just so delicious, Rupert. I'm touched that you have not only arranged for one of my favorite meals, but have given me such a fabulous gift, as well. Thank you, but there is still the matter of last night's events, which we need to discuss, so let's begin now, shall we?" said I.

Rupert placed his folded napkin on the table before him. "By all means, let us begin. But before we do so, Phoebe, I ask that you understand that, as much as I adore you, not everything that is my business is your business."

I could feel Peaches tensing across the table. I smiled at our host while attempting to nudge her with my foot, missed, and knocked the table leg by accident. My facial expression never changed. "That's very true, Rupert, but I think you know that when the business involves stolen art, as head of the Agency of the Ancient Lost and Found, it becomes very much my business."

"First of all, we do not know that anything was stolen, and my second point is that, if something was stolen, it may not have been anything of artistic value."

"What about historic value?" I pressed.

"Actually—" he folded his hands on the table "—as I understand it, the Agency of the Ancient Lost and Found is on a temporary hiatus following the unfortunate attack, and therefore I would postulate that you do not currently hold a position there and therefore cannot interrogate me."

Peaches snorted.

Now that was just outrageous. I smiled broadly. "And I would challenge your postulations—all of them. The agency's London office—as in the actual headquarters—may be under construction but the agency itself is still fully operational, as am I, which I'm certain you know. I just haven't had a case to work on until now."

Peaches looked from one of us to the other as if desperate to interrupt. I caught her eye. *No, please.*

"This is not an agency case," Rupert humped.

"It is now."

"Nonsense," Rupert said, his face reddening in the candlelight. "This does not constitute agency business and is solely a private matter."

"A private matter employing agency technology. Oh, and would that be the private matter of Dr. Clive Hogarth, a reverend and the once Valiant Master of the Temple Church?" I asked. "If so, I'm sure you know that the reverend disappeared in 2020, and that his sudden appearance last night, clutching an object that at least one person might be willing to kill him to obtain, is as suspicious as it is illegal."

"I should have known that you'd discover his identity but, regardless, I state that it is still a private matter, and I ask that you cease investigations immediately."

I sat back. "Tell me why I'd agree to remain uninvolved, knowing that your friend probably stole something from the Temple Church and proceeded to hide it in the wall of the triforium gallery until he could arrange to sneak it out of the building with your help?"

"That's preposterous!" His outrage appeared genuine—at least in part—but I could tell that I had hit a nerve. "While it is true that he hid something—and how the devil did you discover that? Oh, never mind—no doubt with the help of your too-curious mind and my son's brilliant inventions. Nevertheless, that does not mean that the item was stolen. I have reason to believe that it originally belonged to Hogarth himself, who, due to a health problem, found it necessary to hide it until it could be retrieved."

"Hide it in the walls of a historic property? Oh, come on!" Peaches blurted out.

"The church has been extensively rebuilt so it was hardly defacing anything original," Rupert protested.

"That's not the point. And why hide it in the first place if it belongs to him?" Peaches demanded.

I met Peaches's eye, at which point she glowered, got to her feet, excused herself, and stormed from the room.

"That is none of your affair, Phoebe, and I must insist that you stop this meddling immediately!"

"What in the world did Hogarth tell you that was so convincing that you'd assist with something like this?" I persisted, on my feet now. "Do you realize that he in all probability stole that item from the crypts? That is the only area that remained more or less intact following the bombing in the Second World War, and the only place where anything of value might have survived."

"That's ludicrous," he stated, but with far less steam than his earlier protestations.

"There were looters after the bombing as the destruction left the crypt area exposed, but they may not have snatched everything." I held up my phone. "I have evidence that the brickwork blocking the crypts has recently been disturbed, too—recently being sometime in the past few years. The disturbance clearly shows up in the X-ray app, here and here." I pinched open the screen to show a close-up of the irregularity in the brickwork and passed the phone across to Rupert, who blanched noticeably. "You can see how the bricks have been disturbed, leaving just enough room for somebody to enter the crypts and acquire whatever he was seeking, before bricking it back up again. You can see where the newer mortar has been applied."

"I can't believe Clive would do such a thing, or that he would even have the opportunity for an endeavor like that, and besides which, you can't prove that he was responsible for that breach." Rupert passed me back the phone and sat staring bleakly at the tablecloth.

"He had the opportunity. I'm guessing that the theft occurred sometime during the lockdown of 2020. Hogarth, as the Valiant Master at the time, had access to the church and would be living nearby, in the master's residence next door. Nobody would be checking on him given the private, gated area in which he lived, and England remained in lockdown for weeks. I'm guessing that as the Temple Church historian, he knew exactly what he was seeking and maybe even where to look."

"That is all conjecture, Phoebe," he said wearily.

"But you know that I am usually uncannily right-on with my conjectures." I gazed at Rupert, now sitting with his attention fixed on his hands, as if all the wind had gone from his sails. Pity and my fondness warred in me but I forged on. "I'm going to get to the bottom of this, Rupert, so you may as well disclose everything."

"Phoebe," he said after a moment, "I trust you know that I am not a total fool."

"I do know that, Rupert," I said softly.

"So, please understand that I did not enter into this situation lightly and am aware that I may have placed myself in a somewhat untenable situation when I agreed to help. Because of the past, I felt unable to turn the man away and chose to accept his version of events, regardless of my suspicions. Possessing the skills and resources that I do, I realized that I was—*I am*—most likely the only person able to help him work his way free of this predicament. You see, once, a long time ago, Clive did me a great favor, which I am honor-bound to return."

I sat back down and gazed across at my father-in-law. "Honor-bound? Is that like some English public school old-boy's code of ethics?"

He shot me a sour look. "You would not understand."

"If it results in you performing illegal acts and aiding and abetting a crime, I certainly wouldn't. Surely your suspicions boiled over when he retrieved that item from the triforium wall and talked you into helping him repair the damage?"

"Certainly. At that point, it was too late to turn back. I was well and truly in it then. However, Clive brought all the necessary materials and I only had to stand by and watch. He believed that it was his divine right to do as he did. The job was not up to my standards, as you can imagine, but the man is exceedingly persuasive."

I tried not to look too incredulous. "So," I began, taking a deep breath, "it follows that he had enough basic masonry skills to have broken into the crypts and repaired the breach following his theft. He then took the object to the triforium and hid it in the wall, knowing that it was unlikely to be found by anyone without X-ray capability."

Rupert did not reply but appeared to be popping antacid pills from a small gold case he carried in his pocket. "He said that the item was his responsibility to claim, that he had an important task to complete for history's sake."

"Surely you asked him what the object was?" I pressed.

"Surely I did, but he refused to be specific, explaining that all would be revealed once the object had been safely removed. He implied that even retrieving the item was likely to bring unwanted attention down upon his head and, on that point, he was correct."

"He knew he'd likely be followed?"

"Indeed. He told me that he had been under surveillance for some time, but that last night appeared to be the best opportunity to move the item, regardless. At no point would he explain why that was the case. Yes, a great deal of unanswered questions surrounded this situation, but I believed myself honor-bound to proceed, given that Clive had once done the same for me, and that the matter held a certain gravitas."

How I longed to unpack that statement but knew I'd get nowhere at that moment. I proceeded more gently. "What about that mysterious woman who attacked him? Do you know who she was?"

"Certainly not."

I gazed at my father-in-law with incredulity. "Well, your old friend certainly knows her. Recognition passed between them just before she pointed the gun to his head. They know each other with no love lost, it seems. Didn't you ask him for details there, either?" I was probably pushing my luck by then.

"May I remind you that the man had been wounded and was barely conscious at the time." He was getting testy now.

"But since?"

"Though he is recovering from his wound, I fear for his well-being. The doctor has assured me that Clive also has a heart condition and must remain calm, which has prevented me from asking too many probing questions. To simply mention the object he removed from the church pitches him into a state of extreme anxiety, at which point he demands to see it."

That explained the medications. "But you must have an inkling of what it is?" I pressed.

"I do not, as I said. Nor do we know at this point that he did, indeed, steal the item in the first place. I can only say that it is heavy since it is secured in a corroded lead box, undoubtedly medieval in origin, that appears to have been crafted for the express purpose of holding this object, and that the entire package fit very neatly into the wall receptacle."

"It's a book of some kind," I said, "possibly a Bible."

"So I have deduced."

"But you haven't looked at it yourself?"

Totally affronted, he glared at me. "I gave my word."

It was all I could do not to swear. "Assure me that you have not passed the artifact back to Clive as he's requested."

Rupert removed his glasses and rubbed the lenses. "I refer to my original point: I am not a total fool, Phoebe. Clive requested that he be permitted to study the item but I refused, citing the need for proper lab conditions before exposing the contents to air."

I almost sagged with relief. "Then let us find a lab where we can at least discover what it is you have in your vault, and interview Clive right now. I'm sure he's recovered enough to speak. You can't properly help him without knowing exactly what he's got himself—and you—into."

Before he could respond, somebody cried out from upstairs, the sound of footsteps thundering down the front stairs shortly afterward. Rupert and I were on our feet and halfway to the door when Peaches and the Sikh guard burst into the dining room, Sloane in tow.

"He's gone, the conniving Clive Hogarth has evaporated!" Peaches cried.

"But that cannot be!" Rupert exclaimed.

"It is true, it is very true," the Sikh seconded, looking befuddled as if having just been roused from a nap. "I did not leave my post but still he is gone!"

Chapter Seven

Minutes later, we were standing in the upstairs guest bedroom staring at the destruction. The room had been trashed. The dresser had been upended, the armoire lay flat on the floor, the mattress tipped on its side, and the remains of a supper tray smashed on the rug with food strewn everywhere.

"Sloane, have the staff comb the grounds," Rupert demanded.

"Already in progress, sir," the butler assured him.

"And where is Dex?"

"Outside searching the grounds. Shall we call the police, sir?"

"Certainly not," came Rupert's terse reply.

I was taking photos while Peaches strode to the open window, the curtains billowing beside the yawning casements. "He escaped this way," she said. "There's one of those extension ladder things hanging from the ledge but it doesn't look right—none of it looks right."

Rupert turned to the Sikh, who stood straight as a board before him. The man looked so stricken I thought he'd fall on his knife if Rupert demanded. "I did not leave my post, sir, and there was no sound, no sound at all," he assured his employer. "I heard nothing and my hearing is most excellent."

"The rooms are soundproof," Rupert said absently. "You are not to blame, my good man. The chink in our armor lies elsewhere."

"Hogarth couldn't have just helped himself out the window with a wounded arm," Peaches said, turning to face us, "or have brought his own ladder, for that matter, but it wouldn't be impossible to fix a sling in which to lower the guy to the ground. Either way, he had to have had help, or he was kidnapped."

"Surely he wouldn't go willingly? He had to have been abducted," I said, waiting for confirmation from Rupert.

"Yeah, this wasn't a one-person job. Look at those footprints—at least two pairs. But why kidnap him?" Peaches asked, picking her way through the mess. "I mean, where's that going to get them?"

"Maybe Hogarth possesses some critical piece of necessary information." I was still studying Rupert, waiting for a comment.

"Somebody with anger issues. Look at how the room's been ransacked," Peaches continued. "They were looking for something, too. Hey, Addy, let's you and me take a look outside." Addy was the Sikh, it turned out, and he and Peaches appeared to have hit it off.

Sloane spoke up. "We will retrieve the security footage and see if anything has been caught on camera. Shall we activate the Roadside Team, sir?"

The Roadside Team was a group of operatives on Rupert's list who presumably could be called upon to search for vehicles and stake out transportation hubs to catch criminals on the move. How effective they'd be in this instance was debatable, and now that Rupert had retired from Interpol and was cut off from those resources, I wondered how this group would function. Rupert had always depended on Evan to keep the wheels rolling on what had always been a well-oiled machine. That night, it seemed as though the wheels had fallen off at the crossroads and all available mechanics came with questionable credentials.

"By all means," Rupert said, "but they could not have taken their hostage far, seeing as they do not have the item that they so wish to acquire."

So, as I thought: Clive and the artifact were a necessary pair.

"We are presently attempting to determine the entire picture," Sloane said, holding his phone in his hand. "I have staff surrounding the grounds, looking for the guards who have not yet responded to our calls. Also, Robbie just texted to say that one of the circuit breakers in the basement has been thrown."

"Go check it out—all of you. There's nothing to be done here," Rupert ordered. Thus, Peaches and Addy dashed off, Sloane following behind them.

"We probably should check for fingerprints but they'd be stupid not to have worn gloves," I said. I was running my phone across the floor. "Two sets of footprints, plenty of mud—an organized job, for sure, but a shoddy one. These weren't professionals." I took more photos, planning to break them down into essential facts when I had the chance.

"Why would she think that I would keep the object here?" Rupert muttered.

"She?" I looked up. When Rupert declined to provide more details, I continued: "Maybe because *she* knew that Hogarth wouldn't willingly let this thing out of his sight. He insisted on keeping it near him and wouldn't let go of it even at gunpoint, remember?" I now stood in front of Rupert and demanded that he look at me. It was as if he was only half present. "Who is she, Rupert?"

"How the devil do I know? Clive refused to say, and after the doctor's visit, he has been sedated and thus not inclined to talk."

"But you asked him?"

"Of course."

"But he did recognize her?"

"So it seems."

At least he admitted that much. "Where did you secure the object, Rupert —in your private vault?"

"The vault!" he cried suddenly, rousing himself. In seconds, he was scuttling out the door and down the hall, me on his heels.

My first glimpse of Rupert's private quarters—the collection of Roman glass, the halogen-lit display case of gold Roman and Greek laurel wreaths (seriously), the paintings—all went past in a blur as I followed him through the suite to his rear office. The gust of chill air blowing through the rooms heralded what we were to see: another window gaping open. Here, in a small office painted a deep forest green, the desk drawers had been upended onto the floor with papers scattered everywhere.

"How could this have happened!" Rupert exclaimed, losing it now. "I have the security alert activated and guards roaming the grounds!"

"Peaches and the staff are out there at this very moment. If there are clues, they'll find them," I said, studying the room. "These guys are such amateurs."

But Rupert wasn't listening. He had sunk onto a leather ottoman to gaze at a large portrait of a woman hanging on the wall before him. In the style of Gainsborough, only a modern rendition, the subject stood in a large floppy straw hat, wearing a dress fashioned with an abundance of verdant green satin. In the background, the landscape looked very much like Rupert's country estate. I stared from the portrait of Rupert's late wife to Rupert. "I have never seen this painting of Mildred."

"I commissioned it shortly after we were married."

"And behind Mildred is your vault, right?"

"Correct."

And yet, according to my scan app, which clearly outlined the large safe behind the painting, that, at least, remained intact. "I presume the perps ran out of time or failed to bring along the necessary explosives, not that those would have helped them much with this." I badly wanted him to show me that mysterious item right now but that hardly made sense, especially since we could be referring to a delicate manuscript of some kind.

"Apparently so."

"But it looks like this woman discovered where your safe was located, and possibly tried to break into it while her accomplices were kidnapping Clive. This must be a fairly large operation, Rupert, and, if not professional, they certainly are determined. Maybe they had inside information?"

"So I deduced, and undoubtedly they'll return to finish the job," he said, his demeanor unchanged. "I have let Clive down; failing to protect him, despite my assurances, and now I fear for his safety. I am in no way prepared to protect anything in my charge at the moment. How could this have happened?"

I could think of multiple ways this could have happened but chose to keep my mouth shut.

I sat down beside him. "Rupert, I know how upsetting this is but you need to pull yourself together and think. Whoever did this knew the rhythms of the household, knew that the rooms are soundproof, and could identify a weak point in the security system—and there has to be a weak point. There always is. Rupert, someone on staff helped them out."

"I fear that very possibility."

"Okay, then, who knows the inner workings of this household? Who would have known when the guards pass beneath these windows or where you placed the object?"

Rupert sighed. "Sloane, of course, and there were others, many others— indeed, all who were here last night. Surely you're not considering Sloane?"

"No, of course not." Actually, I was considering everybody. I placed a hand on his arm, "Rupert, call the police. Not only are we dealing with an attempted theft—possibly even an attempted murder—but now a kidnapping. These are serious offences. If you don't report these events soon, you will be dragged farther down the rabbit hole and possibly leave yourself open to criminal prosecution."

Evan would know exactly what to do in this situation, and had the connections to protect his father and everyone else in the process. There was a risk that calling the police now would give Chief Inspector Drury exactly the excuse she needed to charge someone, if not everyone, related to the agency with some kind of crime. I could think of several off the top of my head and, at the moment, I was involved in almost all of them. Only Evan, through Interpol, had the authority to keep the wolves from our door.

"No, we cannot call the police, Phoebe. Given what I have already done to deepen my own guilt in this affair, I have now dragged you, Peaches, and my staff into the mire. Surely you understand our untenable position? No, I shall gather the necessary assistance to locate Clive, preserve the object in my charge, and see this affair through to the end. Are you with me?" He turned and fixed me in his gaze as he climbed to his feet and held out his hand.

"I am," I said, standing up. Yes, I actually said that. Marrying into this family meant that I inherited the warts along with the fair prince. "So, do you have a team that you can dispatch to rescue Clive?"

"I do—the Roadside Team."

"And are they reliable?"

"As reliable as I can ascertain."

Which meant little these days. "Then let's get to it."

Getting to it involved a great deal of information-gathering, interviewing the staff, sending out calls for support, and many meetings in the library, where we all gathered to discuss the situation. The security systems were to be strengthened and more vetted staff brought on board, all while attempting not to draw too much attention via police notice.

Rupert ran his household with military precision in some respects but in other ways was remarkably slack. Beneath him, as top dog, came Sloane, under whom a contingent of men and women operated with clearly delineated tasks, including household duties, security detail, and many other aspects. Because of the sheer abundance of precious objects that Rupert had collected over the years, he never relied solely on technology to secure his property, protect his assets, and otherwise ensure his safety, but also on a team of highly trained individuals, including the two guards who patrolled the grounds. One of those guards had disappeared that night and the other was found in the shrubbery with a head injury.

Peaches, Rupert, Sloane, and I sat in the library later that night, reviewing what we had discovered so far. Upstairs, the doctor-on-call tended to the wounded guard who had been on ground patrol while Sikh Aad, now in charge of Rupert's office and private quarters with his own team of fellow Sikhs, stood guard.

"The best I can ascertain," Sloane was saying, "is that Jack Howard was taken by surprise while on the eastern quadrant of his patrol by, I'm assuming, none other than his colleague and fellow guard, Felix Pollard."

"Making Pollard an infiltrator," Peaches remarked.

"Just so," Sloane acknowledged. "Though the man has been on staff for over two months and was carefully vetted prior to being hired, he was obviously compromised."

"Who found him?" I asked.

"Why, Dex, I believe," said Sloane.

"Is he reliable?"

"Well, certainly. I've used the lad countless times and have always been satisfied with his performance."

"Did you thoroughly check his references? It's so easy to fake credentials these days," Peaches remarked. "Fake references, fake IDs."

Rupert looked up. "Anyone can be corrupted if the lure is sufficient. Have I not said that time and time again, Sloane?"

"Indeed, you have, sir." Sloane was looking as exhausted as we all felt. Peaches was periodically nodding off in her chair. "We have just identified another key area in our defense system that we left insufficiently protected. We will need to install a third backup, designed to kick in should the electronic gate be breached, and put additional guards about the estate. Meanwhile, the Roadside Team continues to survey the streets, searching for Mr. Hogarth."

"But I am so concerned about him, Sloane. Clive has underlying health issues and, truly, tonight's activities are enough to addle even a healthy man."

That could be a good reason not to steal precious objects, thought I, at my uncharitable best. "Which brings us back to that item in your safe. When can we take a look at the object so we'll know better what all this is really about?" I asked.

"Tomorrow," Rupert assured me. "It is far too late to tackle such an endeavor tonight, as I'm sure you agree. I am exhausted, as are we all."

"But do you know of a secure lab to where the item can be safely transported? Whoever did this will be watching," I pointed out.

"Indeed," Rupert said. "We have that all under control. Is that not true, Sloane?"

"It is, sir," the butler and right-hand man agreed.

There it was again—the cone of silence—but I was too weary to tackle anything further that night. Let them keep their secrets. It was already past 1:00 a.m. and it was all I could do to keep my eyes open. But not for a minute did I believe that they had everything under control.

Peaches had already lost the battle to stay awake. Striding across the room, I nudged her. "Do you want to stay in my spare room tonight?" I asked.

She sat up and stretched. "No thanks. I have a close relationship with my toothbrush and, besides, I don't want to wake up with nothing but a slinky dress to wear tomorrow morning—I mean, this morning. I miss my tights already. I'll come back first thing. Hey, Sloane, want to call me an Uber?"

"A cab, certainly. We prefer to use city cabs in this household, madam."

"Of course." Peaches yawned and the group dispersed, with me heading straight for bed. One last check of my phone before my head hit the pillow assured me that my husband had not yet messaged. Luckily, I was too exhausted to fret.

Chapter Eight

The next morning arrived far too soon. Still, it was almost ten o'clock before I dragged myself out of bed, dressed, and scrambled down to the breakfast room, only to find Rupert ending a meeting with the security staff, a meeting it appeared he'd held over coffee.

"What have I missed?" I asked as the men and women were leaving the room.

"Come join me, Phoebe," Rupert urged. "Would you like eggs and bacon? I had Cook prepare a full English for all who wished ample fortification this morning, and we could do likewise for you."

"Thank you, but I'm still stuffed from last night. Cereal and yogurt work for me."

Rupert caught the eye of one of the kitchen staff who hastened off to comply.

"Any sign of Clive?" I asked once she had exited.

"Surveillance picked up a black van passing by the estate on at least two occasions last night, and we believe that Clive may have been whisked away in that vehicle, the license plates of which we hope to have scanned through the police database. Admittedly, those services are not easily accessed without Evan's assistance."

A bowl of muesli and a dish of yogurt arrived before me. I smiled at the young woman, who grinned back before slipping away again.

"However," Rupert continued, "we have reason to believe that the van has not left London and, most likely, not even the Belgravia/Chelsea vicinity. We continue to patrol the streets seeking a sign, though no doubt the perpetrators will remain well-hidden."

So, Rupert had recovered from last night's blow, believing himself fully in control of a situation that was clearly wildly out of hand. I took a sip of coffee, noting carafes on the table with plenty of clean mugs for anyone to drop by and recharge.

"Rupert, who knows about your agency smartphone?" I asked.

He looked up, seeming puzzled by the question. "What a query, Phoebe. Why do you ask?"

"Because Dex and Jason knew about the phone's capacity to disarm security systems and disable locked and alarmed doors. In fact, they knew a lot more about our operations than we agreed to disclose to anyone."

"Phoebe, surely you realize that in a house this size, it is difficult, if not impossible, to maintain a vow of secrecy around matters involving a tool of this capacity. Of course, the lads have seen me use it multiple times."

"Don't you see what a security hole that leaves, not only in your household, but in the entire agency operation? Evan has lectured us again and again" (in my case the lecturing always came with side benefits), "about how crucial it is to keep this technology secure, because if it ever should fall into the wrong hands—"

"I keep my phone with me at all times, Phoebe, as I assume do you, and I assure you that it rarely leaves my possession for a single moment, so let us dispense with this irritating discussion, given that we have far greater issues with which to deal."

I almost couldn't believe that he had made such a statement but I knew better than to push things. It hadn't always been like this between us. Once, we had been close to the point of holding Wednesday knitting meet-ups but all that had changed. Was it just because I had married his son or were there deeper issues afoot? "Okay, let's just leave that topic for now. What about the book, or what we assume to be a book? When can we access that lab you mentioned and find out what's really behind this?" I asked.

Rupert checked his watch. "Very soon, Phoebe, very soon. I will call you when we are ready to proceed. Pardon me while I check the status further with my staff. May I leave you alone to dine?"

"I'm fine on my own, thanks. You go ahead and I'll catch up with you."

After he'd left, I sat flipping through my phone before pulling up my email and sending a few hasty messages. When Evan did contact me, what would I tell him that wouldn't worry or possibly distract him from his case? I'd ponder that later. Right then, I decided to wolf down my breakfast and join Rupert to see if

I could urge matters on. By now, I was beyond frustrated at having to wait a moment longer to see this mysterious object.

I almost collided with Peaches in the central hallway.

"I was practically frisked at the door trying to get in here," she exclaimed. "It was all I could do to prove that I am truly me and, seriously, who else could I be? There's only one, right? Dex had to step in and assure the guards that I am on the team. Who are all these dudes, anyway?"

"The new security personnel, hired from a supposedly elite team," I told her, gazing around at the uniformed individuals standing in groups, discussing what looked to be maps on their tablets. "Rupert brought them in because their jobs in the past have included guarding heads of state."

"That's what my Jamaican gran used to call 'shutting the gate after the goat wanders off,'" Peaches said. "Are they trying to find Clive, too?"

"The Roadside Team—some on motorbikes—are on that detail."

"Jeez," she said, "there are so many potential holes in this operation I feel a draft the size of a hurricane blowing in."

"That's not the half of it. I'm worried about the security of the agency technology, too. Come, let's track down Rupert."

But that turned out to be more difficult than expected. For one thing, the mansion was huge and I'd only seen a small part of it during a guided tour by Evan. What rooms we didn't use regularly mostly remained off my radar. The rooms and rooms of antiques, the comfortably well-appointed reception areas, the kitchens, dining rooms, and bedrooms I was familiar with, and now I had become acquainted with Rupert's private quarters as well. After taking Peaches up and down the three levels at least twice, it baffled me where that man had gone. His private quarters were out of bounds, Sikh Aad informed us, but he assured us that Rupert was not there.

"Oh, come on, Addy, where is he?" Peaches asked.

"I do not know this," he reiterated, standing at his post by the door, "but I will ask my team if they have seen him."

After several minutes watching the man on his phone, it was determined that no one had seen Sir Rupert for nearly thirty-five minutes.

"Is Rupert even still on the premises?" I asked the housekeeper when we arrived back downstairs. She assured me that he was, as far as she knew, and that Sloane, too, was present but either couldn't—or possibly wouldn't—say exactly where. I suspected that she didn't have a clue.

We were standing back in the central hall, my frustration mounting, when Sloane suddenly descended the stairs with four guards, one of whom carried a silver tray covered by a dishcloth.

Sloane caught my eye in passing. "Good morning, Phoebe, Peaches. Please do follow me," he said. "We will take breakfast in the back room."

Breakfast? We took off after him, baffled as he led us deeper toward the rear of the house to a set of stairs. I always had believed that they descended to what I assumed was the basement, only once we reached the bottom of the landing, I realized it wasn't the basement I had expected. Though there were laundry facilities along with the usual storage areas, the short corridor ended with an elevator.

Sloane instructed the guards to wait there. He passed the tray to Peaches and proceeded to swipe a keycard to unlock the lift, at which point Peaches and I were ushered in. In seconds, we were descending.

"This thing on the tray is heavy enough for me to figure out that it isn't breakfast we're escorting," Peaches remarked.

I peeked under the cloth to see a corroded black receptacle. My heart pounded in my ears. "Definitely not breakfast, unless we're planning to up our iron quotient," I said. "I believe this is the mysterious artifact which Clive risked his neck to claim."

"A book in a box, right?" she pressed.

"Possibly."

The elevator lurched to a halt, the doors opened, and we stepped into another short hall lit by a row of ceiling lights.

"What is this—a bunker?" Peaches exclaimed, looking up.

"Follow me, please," Sloane urged, which we did, straight down the hall and through a set of electronically locked doors, until we were standing in a large, overbright whitewashed room filled with nothing but broad tables and a variety of equipment like microscopes and high-intensity lamps.

Rupert stood waiting. "Welcome to my lab," he said.

"You have a private lab?" I exclaimed.

"Somewhat outdated, I must say, but yes. When Mildred and I first purchased the house in 1989, beneath the basement lay an old air raid shelter. I turned it into a lab during my Interpol years—before the Agency of the Ancient Lost and Found was created, that is—as a means by which to safely inspect ancient objects without necessitating the involvement of outside agencies. We ceased using it after the creation of the newer facility."

I was stunned. "Why didn't I know about this?"

"Phoebe, I am certain that there are still a great many details about your life that I have yet to discover. Penelope, please don the gloves provided, remove the object from the tray, and place it on the table there." He was referring to what appeared to be a semitransparent table upon which an open glass case rested. A lighting system illuminated the entire surface from underneath.

"And you have an aging, humidity-controlled case over a light table?" Don't ask me why I was so surprised. It made perfect sense and yet I found it unaccountably annoying.

Peaches did as she was asked, carefully placing the object where indicated. "All right, so let's get this party started. What is inside this iron—is it iron?—box."

"It's lead," Rupert said as we gathered around. "In the Middle Ages, they believed that lead would not corrode over time but, as you can see, it will do so in moist environments, which we believe was the situation in which this item once rested, thanks to Phoebe's sleuthing. If I'm not mistaken, this would have once rested inside a wooden chest that has long since disintegrated."

I pulled on a pair of nitrile gloves while studying the receptacle, which was not in as bad a shape as I had expected, despite the corrosion. It had a gold lock set into the side, but it was the cross on the lid that immediately caught my attention. "Templar," I whispered. "It's a Templar strongbox!"

"Okay," Peaches said, "what is a Templar strongbox, besides a chest that the Templars kept stuff in?"

"But that's exactly what's so incredible, Peach—very little remains of Templar belongings, so to find this is fantastic!" I pulled out my phone, hit Record, and began capturing the moment: "Black lead box approximately twenty-eight centimeters long by sixteen centimeters wide and a depth of ten centimeters, or eleven by six by four inches," I said while running the phone over the item. Switching it off, I stepped back and met Rupert's eye. "We really could use a conservationist for this."

"Yes, indeed, but we cannot risk bringing one in," Rupert said. "The last one on the list disappeared without a trace. We shall just proceed on our own, beginning with the lock, which appears to be intact."

Peaches pulled out her phone and pressed the lock app. Holding it over the gold mechanism, she announced: "Simple construction there. Do you happen to have a long, sharp object I can use?"

"Most certainly." Rupert passed her a steel pick. After seconds of jimmying, the lock clicked open and Peaches reached in to lift the lid. The gleam of gold within was unmistakable. "Another box inside, this one of pure gold!" she exclaimed.

Neither Rupert nor I tried to stop her from lifting the gold box out of the lead shell and placing it to the right of the glass case. "Presumably gold is in no danger of suffering from climatic fluctuations so it's still pristine but, wow, look at that—gold, not solid, though, too light—but still, wow! Why would the Templars keep a Bible in a gold container?"

"That, Penelope, is the question," said Rupert while rubbing his gloved hands together. "It may not, in fact, be a Bible, but how can any other kind of book not have avoided destruction along with the Templar persecution? Anything else would have been destroyed as heretical."

"Unless it had been hidden before the dissolution," I mused.

I gazed at this plain gold box, devoid of decoration typical of the time, such as inset precious stones that often adorned containers for special versions of the Bible. All books would have been hand-copied and usually exquisitely illustrated, making them extremely valuable in the first place, but why hide this one? This gold receptacle had nothing on the surface but engraved flourishes and an embossed Templar cross on the lid.

"What's so important that this Bible gets its own gold box and is worth killing someone to get hold of?" Peaches asked. "I mean, I get that Bibles were important, as is gold, but still, wouldn't Bibles have been plentiful in the Middle Ages, at least among the upper classes?"

"Among the upper classes they existed, for certain, but being so costly to produce, they were still not plentiful," Rupert said. "As for value, a Gutenberg Bible, which was the first book printed with movable type and dates from 1455, recently sold for thirty-five million US dollars at auction, a figure which will give you some idea as to the value of these ancient tomes. This book, if it is indeed a Bible, is centuries older, hand-copied, and associated with one of the most enigmatic groups of knights in the history of Christendom, and thus possibly holds even more value."

That caused the three of us to study the gold box with something close to reverence.

"Then there is the Codex Sassoon," I added, "a 1100-year-old Hebrew version of the Old Testament that just sold for thirty-eight million US dollars."

"Holy moly," Peaches said, whistling through her teeth. "So, what are we waiting for?"

I was beyond excited by now. "Shall we unlock the gold box?"

"By all means," Rupert said. "I neglected to mention the case's many features, including ultraviolet light at the flick of a switch. Evan designed that improvement some years ago but Sloane and I can attest to its excellent working condition today." I checked over my shoulder to note that the butler had exited.

"I will turn on the controls," Rupert continued, pushing a button on the side of the glass case. "Penelope, will you do the honor of unlocking the gold box?"

There was no need to ask her twice. Peaches had placed the box inside the case and had the lock picked and the lid open within seconds. She then proceeded to lift the contents with great care, placed it on the flat surface, and shut the glass case door.

The three of us stood, barely breathing, as we gazed through the glass at the leather-bound, gold-embossed book.

"Is it a Bible?" Peaches asked. "It's a lot smaller than I expected."

"I'm almost positive that it's a Psalter!" I exclaimed.

Chapter Nine

"What's a Psalter?" Peaches demanded, staring at the small leather book.

"It contains the Book of Psalms," I said, nearly breathless, "and often parts of the liturgy. The medieval Psalters that survived into modern times contain some of the most amazing examples of medieval art in existence because they were often lavishly illuminated."

"*Illuminated* meaning, in this context, illustrated," Rupert explained.

"I know what illuminated manuscripts are," Peaches remarked.

"Yes, well, regardless," Rupert continued, "I would not be at all surprised to discover that the Templars have fashioned something very unique into this small volume."

"To what end?" she asked, studying the deep-red leather book that, with the exception of the gold embossing, appeared fairly innocuous, if somewhat battered and mildewed. "I mean, weren't they a group of supposedly holy warriors, too busy defending or hacking at something—whatever knights did in those days—to read the Psalms?"

"They were Christian warriors—monks, in fact—Penelope," Rupert explained sternly, "which implies a certain adherence to the Christian faith and, no doubt, to some kind of regular worship. However, since the Order was somewhat secretive in nature, no one has been able to determine the precise nature of their religious rituals."

"Remember that there have been hints of mysterious ceremonies involving kissing among men and who knows what other heinous practices," said I, tongue-in-cheek, "but I suspect most of that was fake news, perpetuated by the forces that wanted to gain control of the Templar wealth."

"And if there was homosexuality, so what?" Peaches remarked.

"For us 'so what,' but for the times, that was a punishable offense," I pointed out, but of course she knew all that but never missed a chance to lodge her outrage. "The Templars were tortured into providing confessions to all types acts, which the society of the time considered indecent and blasphemous. Most supposed confessions were later recanted."

"Nevertheless," said Rupert, "no one would deny that the Knights Templar most likely had something to hide, and what better way to secure their secrets than in what appears to be a volume of a religious or liturgical nature? This little book could, indeed, be worth killing over, if it should lead to some secret trove of riches."

"Even if it doesn't lead to untold riches, the book itself is immensely valuable, especially if we can decipher who hid it in the crypts originally, as well as decode its contents," I said, itching to flip open that cover and get started.

"Decode." Peaches was gazing at me. "Ah, right—the medieval period was notorious for weaving symbolism and secrets into almost everything, even architecture."

"Exactly. Almost every second medieval item holds symbolic meaning. First a person must read the text—should there be writing involved—and then they must study the illustrations, which may ultimately tell another story or even layer one meaning onto another, not that our modern understanding can easily grasp all those nuances."

"But we have before us what might be the only book in existence prepared and illustrated for the Templars, right? No wonder Clive Hogarth wanted to hide it and that mysterious woman wants to steal it. Shall we get started?" Peaches prompted.

I turned to Rupert expectantly, seeing the same eager anticipation in his eyes as I was sure registered in mine.

And yet still we hesitated. Maybe it was because opening that book seemed so momentous—pages that had remained closed under a shroud of secrecy for centuries—or maybe it was because we felt unprepared to deal with either an ancient manuscript or the secrets that probably lay within—Templar gold? How long had that gilded carrot lured treasure-seekers? But, for me, it was something else besides: the book made me feel strangely off-kilter.

"Please do proceed, Phoebe," said Rupert. "I fear that my hands are trembling at the moment but, as you can see, we had long-sleeved plastic gloves fitted into openings of the chamber, so that one can insert their hands inside without altering the humidity controls. I have found the gloves so attached to be quite useful in the past as they did not inhibit the movement of the fingers in the least, albeit those interior gloves are somewhat man-sized and your hands far smaller."

I shot him a look, suddenly just wishing he'd be quiet while I removed the nitrile gloves and stuck my arms elbow-deep into the plastic sheaths. That allowed me to lean over the glass and gaze through the case, which appeared to be shifting oddly. I blinked and things became briefly clearer. "The glass is magnified?"

"Oh, yes, I did neglect to mention that, but we have found that feature amazingly useful in the past."

Carefully—as carefully as possible given that the gloves felt awkward over my much smaller fingers—I lifted the cover and gently eased it open. Immediately, my eyes fell to the frontispiece where a large, blood-red capital T with golden edging lay centered. Beneath the roof of the letter, robed knights riding horses and wielding swords galloped, while a golden dome loomed in the distance.

"Jerusalem," I whispered. A single line of Gothic script lay below. "And Latin text," I said. "It's beautiful!"

"It says: The Book of Holy Psalms, with the capital *T* so captured in that amazing illumination. Astounding artistry! Look at the detail in those red crosses emblazoned on the knights' shields!" said Rupert, leaning forward, nearly breathless himself.

"Yes," I whispered, trying to shake the strange blurred vision that had hit with such nauseating force the moment that I touched the book. Maybe I was nervous or just overwhelmed. "It's written on vellum," I whispered, "probably sheepskin. Okay, here goes another page." With excruciating care, I attempted to lift open the first page, but it appeared stuck to the one below it. "Damn." Actually, I said much worse.

Pulling my hands out of the sleeves, I stepped away, the room spinning. Peaches caught me before I fell backward. "Whoa, Phoebe!" she exclaimed. "Got you, woman. Rupert, grab a chair!"

In seconds, I was sitting on a stool, my head between my knees. It was several minutes before I could even lift my head. "That Psalter is covered in death," I whispered, gazing into Peaches's eyes.

She moistened her lips. "Okay...you mean metaphorically, right? The actual book looks to be in pretty good shape, maybe just a bit roughed-up."

"People have died trying to get hold of that, and more will die trying," I whispered.

"Shit, are you talking woo-woo again? Rupe, Phoebe's talking woo-woo. Hey, snap out of it, woman." She snapped her fingers before my face. "You know how I get the heebie-jeebies when you go into one of these states."

"Of course," I said, rubbing my eyes. "Sorry."

"Do not apologize, Phoebe," Rupert said. "In any event, it is best to allow the book to sit for a period of time in the moisture-controlled environment in order to loosen those pages to good effect. In the meantime, let us retreat back upstairs where you can rest. We can return to this endeavor later."

"Is it safe here?" Peaches inquired, looking at the Psalter.

"So I hope," he said. "We have now equipped the guards—indeed everyone working in this house—with a tracker to ensure that we know exactly where every individual is at all times. If anyone descends in the elevator—the only way in or out of the lab that is commonly known—both Sloane and I will be alerted immediately. No one has been given clearance but the three of us and Sloane. Meanwhile, we will keep five armed guards posted at the elevator doors at all times."

"Is that the agency program that alerts you to where everyone is?" Peaches asked.

Rupert appeared annoyed at the question. "It is. In this instance, the more eyeballs, the better."

I didn't have the energy to argue either way.

"An excellent idea. It is based on the very same technology that Evan devised for our tracker app, and as I deduced, it can be easily transferred to any agency device. Let us proceed upstairs and I will hasten to put this plan into motion. Phoebe, can you walk?"

"Of course I can walk," I said, unaccountably grumpy. I didn't know what was happening to me but it left me feeling disorientated. We left the lab the same way that we had entered—via the elevator. Just before the doors slid closed, I glimpsed the Psalter, bathed in light inside the glass case. I itched to turn that first page while simultaneously feeling desperate to get as far away from the book as I could.

Upstairs, the world returned to normalcy, if normal could be considered a house filled with uniformed, armed people. Even Rupert's regular employees appeared disgruntled. Rupert declared his intention to bring everyone together for what he referred to as a "pep talk." "We will confer together later," he told Peaches and me before scurrying off.

"Peach," I said the moment he had disappeared, "there are far too many unknown people hanging around here and I don't care how well-vetted they are. It's as if we just opened ourselves up to an even greater potential for infiltration. If there was one mole, there could be more."

"I agree one hundred and fifty percent," she told me. "Add to that how Rupe has been commandeering the agency's technology. I'm going to dash home and pick up my kit. I'll be staying here with you tonight. I don't care how many minions Sir Rupe has on a string, as your bodyguard I want to keep you in my sights."

"I'm fine," I protested halfheartedly.

"You are not fine. You had an episode—or whatever you call it—down there and I'm afraid that you'll be talking in tongues soon. I'll be back within the hour." She took off, leaving me to trudge up to my rooms to collapse on my big lonely bed.

So, I thought, as I lay there staring up at the ceiling, something about that book triggered a reaction in me, a sense that time was pressing in too closely, as if all the trauma that book had once provoked threatened to do so again—already had, if the wounded guard and Clive Hogarth were any indication. But why did I feel that—besides the Clive incident, I mean? What was I picking up? I knew nothing about the book for certain except that it had been hidden for years, even centuries, and yet...

And then my phone began ringing. I sat up. "Unknown name," announced my secret caller but I knew at once who it was. I pounced on the phone and hit Talk. "Evan!" I exclaimed.

"Phoebe, my love, I can't talk for long, but I needed to hear your voice as well as tell you that I'm all right, but I won't be able to return home for a while yet. God, I miss you." It was like his voice bathed me in warmth—deep, rich, comforting, and exciting all at once. "Tell me that the weather is fine in London."

Weather used to be our code for potential problems and now had become a kind of joke. I glanced out the window to where the sun shone cold and clear on a London November day. "Clear skies here," I assured him. "How about you?"

"Slightly overcast with a pending storm on the horizon but all is under control, or will be soon. And how is Dad getting along? I don't have time to call him at the moment."

"I promised to keep an eye on him, and I have, but, Evan, I have to tell you something."

"Can it wait, love? I really must dash. I'm making this call on stolen time, as it is."

"Yes, of course."

Endearments, which I'll just keep to myself, passed between us in brief, fleeting words that said everything I needed to hear, emotionally, at least. Suddenly, I felt fortified, as if I could handle anything.

Yes, I could have squeezed in a heads-up about the true events happening in my London microclimate, but to what end? I just wanted to protect that man and worrying about his father wouldn't help. I'd handle things here.

When Peaches arrived later with her suitcase, I was still floating. "Evan called," I told her when I met her at the door of my suite. "He's definitely into something significant wherever he is, but at least I know he's all right."

"And what did you tell him?" she asked, dropping her bag by the door.

"That there are clear skies over London."

"No! You didn't hint at anything going on here?" she exclaimed.

"There wasn't time. Besides, imagine how he'd respond if I told him that his father has gotten himself involved in the theft of a priceless artifact from the Temple Church, which has resulted in kidnapping, assault, and attempted murder? He's thousands of miles away on a sensitive case, Peach, I didn't want to worry him."

"You're married to the man. You each promised to love, honor, protect, and worry the hell out of one another until death do you part."

I laughed a little sadly. "Yes, but there are exceptions."

"No exceptions. The least you could have done was give him a heads-up weather report: 'Hurricane Rupert storming through London. Batten down hatches' or something like that."

"Why, when he can't do anything from wherever he is, and all this would do is distract him from his case? I want him to stay focused on remaining safe and doing his job. We can handle this on our own. Besides, I didn't lie to him; I just didn't disclose the details."

"Hope that doesn't come back to bite you in the butt, Phoebe, that's all I can say. Ev's kind of big on truth and honesty, but I totally get your thinking, even if it's not what I would do. Anyway, enough of that. I was thinking on the way over here: supposing we get back to work on the Psalter, only this time you don't touch the book, I do? You and Rupe can photograph the pages; he can translate the Latin while you decode the symbols, or whatever we'll find in there. What do you think?"

"Excellent!" I exclaimed. "Let's get back to work" and off the topic of deceiving my husband because it had begun to bother me. Though I believed myself completely blameless in the desire to keep my husband safe, I knew he probably wouldn't agree.

Back downstairs, we tracked Rupert to the library where he was sitting at the big oak desk, feverishly researching medieval Psalters with his tablet, his laptop, and several books spread on the table before him, all while occasionally dispatching orders to somebody somewhere. The man was back in his element, and regardless of how dangerous this situation was or the fact that a friend had been kidnapped, today he was clearly feeding on adrenaline.

"Just as I expected," he said without looking up, "very little remains of similar books or, in fact, of most religious manuscripts of the period. It turns out that, contrary to my earlier assumption that holy books such as Bibles and Psalters would be sacrosanct, it seems that many were, in fact, destroyed during the Reformation for possessing illustrations considered to be 'too Catholic.'"

"I forgot how the Reformation razed so much to the ground," I remarked.

Rupert continued. "Yes, truly, can you imagine? By the way, we have come no closer to locating Clive, though the lads have been out surveying the streets on their mopeds for hours now, and yet still I remain convinced that the kidnappers are holed up nearby. They clearly require both Clive together with the Psalter in order to unlock whatever mysteries they hope to obtain. Thus, we are anticipating another attack, possibly tonight."

"Is everyone on staff accounted for?" Peaches asked.

"Well, not completely. Dex said he was to return home to fetch his things yesterday but has yet to return. In the meantime, I trust that the kidnappers are treating Clive in good fashion as, presumably, he will be of no use to them whatsoever if further harm should befall him." He paused to catch his breath as much as anything but, in doing so, he caught sight of Peaches and me fully for the first time. "Phoebe, how are you feeling now? Recovered, I trust?"

"I'm much better, Rupert, thank you. By the way, Evan called."

He swung around on his swivel chair and rose to his feet. "Truly? That is excellent news! Is he well? Will he be calling me also? I fear that my phone has been very tied up today as I communicate with all and sundry regarding this abduction."

"He said that I should send you his love but that he didn't have time to call us both. He's fine, though, Rupert, that's the main thing."

"Oh, yes, very good, very good indeed. I am delighted to hear that the lad is safe. Did you, ah, say anything else to him regarding our present circumstances?"

"Do you mean about the kidnapping, theft of a priceless book, and possible attempted murder?" Peaches inquired mildly.

But Rupert was too fixed on my reply to show his usual annoyance.

"I didn't," I assured him. "I saw no benefit in worrying him, so when he asked how the weather was in London, I simply told him the truth." I pointed toward the windows overlooking the garden, where sunlight lit up the last of the yellow roses.

Rupert nearly sagged with relief. "Most excellent, thank you, Phoebe. I am indebted."

I didn't mention that my decision was more to protect my husband than to collude with his errant father but, in truth, it resulted in the same thing. "One more thing: I want you to turn your tracker on so I know where you are at all times."

"Phoebe, surely you are not implying that I would do something nefarious without your knowledge—" He caught my eye, sighing. "Very well," and used his phone to comply.

I checked my screen to ensure that his dot was transmitting. It was. "Great, now let's return to work downstairs. Peach has a good idea on how to proceed without me becoming confused, or whatever was happening earlier. We really need to forge ahead."

He agreed, and we took a quick lunch in the library before proceeding, though we couldn't even get through our soup without constant interruptions of one sort or another. Rupert and Sloane were head of operations with Addy now leading the security team, and the traffic coming in to provide progress reports along with the constant pinging of Rupert's phone made the food near indigestible. Peaches and I were also busy checking out the new tracking information to assure ourselves that everyone was accounted for. Dex's dot, I noticed, was making its way toward Belgravia. Before we had finished lunch, he was back safely in the fold. I made a mental note to track him down for a little convo before the day was done.

By midafternoon, we were back in the bunker lab. This time, I kept from having direct contact with the book, except to steal quick glances at it through the glass. Still, being that close to it had an effect on me. It was all that I could do to keep focused on the work ahead.

Meanwhile, Peaches managed to carefully separate the pages using one of Rupert's gold letter openers, and the hours spent in the dry environment inside the case had eased the process along. Rupert photographed each page, sent them to me, and I studied them one by one on my tablet.

"We need to carbon date the vellum to be sure," I said, "but it looks as though these entries were made over many decades; there appear to be subtle variations in the inks used, and even in the hand that copied the Latin script."

"I believe the Psalter is, in truth, a kind of Templar chronicle," Rupert said, shoving his glasses farther up his nose.

"I think so, too," I said.

"In the midst of each Psalm, those brilliant illuminations appear to focus primarily on depicting Templar history," he continued, "including battles such as the Siege of Acre in 1191, the reclamation of Jerusalem in 1224, followed by its loss again in 1291, various Crusades along the way, and ending with the arrival of the Mongol and Mamluk conquests in the early 1300s. The greatest example of illumination artistry surrounds the events of 1120 when King Baldwin II of Jerusalem granted the Knights Templar a portion of the sacred enclosure in which to live, thus establishing their title. Indeed, the golden dome of the Temple Mount nearly glows. With so much gold it is almost painful to look at it," Rupert exclaimed.

All the illustrations, with the exceptions of the final entries, were magnificent—large, central, full-page illuminated art with borders of various flora and fauna. Everything was shown in exquisite detail, with four or five illustrations per major event, across several pages of Psalms per occasion. Rupert had no difficulty identifying the events pictured based on his thorough knowledge of the Templar timeline. Background details were so precise that the action could be accurately associated with a certain historical happening in a specific country at a certain time—the Holy Sepulcher in Jerusalem, the court of France, even Notre-Dame, were all easily recognizable.

"This most certainly is a history of the Templars, most likely prepared or commissioned by the Templars themselves," said Rupert. "It is such an astounding discovery that I cannot even begin to estimate its importance." He was wiping his brow with one of the handkerchiefs he always carried.

"It belongs in a museum or an archive," I said, "and must ultimately end up in one." *Once we can determine how to get it there without incriminating my father-in-law.*

"I agree, Phoebe," Rupert began. "Please believe me when I say that at no time did I ever suspect that Hogarth had sequestered such a priceless artifact in the Temple Church. Had I known the true nature of the object so hidden, I would have seen at once that he in no way could be said to have owned it by right. I have been appallingly duped, regardless of the circumstances." He was gazing at me as if desperately wanting or hoping that I would believe him.

Only I didn't. I suspected that he knew the value of whatever Hogarth had hidden, even if he didn't know its exact nature. Otherwise, why had it been hidden in the first place? The two old friends had probably percolated excitement over the possibility of having one more adventure together.

I only hoped that Rupert had not been involved in the initial robbery from the crypt, yet I wouldn't put it past him. His years in Interpol had only come after a lively quasi-criminal past, where he had operated an illicit antiquities business masquerading behind his top-drawer Chelsea shop, now closed. If it weren't for Evan stepping in to firmly steer his father onto the legal track, who knows where Rupert would be right now? No, there was more to this Psalter than a history of the Templars, no matter how incredible that was in itself. Rupert was holding something back.

"Regardless, Rupe," Peaches weighed in, "what I don't understand is why Hogarth wanted to hide this in the first place. I mean, he couldn't possibly sell it unless on the black market, though it's worth millions, right? I suspect there's something else hidden in this book that makes it especially interesting, don't you think?"

"Quite possibly," he said, looking away.

"Oh, you sly dog—you know there is," she pressed. Peaches didn't do subtle as a rule, especially with Rupert.

"Let's get back to work," I said quickly before putting my head into my hands, trying to fight the headache that had been warring between my eyes all afternoon. "We need to study those figures in the margins, too."

"So, we'd better take lots of close-up shots of those," Peaches said. "You okay, Phoebe?"

"Fine—just a headache." What I didn't want happening was for Rupert to close down on us, become defensive, and return to his secretive self—not when we were all working together at last. I knew that there were still plenty of things that he was keeping from us, critical information that he was holding back somewhere. Still, it was crucial that we get to the bottom of this mystery, and fast. I had this terrible sense that everything could unravel without a moment's notice.

Nothing we saw in that first run-through of the Psalter went beyond what was currently known about the Order, according to recorded history, at any rate, and yet there were plenty of baffling figures, as well as ornamentation in the margins and under or within capital letters, that appeared to hint at a much deeper tale.

Our goal that afternoon was to photograph each page for further study, as it would require far more than a few hours to decipher what secrets the book might hold. To that end, the work progressed quickly; each two-page spread carefully photographed and added to an electronic file that only Rupert, Peaches, and I were to share for the time being.

"From the best I can determine, this chronicle of the Templars so illustrated in Psalter form ends around the early 1300s, prior to the Order's dissolution," Rupert said, cleaning his glasses before gazing down at the final page. "I say this based on the fact that the history ends abruptly with a half-completed illustration and an incomplete Psalm. The last recorded Psalm is number 146, which ends mid-verse with the line: *May the praise of God be in their mouths and a double-edged sword in their hands, to inflict vengeance on the people, to bind their kings with fetters..."*

I looked up. "What is the illustration accompanying that one?"

"It, too, is incomplete," Rupert told me, peering into the case. "It appears to be the outline of a large castle or stone building, positioned on a hill."

"With a valley in the background," Peaches said. "Here, the photo is on its way to you now."

"What if whoever recorded that last page of the Psalter hid the book in order to preserve it?" I asked.

"And endeavored to preserve the book because it contains some Templar secret that the Order was desperate to keep safe?" Rupert suggested. "If they were in danger, or possibly threatened in some way, they might take their Psalter with them because, I assume, they had something to hide."

"Because a Psalter would attract no notice, whereas something like gold or other valuables definitely would," I said. My phone pinged and I stared down at the picture, which was exactly as Rupert had described: incomplete, as if both the illustration and the scripting of the Psalm had been cut short. "That castle could be anywhere, whereas all the preceding illustrations are clearly identifiable by the landscape features," I said. "It's as if the recording of this book was suddenly interrupted."

"Maybe the recorders knew that the Order was doomed," Peaches suggested. "Maybe they stopped writing and illustrating the chronicle because there was trouble afoot."

"But where were they at the time?" I asked. "And who was responsible for writing the text and painting those illustrations?"

"They could be based anywhere," said Rupert, "as the Templars had estates and strongholds all over Europe and the Middle East. However, Jacques de Molay was the Grand Master at the time—the last Grand Master, in fact—so we must assume that he was responsible for the final entries. He most likely did not pen them himself but had others in his Order do so."

"So, if we could find out where this last entry was made, perhaps we could locate whatever the Templars hoped to keep safe?" I asked, getting to my feet.

"Most certainly," said Rupert, his attention fixed on me. "Yes, indeed!"

"If this aborted entry was made under the jurisdiction of Jacques de Molay, where was he when he suddenly stopped the recording of the Psalter?" I asked, my headache thundering side by side with the fever of discovery.

"What became of him again?" Peaches asked.

"He was arrested, tortured, and later executed by Philip IV of France, who, in 1307, in order to lay claim to their property in France, had every French Templar arrested and handed over to the Inquisition," said Rupert.

"So, de Molay was in France at the time?" Peaches asked.

"Indeed," said Rupert. "He was burned at the stake in front of Notre-Dame Cathedral."

Peaches gazed from Rupert to me. "Well, I wouldn't think that France would be the best place to hide anything, given that the king was busily trying to crush the Order and had all Templar property under his fist. Would Jacques have had a heads-up for that?"

"In a manner of speaking," Rupert said, as if the sudden spark that had briefly fired him up was dissipating. He sat down heavily in one of the wooden chairs across from me. "De Molay was striving to reform the Order as support for the Crusades was waning and, additionally, he desired to fund another focused attempt to win back Jerusalem for the Christians. To enact these endeavors would grant the Templars the authority with which the Order had begun, and strengthen their case for continuing. He must have known that there were forces afoot attempting to disband the Order, and that there had been discussions centered on unifying the Knights Templar with the Knights Hospitaller. And yet, I believe he was unaware that any power would dare strike the death blow to what had been such an honored institution."

"In other words, he had a sense of false security," Peaches said.

"Very likely." Rupert rubbed his temples. "He was an older man by this time, in his late sixties, when first he became the Grand Master and soon after the trouble began. Let us rest for now. We are all quite spent. Let us retire upstairs for the duration of the day, give our minds a reprieve, and then come back to the task at hand after supper this evening, when we are well-fortified. Though there is much work to be done, our bodies are only human and, I fear, I must attend to matters upstairs, in any event."

"Someday, I just want him to say: 'I'm knackered. Let's take a break,'" Peaches whispered as we headed for the elevator.

"Maybe you and I can keep working down here?" I suggested, thinking that I didn't want to be parted from that Psalter for a moment.

"It's musty, damp, and probably bad for the health, not to mention that you're feeling bad effects already. Let's take our tablets upstairs. We have everything in photograph form, anyway," Peaches insisted.

For some reason, I was reluctant to leave the Psalter alone in its bunker home, though the protections put in place seemed foolproof. At the same time, nothing was ever truly foolproof, especially if one assumes that people could be fools, but I was powerless to do anything to fix things. I was experiencing a strange push-pull toward that book: I couldn't touch it yet didn't want to abandon it, either.

Peaches and I remained holed up in the library, researching for the rest of that afternoon until, several hours and a light supper later, Rupert joined us to resume our work. By then, Peaches had worked up a Templar timeline cheat-sheet to which we could refer while working on the decoding. Already, it was nine-thirty and the three of us were almost too exhausted to continue. I gazed down at my tablet where pictures of the illustrations and border ornamentation swam before my eyes. I'd been tracing an odd curlicue that seemed to trail in one unbroken though twisted line from page to page.

"Most likely a Templar Grand Master launched the chronicle," Rupert said, stifling a yawn. "Hugues de Payens was the first master appointed by the knights, but, across the 192 years of the Order's existence, of course there had been many others, ending with the aforementioned de Molay."

"So, Hugues de Payens probably initially commissioned the chronicle, which explains the variations in inks, scripts, and even the style of the paintings," I said, looking down at the illustrations accompanying the first Psalm.

"Quite possibly," Rupert agreed. "Certainly the illumination showing the Templar knights receiving the keys to the Temple Mount are some of the most magnificent of the entire Psalter, as well as being the event to which de Payens is most closely associated. If you scroll down three pages, you will see de Payens being given the land in Holborn to establish the first Temple Church in London."

"Boy, those guys got around," Peaches marveled, "from Jerusalem to London and everywhere in between."

"Indeed, it is a common misconception that people in the Middle Ages did not travel far because they lacked modern transportation. However, pilgrims journeyed to many holy sites throughout the Middle Ages, including to European cathedrals to view holy relics, and to Jerusalem, of course," said Rupert. "They believed that in so doing, they would guarantee themselves a place in heaven, or that it would cure an ailment."

"It gave them a bit of a road trip, too," Peaches remarked.

"Let us not forget *The Canterbury Tales*," I said, "one of the first recorded road trips in English literature."

"'The Wife of Bath is my fave," Peaches added. "I consider her a fun gal."

Rupert cleared his throat. "Yes, well, the Templars were initially established to protect these pilgrims journeying to the Holy Land, as the way was fraught with thieves and murderers that attacked and killed the travelers, and then later, the Order fought to win back the city of Jerusalem from the Muslims," Rupert continued, as if we didn't know all this.

I was barely listening as a message from Margaret had just popped on my screen, responding to a question I had posed earlier:

A chronicle of the Templars? If only such a thing existed or, if it did exist, if only it had survived! There have been rumors of a history of the Templars having been compiled and added to by successive generations of Grand Masters but, if such a thing really did unfold, it's been long lost. What are you up to, Phoebe? Tell Margaret.

I was about to respond when Peaches interrupted Rupert's rumination with: "What's with all these snails?"

I looked up. "Do you mean those little mollusks crawling among the foliage throughout the Psalter's borders?"

"Actually, they first appear about halfway through," Peaches said, "and they strike me as so odd. I mean, look at this one." She held up her tablet to where she had pinched out the photo of an illuminated border to better reveal a snail peeking out from under a forest of trailing vines. "They're almost jokey-looking, only who'd have thought of the Templars as a bunch of wild and crazy guys? Is this like some kind of medieval Wile E. Coyote?"

I aborted my intended response to Margaret and zipped back a question concerning the symbolic meaning of snails in medieval art instead. When I looked up again, I said: "They did have their own odd-to-us sense of humor but this isn't intended to be jokey. Besides which, humor would vary according to whoever is the illustrator. The Templars probably had their own scribes, as did all monastic orders of the time, and maybe they decided to lighten things up?" I said, switching to my photos and scrolling through the illuminated pages until I found the one Peaches had identified.

That page began with what appeared to be the story of a snail, or snails, as they kept appearing after that. "I've seen snails in illuminated manuscripts before," I said. "I always thought of them as humorous ramblings of the scribes, since they often appear with other wild little doodles, like bare bottoms or grotesques breaking wind."

My phone pinged as Margaret's response came in: *Snails can have multiple meanings, depending on the context. Possibly they represent the Lombards; some say they stand for social climbers or even cowardice, and still others suggest that snails represent strength. In many cases, their presence is satirical in nature so it's necessary to consider the manuscript as a whole. I had a prof once who was convinced that, in some instances, snails stood for housewives because women remained mostly inside the family home at the time, and snails carry their houses on their backs. In other words, who knows for sure? Phoebe, what are you looking at?*

I looked up. Snails could equal women?

"People in the Middle Ages did have a very crude sense of humor, very crude indeed," Rupert was saying, warming to the topic. "Consider, if you will, the abundance of carvings present in even the most exalted cathedrals, where they are tucked away in various places and border on the obscene."

"Well, these snails aren't obscene, just weird and persistent," Peaches stated before Rupert could take another breath. "It's as if there's a story of a snail being told throughout the pages of the Psalter—a snail half-hidden in the foliage, a snail going about its slimy business. Here's one of a knight riding a snail. Now, what's that about?"

"Definitely symbolic of something," I said, cold shivers coursing down my spine.

"And then there's the foliage," Peaches continued. "It changes from page to page. When the illustrations show a French castle, the flowers in the margins are bluebells and buttercups, but a few pages over, they turn to berries and acorns."

"So, the vining foliage actually indicates both place and season," I said. "It must be—from spring to fall, from France to—?"

"There are palm trees in the Jerusalem illustrations, and the curling vines are like nothing we see here in England. The flora sets the place as much as the buildings do, only much more subtly," Peaches said.

"So, what is the foliage like on that last entry?"

Peaches pinched out the screen. "The drawings are unfinished but it looks like a weird flower of some sort—maybe a cyclamen?"

We were getting close to discovering something important. Even my fingers were tingling. "Rupert?"

But Rupert wasn't listening. He was fixed on the two men who had entered the room. An exhausted-looking Sloane stood accompanied by a stricken-looking man I did not recognize.

"Sir," Sloane began, "a terrible thing has occurred. Clive Hogarth has been located—dead, sir, quite dead."

Chapter Ten

"Dead?" Rupert exclaimed, getting to his feet. "But this can't be! Where? How?"

"Perhaps it's best if Louis, head of the Roadside Team, provides the details." Sloane turned to the man beside him, a thin man approximately fifty years of age with short gray-streaked hair, who gazed at Rupert as if reluctant to utter the words he was obliged to speak.

"Ah, sir, well, sir, we were driving down Fleet Street—"

"Fleet Street!" Rupert erupted. "What the devil were you doing on Fleet Street?"

"Ah, well, me and my team were seeking the gentleman we were tasked to find—one Clive Hogarth, sir—and one of the lads suggested we look there on account that Mr. Hogarth had been seen in the vicinity just days before."

"Who is this 'lad' that suggested such a thing?" Rupert demanded, his face turning redder by the minute.

"His name is Dex, sir. He was working with me tonight and—"

"And?" Rupert prompted. "You and Dex were on Fleet Street?"

"And Dex suggested we take a quick squint around the Temple Church, sir, and that's where we found him, on the grass, like. Real peaceful looking, as if he had just laid down and went to sleep—hands folded on his chest and everything. Oh, and a rose between his fingers."

Rupert began to pace. "This is unbelievable! Where is Dex?"

If possible, Sloane's expression became even more grim. "Apparently gone, sir."

"Gone?" Rupert stopped dead. "Gone where? Bring him back immediately!"

"He is not responding to our calls, sir, and his signal has disappeared off the tracker screen," Sloane explained.

"After he had apparently located the body, he slipped through the buildings and was gone before we noticed," Louis said.

"What do you mean 'before you noticed'! Was he not under your charge?" Rupert demanded.

"Ah, yes, sir, but we were too fixed on the body. There were three of us, all stricken with the sight of a dead man laid out before the Temple Church and, well, we didn't notice Dex leaving, sir. The other man with us was a bloke named George."

"What's wrong with you? Haven't you or George seen a dead man before?" Rupert erupted. "And what if you end up on CCTV?"

Peaches and I exchanged glances.

"We studied the blind spots, sir, and the body was placed in a blind spot. As soon as we saw the body, we took off."

"Well, you'll be caught on camera, won't you?"

"We were careful, sir. There was no sign of violence, other than the bullet wound from last night, but he looks as though he was laid out for a funeral."

"What about his complexion, his facial expression—did you note anything at all?" Rupert demanded.

"It was dark, sir," the man explained, "but I don't think he was shot or anything—a second time, I mean."

Rupert turned away, looking so distressed that I was afraid for his health.

I stepped up beside him. "Try to stay calm, Rupert."

"Do not presume to suggest I stay calm, Phoebe!" He turned to me. "This entire affair just goes from bad to worse!"

Sloane quickly dismissed Louis from the room. "Sir, security has been intensified and there is nothing more to be done this evening. I have recalled the remainder of the Roadside Team and told everyone to lay low until the police retrieve the body, which will doubtless be soon enough."

"And we can only hope that they don't trace Hogarth back here," Rupert said.

"May I suggest that you retreat to your rooms and rest?" Sloane said, taking on an authority with his employer that I had yet to gain with my father-in-law. "I shall send up a pot of tea along with your medications. Please do try to calm yourself, sir. Come along."

We watched as Sloane steered him upstairs, Rupert shooting him instructions the whole time.

I swore under my breath.

Peaches leaned over and whispered: "Are you thinking what I'm thinking?"

"That this whole abysmal situation has just gone from being a total mess to being a complete and utter disaster that is growing worse by the minute? I almost wish I'd told Evan the whole story."

"Forget about that for a moment. Now we know that Dex was an infiltrator and, if he was compromised, there are probably others."

"They're after the book, Peach, and I'm afraid that Dex and others have enough of an inside track to know where it is located, and maybe even how to get it. Let's go upstairs and keep working on decoding the Psalter. The key is to decode it before, or if, somebody snatches it."

We trudged back upstairs, past the numerous guards patrolling the house, none of whom made us feel any safer, and into my suite, where Peaches proceeded to barricade the door.

"Any one of those hired bozos could be on the take," she said. "What was Rupe thinking by hiring them?"

"He's getting desperate and starting to make mistakes." I watched as Peaches propped a chair under the door handle. "Ever since his illness in 2020, his judgment has been slipping. How's barricading the door going to help?" I asked.

"If anyone does try to get in, at least we'll have another warning." She turned to face me. "When was the last time you ran a bug scan in here?"

I shrugged. "Never—I am living under my father-in-law's roof and, until recently, with Evan." I stopped and gaped. "Damn—let's do a bug scan."

We set our phones and scanned every inch of my suite, finding no hidden surveillance devices, but Peaches wouldn't let that be a reason to relax. She took my phone and tablet out of my hands and went into the agency settings. After several minutes, she handed my devices back and said: "We are no longer transmitting through the agency satellite. We have gone dark. I notice that Rupert has turned his finder back on."

I widened my eyes. "I asked him to. I'm glad he's listening to me for once. So, you think Dex and that woman have been tracking us and listening to everything we say?"

"Maybe."

"So they could be working together."

"It would explain a few things, right?" she said. "And what if Dex had access to Rupert's devices? Didn't you say that he knew Rupe could disengage the CCTV cameras through his smartphone that night they stole the Psalter?"

"Dex did know that, though there's no way he should have. I brought the matter up with Rupert but he shut me down. Still, when Dex and Jason brought Clive here that night, they had plenty of opportunity to spy and even plant their own surveillance devices—so many damn ways to infiltrate Rupert's systems, when you think about it."

"What about Jason?"

"Seems legit. He went home and, as far as I know, went about his life. Dex is another story."

"So, the bad guys may already know that we're decoding the Psalter and that we may be getting closer to figuring it out."

"We *are* getting closer—I can feel it. All we have to do is discover where de Molay was physically when the Psalter pages ended. There were more Psalms than recorded in the chronicle so presumably he expected to record more entries. Rupert would have figured that out if he hadn't been so distracted."

"Well, de Molay couldn't have been in France because none of the flora trailing along the borders looks remotely French. Maybe Jerusalem?"

"Jerusalem was no longer in Christian hands by de Molay's time, so I doubt he could have left from there," I said.

"Wherever he was, he left in such a hurry that he never finished the last entries."

"But he didn't leave the book behind because eventually it ended up in London's Temple Church. That's important. I'm thinking that he probably took the Psalter with him, planning to complete the final Psalms while illustrating what he hoped would be his final contribution to the Order—fortifying its reputation by lobbying for another Crusade."

"Only he never had the chance," Peaches finished.

We stared at each other, our brains working furiously. "Maybe he gave the Psalter to some trusted person who managed to transport it to England before the proverbial ax fell," I added.

"Yeah, so maybe he took the Psalter with him but left something of great value behind, something that he couldn't risk taking to France, something priceless and difficult to transport," I said, a little breathless.

"Something that every Grand Master knew of through oral tradition—"

"Or through coded hints hidden in the Psalter," said I.

"Something like a priceless treasure," Peaches finished.

We stood gazing into space for a few minutes, deep in our own thoughts, before I continued: "What if Clive Hogarth, as former honorary Valiant Master

—a master who had no problem mucking around in the tombs of his predecessors and was supposedly a Templar historian— discovered the Psalter and knew enough about the treasure myth to believe it to be true?"

"So, he hides the Psalter in the Temple Church during the lockdown and bides his time, waiting for the perfect moment to make his move. He contacts his old bud, Rupe, and dangles the prospects of a great adventure before his eyes and—bingo—Rupe is in, hook, line, and sinker."

"Maybe heavy on the sinker part. Anyway, Hogarth is oblivious to the fact that he's attracted the attention of somebody who also knows about the treasure—maybe even through him. Either that, or he knows somebody is keeping an eye on him but thinks he can stay one step ahead."

"You mean Dex?" Peaches asked.

"No, I mean that mysterious woman. She and Hogarth knew each other, remember?"

"Okay, so all this is making sense," Peaches said, "at least enough to form a working premise. So, what do we do next?"

"We discover the location of the presumed buried treasure before Dex and the mysterious woman do, and then we go there and find it."

Peaches shook her head. "Just like that? Only Phoebe the Lost-Art Sniffer Dog can make that kind of glib statement and not sound ridiculous."

"What other option do we have?" I whispered. "We'll get nowhere staying here."

"That's for sure. If Clive Hogarth has expired, there is only one person left who can find the treasure, and that's you. Maybe Dex knows all about your special gifts like he knows about everything else. If that guy was in this whole thing from day one, soaking up all the information as one of Rupert's trusted 'lads,' I bet he knows plenty. If we could squeeze the info out of your sneaky dad-in-law right now, we'd probably discover that he's been plotting something with Clive for months, with the 'lads' part of the inside track."

She tossed her backpack onto a chair. "It just makes me so furious! Like, from now on, every time Rupe gets involved in something, he'll be using agency technology if Evan's not around to keep him in line."

My stomach lurched. "I hope Dex doesn't know about me."

"Don't count on it. Half the criminal world knows about you, Phoebe. Okay, let's get to work."

And we did, sitting in my lounge, flipping through our tablets, trying to identify more clues from the tangle of symbols locked inside the border foliage that trailed through the Psalter.

Peaches kept the timeline cheat-sheet in front of her. "The last recorded location of de Molay was in France, but the last Psalter entry is not based in France."

"Then our timeline is probably incomplete. Seems that this one only highlights the main events of the Order as a whole, but not all the smaller events along the way. Any luck in identifying that flower in the margins on the last page?" I asked.

"No, it's boggling." She looked up. "What are you doing?"

"Messaging Margaret. She'll know where de Molay was holed up before he headed to France and met his end."

Margaret must have been keeping her phone close by in case I contacted her because her one word response came through immediately. I looked across at Peaches. "Cyprus," I whispered.

"Cyprus?" Peaches glanced back to the half-finished Psalter drawing. "Then that strange flower *must* be a cyclamen!"

In seconds, we were both tracking down everything we could find online concerning the Templars in Cyprus.

"They briefly owned the entire island," Peaches gasped.

"They bought it from Richard the Lionheart."

"They had a large manor on a hill overlooking the bay, along with a fortification." I placed the half-drawn Psalter illustration next to the online photo. "The village of Foinikas became the seat of the Templars, built in a strategic location in order to defend critical trading routes. That's it!"

"I've never even heard of the place," Peaches marveled.

"Me, either, but it says here that it's a ghost town now. You know what that means, don't you?"

"We're going to Cyprus."

But going to Cyprus would be a logistical nightmare. There wasn't just the business of booking plane tickets—that was the easy part. Escaping Rupert's house without being detected, or even worse, being stopped, was by far the biggest issue. We suspected that the house was overrun with infiltrators and the thought of abandoning Rupert was wrenching.

"Look, they're not going to harm him now that Hogarth is gone," Peaches said.

"They won't hurt him if we take the Psalter, for certain. That's what they're really after."

"We're taking the Psalter?"

"What else can we do? Once it leaves the property, so does the reason for all this craziness, so we can't let it fall into enemy hands. Whoever has possession of the book could figure out the possible hiding place of the treasure, just as we have. It's not all that complicated once you know the Templar history."

"But we can't physically take it to Cyprus with us, can we?" she asked.

"No, of course not. Instead, we'll have to drop it off at the British Library on our way to the airport. That will check the repatriation box." Which just added another layer of complexity to our already fraught escape plans.

"Which you also make sound oh-so-easy," Peaches muttered. "Let's just drop it in the night deposit box marked 'Priceless Manuscripts Deposit,' shall we?"

"I'll think of something."

We booked our tickets using false identities from the selection of fake agency passports Evan kept locked in our safe. "Evan will know that we're using these," I told Peaches. "Every time that safe opens, it triggers an alert, but he'll notice that our trackers have gone dark long before then. He sets up an alert on his devices for that kind of thing."

"Bit of a control freak, isn't he? Anyway, my signal hasn't been reengaged since my return from Africa so it will be just you that he'll see disappear off the map and, yeah, that will worry the hell out of him. He'll know there's an emergency afoot but—" and she took a deep breath "—if he's on a job, he sometimes mutes those signals so he can concentrate, right?"

She caught my expression. "Don't look at me that way: Ev's been training me on the technicalities of these devices because he knows that you're so not into it, and you did tell him that the weather was fine in London, didn't you? He'll be unsuspecting."

"Yeah, okay, but it's enough trying to keep everything else straight," I complained, "like all these timewalking events playing with my head." I paused for a moment. "Does that sound like a whine?"

"I can almost hear the violin accompaniment." Then she broke into a grin. "Right, so you don't have to do and be everything, Phoeb. It's enough that you have all these special gifts. Let your security detail—" she thumbed her chest "—as in me, take care of most everything else."

I expelled a lungful of air that I hadn't realized I'd been holding. "Okay, so we can justify what we're doing here because we're trying to right a wrong, trying to solve a murder, attempting to protect my father-in-law by using ourselves as decoys, oh, and tracking down a possible treasure before the bad guys get hold of it. Did I cover everything?"

"That's enough. Now, let's get some rest, and you still need to pack, too. Tomorrow's going to be a long, long day. Recharge your devices, bring your auxiliary battery charger, and anything else you think you'll need."

I did as she suggested, and I always recharged my phone, anyway. That thing was my lifeline—communication central, defense system, alarm, everything. Yawning, I headed toward my room to pack, wondering which items of my gourmet wardrobe I'd take. "The guest room's all made up. Make yourself at home, Peach."

"Are you kidding? I'm sleeping in your room tonight. Just don't snore."

"You're always welcome to—it's a big enough bed—but what are you worried about? I don't have the Psalter in my care and, for once, I'm not really the center of this particular acquisition."

Peaches dug her toothbrush out of her kit bag and looked at me agape. "How can you be so obtuse for a very bright person, Phoeb? You keep forgetting that now that Clive is dead, maybe these slimeballs will realize that only one person can help fill in the dots leading from the Psalter to the treasure, or whatever the hell is behind this: you. Don't get complacent."

"I'm not complacent, just hopeful." At that moment, I felt so weary, so overwhelmed, and consumed by a headache that wouldn't abate. I could barely stand up, let alone think straight. "I'm hoping that I'm not on their radar."

"Don't count on it. They know about the phones. Who knows what else?"

"I just can't deal with this tonight, Peach. You're probably right about everything, as usual. Let's rest and hopefully I'll be in better shape in the morning. Our flight is so early."

I fell into a deep sleep as soon as my head hit the pillow but my brain didn't stay still. Images of snails slithered inside my dreams—snails riding horses, snails fighting with knights, snails sailing across the ocean blue. Finally, something jerked me awake. I thought for a moment that a snail was pounding on the inside of my skull with a baseball bat, but when I sat up, all was quiet except for Peaches's soft breathing—no perimeter alert, no beeping alarms, no snails, either. But what woke me? I checked my phone: it was 3:30 a.m. and our wake-up alert wasn't due for another thirty minutes.

I sat up. "Peaches," I whispered, giving her a nudge. "Wake up."

"No," she mumbled, burying herself deeper into the covers.

"Yes. Something's wrong. Wake up."

She rolled over onto her back. "Everything is wrong around here. What else is new?"

"Someone's making a move on the Psalter in the lab."

She bolted upright. "Now?"

"Right now."

"How do you know? Forget I asked that—you just do. Shit!" She stumbled out of bed and started pulling off her nightshirt. "Okay, so let me get dressed."

I was putting on my leggings and a hoodie, sneakers and a jacket—my travel ensemble. Stumbling over to my coffeemaker, I poured the dregs of a pot of cold coffee into a couple of mugs and passed one over. "Drink up."

"This is nuts!" she complained, downing the coffee in one gulp. "Our escape plan wasn't supposed to be enacted until the security detail shift change at 4:00 a.m."

"We'll have to take our chances." I pulled out my tablet and tapped the security tracking monitor app. "With all the personnel supposedly on duty, there should be a constellation of dots on this screen. Why are there only nine and three of them are in Rupert's quarters? One of them must be Sloane, and maybe the other five are the guards in the basement."

Peaches took the tablet from my hand and stared. "Shit. Let's go to plan B."

Chapter Eleven

nly, plan B was the escape plan least likely to succeed. It involved somehow making our way to the lab elevator while lightly stunning everyone along the way, including the good guys because we couldn't accurately identify one from the other at this stage—anybody could be an infiltrator.

However, plan A wasn't much of an improvement since it involved using an alternative route to the lab that we weren't sure even existed. Rupert had installed an elevator descending to the air raid shelter lab but had casually mentioned that another, presumably older, entrance remained somewhere. It had to be either a tunnel or a staircase, but my efforts to find a blueprint of Rupert's house during the war years had come up empty. Knowing my father-in-law, he probably had all such diagrams deleted in the name of privacy.

"It's probably near the original staircase descending from the kitchen to the basement," I whispered. "I'm hoping maybe he just had it blocked off."

"And if that's true, are we just supposed to knock down the walls in a timely fashion and hope nobody notices? No, let's do plan B and take the elevator. At least we'll get there quickly. Let's go."

We set our phones on stun, slung on our backpacks, and stepped from my suite into the third-floor hall. Everything was still—too still. With the number of supposed rent-a-guards on-site, there should have been a person standing watch on every floor at least. By the time we had reached the second level, we hadn't seen one. Rupert's quarters were behind several doors, putting his guard

JANE THORNLEY

team out of sight, but at least there were three signals coming from that direction. We took that as a good sign.

Our descent to the first-floor hall met with no resistance. The security team had to have either vacated or been disabled. We were shocked as we proceeded through to the kitchen without challenge, our perimeter alarms silent. That just wasn't right.

"It's like the whole house has emptied except for Sloane, Rupe, and a few others," Peaches whispered.

"The housekeeping staff only come in the morning," I told her as we descended the basement stairs. I ran my X-ray app along the walls as we went, surprised to find no hollow areas. I had wrongly assumed that an old secondary staircase must run parallel to the modern addition. "So where is the original entry?" I whispered.

"Maybe it has an outside access?" Peaches suggested.

We continued all the way down the stairs and paused. Ahead along the hall, five Sikh guards were either slumped against the wall or lying curled up on the floor, apparently asleep under the bright overhead lights.

Peaches ran up to each man and checked his pulse. "Strong heartbeats and no wounds. It's like they're dozing." She shook one, who just slid down the wall to the floor and started snoring.

I strode up to him. "They've been stunned, probably by using the Sleeping Beauty app—" I held up my phone "—as in one of these. How else can you send multiple people into a deep sleep without poison or drugs?"

"They don't appear to have been poisoned or drugged."

"Peach, one of those bastards has a hold of an agency smartphone!"

"But how in hell could they even get it to work—it's fingerprint operated."

"Maybe they used an imprint of a finger or something? This house has to be plastered with Rupert's fingerprints and, if a phone's missing, it could be his. Everybody else's is accounted for, right? Those phones were only issued to agency members and I'm sure the Italian office is in possession of theirs. I've got to call Rupert to make sure he's okay." But I hesitated, my finger hovering over the speed-dial button. "I'll ring the house phone instead."

"Then you'll wake everybody in the house."

"At this point, I'm just hoping that there's someone left in the house to wake." I rang Rupert's landline, which rang and rang. We could just hear the ringing upstairs. It was just about to go to voicemail when someone picked up. A soft thump sounded on the other end, like something had fallen to the floor and been retrieved. Heavy breathing followed. "Good evening—morning—hello? Who the devil is this?"

86

I was nearly delirious with relief. "Rupert! Are you okay?"

"Is that you, Phoebe? And why are you calling me on this phone at this ungodly time of the night? And yes, I am perfectly fine, all things considered. Why would I not be? Well, yes, of course I know why that may not be the case, but I am extremely befuddled as you have awoken me from a sound sleep. What the devil is going on?"

"Try to wake up pronto, Rupert. Peaches and I are down in the basement with the guards you put on watch by the elevator. They've been stunned by something. Quickly, where's your agency phone?"

"Ah, it's right here. I must switch on the light first, however." I could hear him fumbling in the background while Peaches and I headed for the open elevator door. "Now, where did I put it? It was right here. No, I—"

"Rupert, listen carefully: someone, presumably somebody working with Dex and that woman, have commandeered your house, taken your phone, stunned your guards, and made off with the Psalter."

Peaches widened her eyes at me at the last part.

"Taken off with the Psalter!" he gasped.

"Yes. We're heading down to the lab now, but I already know that it's gone. If you go to your rooms' vestibule, I think you'll find that your guards have been stunned, too. I'm guessing that a similar fate has befallen everyone in your employ tonight, and I'm damned glad that they didn't do something to you, too." Though I was guessing that after they nabbed his phone, he was the first to be zapped and, it follows, the first to rouse.

The elevator was descending when he returned to the phone. "You are correct: my dear Sikhs have each been stunned and my phone has vanished! I found Sloane on the floor of his room, quite out cold—"

The elevator doors opened. "Rupert, please listen carefully: I'm hoping that no one in the house is in further danger. The Psalter is gone and that's what they were after." Of course, I had been known to be wrong.

Peaches left the elevator and headed for the lab. "It's gone!" she cried as she stood at the door.

Sharp pangs of regret, panic, and relief hit me at the same time. I knew that the book had been stolen but I still hated to hear that a verified fact. "Rupert, are you still there?"

"Yes, still present." I could hear him breathing heavily.

"We've confirmed that the Psalter has been stolen and we're going after whatever it was hiding. Don't follow, understand? Absolutely do not follow. We're off the agency grid now and plan to stay that way. Remember that you are virtually defenseless without that phone."

"Nonsense," came the gruff reply. "I've worked in an age that predates these technological advancements."

I squeezed my eyes closed. "But the enemy is in possession of your phone now, which makes that a game-changer."

Peaches whipped the phone from my hand. "Hey, Rupe, listen up: if they've got your phone, which they clearly do, then everything you say or do on your tablet or desktop will be accessible to them. You need to go into Settings on your tablet, tap General, and disengage the 'synch among devices.' Got that?"

I took back my phone. "And stay home and stay safe." And I clicked off.

"Do you think he'll listen to us?" Peaches asked, striding up to the empty humidity-controlled case. The light was still on, the controls still activated, though the sliding door was open.

"Probably not, since he'll figure out where we're heading soon enough."

"Look at this. It's like they just breezed through the house, stunning everyone, and took the Psalter like it was a walk in the park."

"Hopefully, they won't treat the book the way they did Clive Hogarth. Anyway, matters just became a whole lot worse now that one of our smarter-than-brilliant phones has fallen into enemy hands."

"So, how's that going to play out when we get to Cyprus?"

"I have no idea." I checked my watch. "Let's get out of here. We have a plane to catch."

But then the power went off. For a moment we just stood frozen in disbelief.

"This is no coincidence. It's like they've been listening in on everything we say. Did you activate your phone's Privacy Close Contact setting?" Peaches asked.

"What's that?" I asked, fearing that I'd messed up somewhere.

She whipped the phone from my hand again and fiddled with the settings, her expression furious in the screen light. "It prevents anyone on the agency network from listening into our private convos."

"But we've gone dark so how can that happen?"

She turned my screen to face me. "That's how it happens, Phoeb. See the red flashing dot? That means you're sharing live info with another agency member, which could be anybody with an agency phone within a two kilometer radius. That means whoever has Rupert's phone could have been listening in, see? It must have just happened and I should have noticed it myself when I went into your settings—damn! Evan set it up to act like a walkie-talkie when we're on a case but you're supposed to turn it off otherwise. He sent us info on when to disengage it weeks ago!"

"I was busy weeks ago."

"Now these bastards know that we're down here and where we're heading next." She looked around the high-ceilinged, vault-like room. "Shit, and they must still have access to the house's power controls, too. Now the elevator won't work! I've got to send an SOS to Evan. Only he can deactivate that phone."

I waited while her fingers flicked through the phone's settings, her expression fierce. In a few seconds, she looked up. "So, how in hell are we going to get out of here?"

"Maybe exit through the barricaded tunnel?"

"Is that the one we can't find?"

"I get that you're mad at me but that's not helping." I snatched back my phone and switched to the X-ray app to begin running it along the concrete walls of the lab. "Try the hallway," I said, the whole time searching my memory for exactly what we had said and when.

They must have commandeered Rupert's phone last night, making every comment made since we awoke this morning up for grabs. Did I say anything to Peaches about my lost-art sniffer-dog capabilities? I'm sure I didn't. There was still a chance that they didn't know about that—yet. If they had full access to Rupert's phone and could read through all our past messages, they might soon discover my secret, if they didn't already know.

Peaches strode out the door to check the walls leading to the elevator. I ran my phone around the lab looking for openings behind the concrete, finding nothing. I was halfway around when I sniffed something strange, almost mustardy. Covering my mouth, I ran out to the hall. "I smell something!"

Peaches sniffed. "Could be sarin in a crude form—nerve gas. These guys are more lethal than I thought. We've got to get out of here!" She pulled her turtleneck up over her nose.

I thumbed toward the lab. "They must be sending gas in through the air vents," I said, shutting the hall door. "Maybe we found where that old entrance was, after all—today it's an air vent. We've got to get that elevator to work." Already I was feeling faint.

"Bastards!" Peaches tugged me into the open elevator and leaned me against the wall. "Stay there."

The sound of glass shattering followed: she had smashed the fire alarm box in the hall, activating a screeching alarm that would alert the entire house, along with the fire department. She immediately returned with the fire ax and began hacking at the ceiling until a large, ragged opening was exposed overhead. Then she shimmied up to the elevator roof and reached down to offer me a hand. "Smells a lot fresher up here. Pass me your backpack, then take my hand."

Whiffs of grease and oil also came wafting down the shaft along with a fortifying blast of cool fresh air as she hoisted me up to the top of the elevator roof. There we crouched for a few moments, catching our breath.

"What if they sent that gas through the whole house?" I gasped. "What about Rupert and the others?"

"Why would they need to do that? They already incapacitated everyone else and they don't think Rupert is any threat now that they have his phone and the Psalter," she replied. "No, they were trying to stop just us—permanently."

I hoped she was right. "The elevator shaft must exit on the roof," I said.

"That's my guess, and the original access to the old air raid shelter must be somewhere at the back of the house. Ready to climb?" she asked.

I shone my phone light up the thick, greasy cables trailing down the filthy shaft. "Up there?"

She flashed her own light to the right. "No, up there." I stared in relief at the skinny stairway leading into the shadows above. "It's designed so that the mechanics could get up and down for repairs. Man, I love these kinds of elevators. The older ones are always the best. Come on, let's move."

So we did, but with our backpacks rubbing against the cables and everything coated in decades of grime and grease, it was all I could do not to sneeze all the way up to the top.

"Are you okay down there?" Peaches called a few minutes later.

"Sure!" I wheezed. "Keep moving."

Meanwhile, the fire alarm was reverberating in our ears, but since it meant that the house would soon be overflowing with trained personnel who could deal with noxious gases and possible incapacitated people, it may as well have been music. If Rupert or the others were harmed, help was on the way. I wanted to call the house again to make sure he was all right but that would have to wait. Right then, we had to escape.

When we reached the trapdoor at the top, Peaches pulled her phone from her pocket and zapped the lock followed by a firm kick to open the thing. We crawled out onto the roof and collapsed, gasping for breath in the cool damp air. Sirens ripped into the dawn and flashing lights pulsed below.

We crawled to the edge of the roof, gulping in oxygen while gazing down at the two fire trucks and multiple police cars pulling up to the house.

"Rupe will have a lot of explaining to do," Peaches said.

"As much as I'd love to hear that, let's catch that plane. We should have time to reach the back fire escape before they surround the house."

Chapter Twelve

Whoever was behind this robbery/kidnapping/murder would be heading to Cyprus, too. There was a possibility that they were even on the same plane as we were, though there was no way to tell for certain. I had never seen the vicious woman's face and Dex would likely take another flight—or I would, if I were him—but there had to be others in the gang. That left Peaches and I sitting in the eighth row, scrutinizing everyone who boarded our flight.

"What about her?" Peaches whispered as a woman wrapped in a pink puffer coat squeezed past.

"Too tall and too pink," I said. "Vish would be about five feet eleven inches, maybe, and she just couldn't be into pink." We now referred to the vicious woman as "Vish" for short.

"How do you know? I mean, I get that you can sometimes superhumanly intuit past events but where did this insight come from?"

I considered the question. "Probably just a guess, one which isn't any different from what a lot of people experience, if they let themselves. Vish just seemed so focused and angry—cruel, even. To me, that just doesn't spell pink."

"But I wear pink and I'm no pushover," she pointed out.

I smiled. "Pink is your power color."

Meanwhile, everyone who boarded was a Goldilocks of possibilities from being too short to too wide. When we found ourselves studying women passengers' facial expressions, looking for signs of deviousness or guilt, we stopped. That wasn't getting us anywhere.

By the time the plane was on the runway waiting for takeoff, we had briefly sunk into our own thoughts. Though I felt horrible about not engaging the privacy feature back at Rupert's, at the same time I couldn't waste energy on self-recrimination. I was too busy worrying about Rupert and Evan, what may lay ahead of us in Cyprus, and a plethora of other concerns too numerous to mention.

"I can't believe that Ev didn't pressure you into studying your phone features more carefully," Peaches said, beside me in the aisle seat. I prefer the window and we had booked business class for the two-seater experience. She was still annoyed with me, apparently, and maybe with herself, too. I got that, I really did, but she wouldn't let it go. "I mean, yes, his manuals and updates are usually pages long but it's critical stuff, and every time he runs an update, you need to pay attention, Phoeb."

"I actually do pay attention to Evan in great detail. I try to focus on the man rather than the manual—get it?" If I was hoping to wiggle out of this one with humor, it wasn't working.

She threw up her hands—literally lifted them into the air. "I mean, you're married to the developer. That's got to flatten the learning curve for you somewhere. He must have given you private lessons?"

A memory of Evan's most recent private phone lesson came to mind. We had been sitting on our hotel room balcony in Hawaii, hours away from hopping a plane to an island off Fiji. A balmy ocean breeze was ruffling his hair while he patiently went over his latest thirty-page update document. I'm sure he had mentioned that particular privacy feature amid the other details, but I wasn't certain. His glasses kept sliding down that perfect nose of his and I found the way he pushed them back into place with one long finger very distracting.

He'd developed a tan by then and had taken to wearing a T-shirt that molded everything worth molding on his impressive chest, as well as the biceps I admired so much. I recall him looking at me with that intensity he sometimes assumed when explaining some finicky detail of one of his latest designs. In those moments, he became so deeply involved that his hazel eyes seemed to turn almost sea-green, as if he'd gone deep-diving inside his own head. When that happened, all I want to do is take the plunge and pull him to the surface.

That day, weak woman and terrible student that I was, I ended up removing those glasses to anchor the man's attention fully on me. I loved observing how his concentration shifted. It's as if his viewfinder swerved in an instant, zeroing in on the woman rather than the device. He gazed at me as if I was his entire world and, in that single moment in time, I was. Leaning forward, I kissed him. Lesson over.

"I do get private lessons," I said aloud, bringing myself back to the present, "but as I said, I'm easily distracted." The bell was dinging, the Fasten Seat Belts sign blinking. We were getting ready to take off.

We had just reached cruising altitude when she said: "At least they couldn't know about your sniffer gifts, otherwise they wouldn't have tried to kill you back there—I mean, kill us."

"I suppose that's some consolation."

"Man, nothing makes me angrier than someone trying to kill me."

"Not my favorite situation, either." But I had a feeling that we were in for more of the same. We should have been used to it by now.

"So, what's our game plan when we arrive in Cyprus?" she asked next. "I meant to ask you earlier, but we were a bit preoccupied."

"We arrive in Larnaca, we head for our hotel—we don't want to be driving up to Foinikas in the dark. From what I can tell, the way is isolated and the going a bit rough—hence the four-wheel drive I rented. Then, tomorrow morning, we find a hardware store and buy tools and gear, including a tent. We have no idea what we're in for, so we best be prepared for anything."

Her eyes widened. "We're going camping?"

"In a manner of speaking. There are no accommodations close by Foinikas so this makes the most sense." Our so I hoped. I only knew that driving back and forth to some bed-and-breakfast hardly seemed practical.

That seemed to satisfy her, at least for the short term. Stifling a yawn, she pulled out her travel pillow and bid me good day/good night. I was relieved not to have to probe our next steps in too much detail, since I really didn't have much in the way of specifics.

Two hours away from our destination and at least I'd managed to get in a couple of hours of sleep, waking up disorientated and anxious. Peaches was dozing beside me, a half-eaten sandwich still on the flip-down tray before her.

I pulled my backpack out from under the seat and took out my iPad. If we had those photos, presumably so did the enemy. Could Vish and her crew be a band of rabid Templar scholars searching for the Order's secrets? Since they had Rupert's phone and thus the photos, too, I needed to figure out whatever the Psalter hid sooner rather than later.

I began flipping through the Psalter images and ended up focusing on any page that featured a snail. Those things had to be the key to something. The mollusks began appearing about halfway through the Psalter. The first ten or so times one appeared, it remained tucked in amid the foliage of an illuminated border, usually peeking out from under a leaf or a clump of berries.

In later pages, snails began crawling on top of the foliage, slithering along in apparent nonchalance. As best as I could tell from the photos, the creatures' shells were each painted with different pigments and often in a different style as the chronicle progressed. By the last entries, the shells became more detailed, even ornate. Perhaps the snails were added after the chronicle had been nearly completed? One snail in particular sported what looked to be an ermine mantle around the shell opening—a collar for a noble snail? How baffling!

But then the snails became even more extraordinary. In fact—and I flipped through the Psalter photos quickly at this point—they eventually began looking the same from page to page, as if this had become the story of one particular snail. These creatures sported a long sepia-colored body with an ornate golden shell, the antennae sticking straight up as if in curiosity or fear, sometimes even consternation.

The more I studied the illustrations, the more extraordinary they seemed, as the creatures registered emotion in a combination of antennae, eyes, and mouth openings. By the last page, before the chronicle suddenly ended, one snail had emerged from its shell entirely and appeared to be wielding a sword. Since I had seen many medieval manuscripts where knights rode snails, one bearing a sword seemed almost comical—only, this one didn't appear to be a joke.

The snails had to be significant, but how? I searched the Internet for Cyprus+snail and discovered that the island did have a large indigenous species with a worldwide reputation for deliciousness. There were similarities in the shell markings with the later snail appearances in the Psalter but their presence still didn't make sense. Were the Templar scribes recording a favorite edible in the margins? If so, why this one and not other favorite foods? Had the Grand Masters been fond of escargot? But that made no sense.

I turned off the tablet and rested my eyes, hoping that an idea would coalesce in my brain. So far, I had nothing. Would I find the answers in Cyprus, or would they remain locked away in my subconscious, waiting to jump in some terrifying way? My biggest fear—and I had plenty to choose from—was that I would slip into some sort of timewalking event that would drag me down a path I was powerless to stop.

These episodes terrified me. I ceased being myself and literally became someone who had lived—and died—hundreds, sometimes thousands, of years before. The dying part was key. I'd had experienced another human's trauma more than once and it had left me raw and a bit traumatized. I had to prevent timewalking episodes at all costs and rely on my super-active intuition to lead the way.

We went through customs at Larnaca International Airport, reminding ourselves that we were Jennifer MacDonald and Lucy Jones, two friends off on a holiday together. Now that the enemy knew our destination, the false identities hardly seemed necessary. However, we were in it now and had to follow through. Apparently, our credentials were convincing, either that or the customs officials were more interested in drug smugglers. Still, it was aways a relief to pass into the country unimpeded.

"We've rented a Land Rover, like I said," I told Peaches-cum-Lucy as we headed for the car rental desk. "We need something robust. Do you want to drive or shall I?"

Peaches kept an eye out for suspicious-looking characters and wasn't having any more success with that than we had on the plane. "You drive and I'll watch out for trouble," she said.

That settled, we filled out the appropriate paperwork at the rental desk, showed our phony driver's licenses, and proceeded out the door to the car park. Even though the sun was hanging low in the sky by then, the temperature was warm enough to be comfortable with a light jacket, the air clean and fresh, and the sky an incredible deep cerulean blue. Just being someplace different gave a positive charge to our mood.

"At least we get to drive on the left-hand side like we do in England," I remarked. I could switch to a right-hand drive state of mind easier than most since I'd grown up in Canada but I'd rather not have to constantly remind myself.

"Think I'm going to like this place," Peaches remarked as she donned her sunglasses. "Just as long as somebody doesn't try to kill us—did I mention that already?"

"At least once."

She turned to me. "Where are we staying, anyway?"

"Here in Lanarca, at a little boutique hotel only 500 meters from a beach. We need to rest up before tomorrow since we have no idea what's ahead. Let's enjoy a brief reprieve while we can."

"You'll get no arguments from me." Peaches beeped the key fob looking for our rental. A white Rover flashed its lights at us from across the parking lot.

"What are you hoping to find in Foinikas specifically?" Peaches asked as we headed toward the vehicle. "Wait—let me rephrase that: I know what we're hoping to find—sort of—but how are we going to find it? I mean, we can't very well just drive into this ghost town, or whatever it is, and start digging. I know you want to avoid timewalking."

I tapped the phone in my pocket. "We'll scan the ground and foundations with our ground-penetrating X-ray app first."

"Yes, that's a place to begin but I'm just hoping you can sniff out something interesting before company arrives." She checked over her shoulder. "They either have to be here on the island already, or on their way."

"With a little luck, the app will detect something that no one's yet discovered and we'll go from there. Maybe my intuition will kick in and I'll find the cache quickly." Sometimes it seemed that I survived on hope alone.

"The key thing is to ensure that we're not being followed." Peaches gazed around the parking lot. Someone had just dropped off a car and was heading into the rental stall but, otherwise, the area with its parked cars was empty.

"If this gang is as large as it appears to be, we need help, Peach," I pointed out, "so I've messaged the Rome office to ask if Nicolina and Seraphina could join us."

"And?"

"I'll just see if they've answered."

"While you're doing that, I'll check if Evan answered me or if Rupert followed the instructions I sent to lock down his linked devices."

We sat for a moment in the Rover while checking our phones for messages and calls. Even though our signals had gone dark, that didn't mean that we couldn't receive or send. Everything went into kind of a holding tank in the cloud but our signals were near impossible to trace—unless you were Evan.

"Nothing from Rome yet." I looked up, my anxiety stoked again.

"Nothing from Ev, either. How about you?" Peaches asked.

"No Evan, and that makes me concerned, too, but a bit relieved all at once. Rupert, however, sent me this, presumably from his tablet," and I read:

Phoebe, where the devil are you? The house is filled with police and Chief Inspector Drury appears to be reveling in the opportunity to skewer me to the wall. She has concluded that I may be involved in the demise of Clive Hogarth, whose body, she informs me, has been found near the Temple Church. Though the man has suffered a recent gunshot wound, he, in fact, appears to have expired from a heart attack. This last piece of information I only managed to extract from a police coroner still responsive to my queries—and my billfold. Meanwhile, Drury has located the lab and is asking exceedingly annoying and distressing questions that I fear I cannot easily answer. And what is worse, I have been forbidden to leave the country!

Peaches and I looked at one another. "Hogarth died of a heart attack? Then why would they have laid him out the way they did?"

"It almost sounds ritualistic, doesn't it?" I said. That was only one of the countless unanswered questions mounting around this situation. "Oh, the last thing that Rupert wrote here was to tell you that he followed your instructions to delink his devices but he's still trying to figure out how to delete the Psalter images along with all his correspondence."

"Damn—that part is important."

"And Drury may confiscate his laptop, so hopefully he can figure it out before then."

"Anyway, as much as I feel badly for all the inconveniences he's going through, at least we know he'll be safe," I said. "Drury will probably have him watched, at the very least."

Peaches smiled. "Poor Rupe. Karma can be such a bitch. Okay, then, let's go."

I started the Rover and we rolled out of the parking lot. "Did I mention that Cyprus is the supposed birthplace of Aphrodite?"

"Since one part of the country is run by Greece and the other by the Turkish Republic of Northern Cyprus, nothing would surprise me—why not Mount Olympus, too?"

"We'll be staying in the Grecian part. Oh, and Cyprus was also once a British colony, and before that was fought over by the Mycenaeans, Egyptians, Assyrians, Persians, Ottomans, and the Greeks, among others. I think even the Venetians had a go for a time, too. The island is seething in history."

"And then the Templars bought it from Richard the Lionheart, which is extraordinary enough."

We used the car's GPS to direct us to the hotel, winding our way through the modern streets of what appeared to be a thin strip of a town that mostly followed the shoreline. White buildings no more than a few stories high mixed with mosques and red-tiled churches, making the town a pleasant little hodge-podge of architectural history. We reached our hotel without difficulty, booked in, and headed for our suite.

"Oh, wow!" Peaches exclaimed, taking in the large light-filled space over-looking the ocean. "Hot tub on the patio?"

"We're going to be roughing it for a few days so let's enjoy the luxury while we can," I said. "I'm changing into my swimsuit and heading for the beach. Want to come?"

She came but with no intention of swimming. Instead, she watched from the shore, up to her ankles in surf, but refusing to go farther. As an island girl, her statute of limitations excluded what she considered to be freezing water. As a Nova Scotian, my definition of cold differed. It seemed that most of the other beachgoers agreed with her since I was the only one actually in the water. Everybody else was walking their dogs or out for a late-afternoon stroll.

Splashing in the ocean on the nearly deserted beach was the best time I'd had since my honeymoon. For a few minutes, I reveled in the crisp bite of the ocean on my skin, indulging in the feel of the sea, completely in the moment. It wasn't until later that I returned to my head instead of my senses.

Peaches and I were sitting in the hotel restaurant overlooking the ocean, glancing through the menu, half of which featured Greek dishes, the other half Turkish, which were much alike in some respects.

"I'm starving," Peaches announced as she dug into our shared plate of flash-fried calamari.

"Me, too. I'm going for the moussaka platter with a side of fried Halloumi." I looked up to scan the restaurant, something we hadn't stopped doing since we'd arrived. Fellow diners appeared to be older couples enjoying a holiday with no one remotely resembling Vish or Dex in sight. I had begun to relax, at least to the point of allowing my neck muscles to unclench. We sipped wine and ate with gusto, so stuffed after we were finished that we decided to walk off our meals.

We strolled across little plazas, down narrow streets, beside old stone walls that we guessed dated from the Ottoman age, almost relaxed enough to enjoy ourselves. Overhead, the stars were twinkling against a near perfect night sky. Nothing tugged at me here, no sense that time was scratching at the portal between centuries.

We were almost back to the hotel when Peaches turned and stared behind us. "I'm sure someone's following us back there."

"I know. I can feel it, too."

Chapter Thirteen

We were going forward on this quest knowing that every move we made would probably be scrutinized. Even driving through the town following leads to the one source of camping supplies could be under observation. Still, we persisted, hoping that agency reinforcements would soon arrive. With Rupert out of commission and Evan offline, everything rested on Nicolina and Seraphina responding to my SOS. In the meantime, we resolved to keep on keeping on. What else could we do?

We had decided to use an old-fashioned paper map to guide us initially, instead of using our GPS. Niko, the guy in the outfitters shop where we bought our supplies, informed us that part of the road to the ghost town was an often flooded, mostly off-road track, so that Google Maps probably wouldn't be able to keep up.

"You need good skills," he said in broken English, tapping his skull for emphasis. "Way very hard. I hire guide to lead way?" he asked hopefully. We assured him that we would manage, thank you, but if he would just mark the map at the key points, that would be very helpful.

"Asprokremmos reservoir floods, you understand? When rain comes, very dangerous. This rainy season." His finger rested on the body of water I had assumed to be a lake.

"It's not raining now. Anyway, we'll be careful," Peaches assured him.

The shop primarily outfitted tourists and day-trekkers and, just in case the fellow spread the word about these two strange women intending to go camping in a remote area, we bought far more gear than we needed and added a monetary bonus just for him. We said that it was important to keep other possible happy campers off our tail, letting him figure out the reasons for himself.

"Others come?" he asked.

"We hope not," I responded, smiling and hefting the sleeping bag over my shoulder. We made several trips back to the Rover to load up the propane heater with extra tanks, cookstove, and the tent. Our last stop before hitting the road was to stock up on food. By then, we may as well have been preparing for an expedition.

"Do you feel anything so far?" Peaches asked as we took the highway toward our destination, admiring the incredible turquoise blue of the ocean, the glimpses of boats plying the waves, the far-off ruins on the hillsides.

"No, nothing—not even a glimmer," I replied. "I'm not sure whether that's a good or bad sign, considering that we're hoping my sniffer capabilities will kick in somewhere."

For whatever reason, so far Cyprus had not awakened any sleeping ghosts for me. Perhaps that was because there were so many layers of habitation and civilizations here. Unless I touched a key artifact, my bloodhound capabilities remained dormant.

We carried on along a coastal highway for about an hour while Peaches read about Foinikas from a brochure. "So, the settlement was built inland to protect a strategic valley, now flooded by the reservoir. Seems like Cyprus has a serious water problem, making the reservoir necessary," she said. "Says here that the Templars originally settled in Nicosia back along the coast, but later established their administrative capital in the village of Foinikas in order to protect said valley. The place was also once known for sugar plantations, and the Franks established a profitable silk trade there, too. The last people to occupy the town were the Turkish Cypriots."

"So, what caused it to become a ghost town?" I asked, keeping one eye on the rearview mirror. So far, any vehicle we thought might be following us had pulled off the road in another direction.

"Says here that the village was abandoned after the Turkish invasion in 1974. The Greeks regained this part of the island and briefly settled in Foinikas, but that after the reservoir was built two years later, they were forced to relocate. Turn here."

I took a right-hand turn down a narrow little road that appeared to be climbing upward through grassy meadows and rocky outcrops. Shortly after-ward, she pointed the way to the next turnoff, a dirt road climbing up amid bushes and shrubs, everything rocky and deserted but for occasional modern concrete buildings.

"Take a left here," Peached prompted.

Now the road became even more track-like, to the point of barely seeming like a road at all. What looked to be a riverbed with a trickle of water lay to our left, rocky, everything desolate. At least we had nobody behind us—that much was obvious since everything appeared empty in all directions.

And then the road ran out completely. I stared ahead at the stream flowing just beyond our wheels.

"This is the Xeropotamos River. Keep going."

"But this is the rainy season," I remarked. "I thought it was supposed to be flooded?"

"It says here that a bridge was washed away so there definitely was rain recently. Anyway, this is a good place to cross since it doesn't look deep enough to cause us any grief."

Putting the vehicle in gear, we splashed across the rocky streambed to the other side and forked right until we were once again on dry, stony ground. We followed the stream until we crossed it once more to connect with a track climbing up a steep little hill.

The rest of the route continued through the scrubby landscape until the reservoir appeared on our left-hand side. The remains of ancient stone walls could be spotted on the hillside along with equally old olive trees until, finally, the track dipped down beside desolate ruined walls and the remains of multiple stone buildings. I parked beside one of the crumbling walls and climbed out.

"Welcome to Foinikas!" Peaches exclaimed, joining me.

My spine tingled. Everywhere one looked, deserted, crumbling stone walls and buildings emerged from the low vegetation. The remains of a cobbled street could be glimpsed climbing ahead but soon even that became obliterated by sweeping grasses.

Peaches held up the map. "This is the remains of the village but the ruins of the actual Templar fortress are over there."

I gazed in the direction she was pointing, toward a grassy promontory overlooking the reservoir where ruined fortifications marked the earth with square walls, roofless structures—including what might once have been a watchtower —and mounds of grassy earth lying open to the elements.

"That's Templar land," Peaches said.

"Let's see how close we can get by car."

We carried on, jostling over what was left of the road as it crawled through the village, past modernish square concrete houses positioned by the remains of structures far older. Many of the ancient foundations had been incorporated into the newer buildings, but even the latest houses had decayed under the assault of time and nature.

I drove the Rover up the grassy hill until we were within meters of the fortification's remains. Parking the vehicle, we climbed the rest of the way on foot until we were deep into the area of what had been the Templars' fort.

More walls remained standing than I had expected, including one that still had the original roof timbers.

"Wow," Peaches exclaimed, gazing at the structures. "The mostly dry climate and lack of humidity has really preserved this place, considering these walls were built back in the 1300s."

"Probably whatever group of conquerors who took over the place chose to occupy the fortress rather than razing it to the ground." I was still gazing at a wall that clung to its partial roof. A timbered crossbeam supported many of the ruined walls every six or so feet from the ground, similar in style to crossbeamed medieval European buildings. Pebbles served as mortar tucked in among the fieldstone, and evidence of early plastering could still be seen here and there. Though the building techniques used were less refined, they were no less skilled than their European counterparts.

Despite everything, it was clear that the fortress—in fact, all of Foinikas—was slowly falling apart. Jungles of foliage fought for dominance between the walls and crawled up the sides of every visible building.

"No cell signal. Wouldn't you know it?"

"So we're literally off-grid," I remarked, peering through what remained of an ancient window.

"There'd likely be snakes in there," Peaches said over my shoulder. "Three venomous varieties exist on the island. They'll be a bit sluggish this time of year but why tempt fate? We should wear our waders when we scan in deep grass." We had even outfitted ourselves with rubber waders just in case.

"We'll run the ground-penetrating scanner app across every bit of Templar-occupied land but we need to find a camping spot first. What about up there?" I was pointing to another rocky hill even higher up, where yet another ruin hunkered. Behind that lay nothing but a rough-scrabbled hill. "If I'm not mistaken, that's the Commandaria della Finicha, where the Grand Master lived." I didn't try to keep the excitement from my voice. "That area has the strongest possibility."

"Of what—holding Templar secrets?"

"Yes," I whispered.

"Is your Phoebe Meter jangling?" she asked.

"It is, actually. Jacques de Molay would have lived there just before he sailed back to France and to his eventual demise. I feel the strongest energies emanating from up there."

"You mean that the big boss Templar didn't reside with his Order?"

"This was a hierarchy, Peach. Let's go!"

"So," Peaches said as she climbed ahead of me toward the stone ruins. "It looks like this building may have been deliberately destroyed. See that wall to the right? Somebody used a battering ram to knock a hole in it."

I paused to shield my eyes with my hands. The sun had fallen low in the sky by now, sending long shadows across the grass to gather in dark masses at the walls. "Apparently, the Ottomans destroyed this house but not the fort. I wonder why they saw it as such a threat?"

We continued without speaking, something about the atmosphere affecting us both. The higher we climbed, the more the wind whistled through the stone, rustling the grasses as if with an agitated hand. When we reached the first wall, I turned to look back over the terrain. The Rover sat down in the shadows at the base of the fort, but other than a bird flitting by the edge of the reservoir, not a single living thing was in sight. I suppressed a shiver.

"I'm beginning to feel the ghosts," I whispered.

"Oh, just stop," Peaches chastised with a laugh. "It's way too soon for ghosts. At least wait until midnight. Maybe it's human creepos that you're sensing."

"Yes, maybe Vish and the gang are already here somewhere," I said, stepping to the crest of the hill to survey the village in all directions.

"Maybe," she said, following my gaze, "but if they are already out there, they'll keep well hidden, until—"

"—until we find something. Then they'll pounce."

"Yeah, that's what I'd do. Keep your perimeter alert on at all times."

"The ground-penetrating radar app won't work when the perimeter alert is engaged," I reminded her.

Peaches sighed. "I forgot about that. Ev hasn't got to that one yet, has he? Have you been distracting the poor man, Phoebe? We'll just have to stay together—one of us on watch, the other using the app. It will be slower but I don't see what choice we have."

She trudged a few yards farther up the hill. "What if we make camp here?" She was standing on the other side of the ruins where two six-foot-high walls met, forming a sheltered corner. "It's protected from the wind and hidden from the entry to the village both by road and by water, making it the best option."

Carefully, I picked my way through the thick grass to stand by her side. This section of the building must have once led into a courtyard because a large door-like opening yawned into the remains of a thickly vegetated square, open to the elements. Across the space, a Gothic-style arched window could still be seen—no glass or shutters, of course, but amazingly intact.

"Okay," I said slowly. "It's been a long time since I pitched a tent—actually, I've never pitched a tent—so just tell me what to do."

"These ones practically pop up by themselves. It won't take long."

First, we cleared the brush away from the corner space we were to occupy while wearing gloves and thigh-high rubber boots, just in case. After that, we hefted the gear up the hill and set up camp, me following directions every step of the way. In fact, I was relieved to be focusing on physical activity that did not require me to probe too deeply into Templar anything. Already, I'd felt something tugging on my psychic senses but I wanted to stay as far away from all that as I could, and for as long as possible.

Peaches instructed me to use fallen stone to form a makeshift firepit with a low wall at the back that would reflect heat into our little corner. While she tidied up and arranged our camp to her specifications, I trekked back down to the Rover to collect our two backpacks.

The light was fading fast, casting long shadowy fingers across the landscape. That unfamiliar bird still screeched from the water's edge but otherwise only the wind interrupted the peace.

I hauled out the backpacks, locked the car door, and huffed back up to the hill, resisting the urge to glance over my shoulder every few steps. Halfway up, I paused, thinking that I could hear a bell clanging from somewhere. Turning, I gazed back, listening. Gongs reverberated faintly as if from a long way off. Church bells here? Maybe the wind carried the sound over the hills. Turning, I continued.

When I arrived at the crest, Peaches was gathering twigs to feed the fire.

"Let's do a quick scan inside the Grand Master's house before we lose all the light," I suggested.

She looked up. "We've already lost most of the day. Are you sure you want to do a first run in the dark?"

"Absolutely. Besides, we bought those two big spotlights that will help brighten it up in there." I was indicating the gaping door to the last Templar master's mansion while trying to think past the gloom. The last thing I wanted was to start searching inside that enclosure. "Time is running out, Peach. Let's get a head start before tomorrow."

She didn't put up much resistance in the end but insisted that we outfit ourselves as if we were wading into piranha-infested waters. I was to stand by the inner wall with the perimeter alert activated while she paced inside the walls with the ground-penetrating X-ray app, the two mega-spotlights beaming into the interior.

As soon as I stepped into the vines choking what once would have been the Grand Master's courtyard, I felt something inside me shift. It was so subtle at first that it would have been easy to ignore—a heightened sensitivity to sound, slightly blurred vision, which could be easily attributed to allergies or fatigue.

I took a deep breath, blinked, and steadied myself before plunging into the thicket to stand more or less in the center of the space. "How's this?" I called.

Peaches was already on the opposite side beside the Gothic window, her shadow exaggerated against the wall, her phone screen brilliant even in the spotlights. "Good," she called.

The perimeter alerts could detect human or large animal heat signatures within a fifty-foot radius but worked most effectively when the device was placed in the center of an imaginary circle. I found a pile of stones on which to perch while focusing on the screen. "See anything?" I asked.

"Nothing yet," she said. "Plenty of depressions in the earth. Looks like there may have been a cellar below this but it's collapsed, of course. No sign of shiny metals, either."

"We may not be looking for shiny metals," I told her.

"I know, but they are the sort of thing that show up best on the scanner. Hey—" she paused, gazing around "—look at all the flattened foliage. Somebody was scouting around here already and not long ago, either."

It's true that under the bright spotlights the shrubs did look recently disturbed.

"Damn. Maybe they're steps ahead of us, after all," I said.

"Maybe."

"Keep looking, Peach. That cellar could be interesting. See any sign of stairs?" I called. Really, I just wanted to keep her talking. The minute I was left alone in my head, I felt something scratching away at my consciousness, something fearful, something not my own.

My screen began flashing red. "Intruder alert!" I cried.

Peaches bounded through the shrubs toward me. "Where, what?" Taking my phone from my hand, she stared. "About four feet tall and maybe forty feet to the right and coming up the hill," she whispered. "Could be a person crouching. Let's go."

We bounded out of the enclosure, taking one of the spotlights with us, Peaches switching her phone to stun, me keeping mine on the heat signature. Whatever it was, it appeared to be moving slowly as if stalking us.

My heart was throbbing in my chest. On one hand, I badly wanted to confront Vish and her gang, but on the other hand, I in no way felt ready. In fact, the effect of this area was knocking me off my game.

Outside, on the other side of the ruins, something white was just cresting the hill. As Peaches lifted the spotlight, the creatures baaed. "Holy shit, a goat!"

I doubled over in laughter, or maybe that was hysterical relief. "Let's call it a day."

Later, once the fire was blazing, fueled by dried grasses and branches, and with our tent facing the warmth, things were beginning to feel almost cozy. Inside the tent, two comfy sleeping bags awaited, and Peaches had insisted on us buying a propane cookstove on which to warm our store-bought supper—stuffed peppers and spanakopita served with a side salad.

A loneliness had begun to affect my mood. Though I assumed it had something to do with being cut off from everyone, especially Evan, it felt foreign, too, foreign as if these feelings weren't mine. I was experiencing a deep, penetrating sense of loss.

We ate while sitting on the remains of a crumbling wall, gazing out over the reservoir, now luminous under a mass of stars. "I'm starting to feel this place working on me," I said.

"Yeah, I know." Peaches scraped up the last mouthful of salad and placed the foil container in a plastic bag for cleaning up later. "So, I'm putting you in protective custody. Tonight, I'll sleep by the tent door with you against the back so, if you should sleepwalk or ghostwalk or whatever might happen, I'll be there to stop you." She checked the charge on the phones. "Almost fully charged now but we'll need to boost these using the Rover's battery tomorrow. Are you ready to hit the sack?"

"Hitting the sack" was hardly a hard fall considering how comfortable those sleeping bags were. We were both so exhausted that we fell asleep instantly and I might have made it straight through to the morning if it weren't for the bells.

I jolted awake before dawn. The deep donging was so noisome that the belfry could have been right overhead or maybe lodged inside my very skull, those bells so plagued me. To ring them so early must surely rouse the entire town.

But I could not remove the blanket from over my body. It was as if it had been wrapped around me like a swaddling cloth. Had I been restrained? I kicked and struggled, fighting to be free. Had we been attacked overnight and taken captive? Were the bells but a warning?

I could not—would not—scream. Father was adamant that in order to survive, silence was critical, as was invisibility. Rolling on the ground, I made to break loose, but something was shaking me.

"Wake up, Phoebe!" a woman cried, but that could not be—no female but I lived on these premises.

I attempted to kick her away. "Leave me!"

Had not my arms and legs been so bound, I would have grasped my sword and threatened to skewer her to the ground, but alas, she slapped me hard.

Chapter Fourteen

"Here, drink up." Peaches poured more hot coffee into my mug. I sipped, struggling to clear my mind as dawn broke over the horizon.

"Tell me what just happened," she asked gently.

I kept my eyes fixed on the sun's red glow bleeding into the hills, my head still foggy and confused. "I heard bells," I told her, "and not for the first time. But last night—or early this morning—they were so loud that they woke me up —I mean, woke *her* up." I gulped more coffee.

"So," Peaches said slowly, "you—*she*—awoke from a deep sleep? And in this timewalking moment, you became someone else? A woman?"

"Yes, definitely female, but I sensed that she was trying to move about the house as unobtrusively as possible. She was thinking that she had to get up because there was much to do, but she panicked when she found herself constrained by the sleeping bag."

"Do you know what time period this was? Could it have been Ottoman or later?" Peaches was staring at me in the half-light.

"I don't know. It was dark so I couldn't see anything that might provide a clue, but since the Ottoman invasion destroyed the Grand Master's house, it had to have been before then."

"But it couldn't have been during the Templar occupation, though, right? Surely women wouldn't have been permitted among all those godly sword-wielding monks, right?"

"We don't know, do we? History makes assumptions based on whatever evidence is available at the time but there are always exceptions—always. There's a woman involved here, that's for certain, and she's connected to the Templars somehow." I leaped to my feet. "The snails!"

"What?" Peaches watched me bound into the tent, emerging with my iPad seconds later. My intuition was crackling like an electrical storm.

"I knew they were important, I just didn't know how." I sat back down beside Peaches and began scrolling through the Psalter images. "When we first saw the snail, it was peeking out from under the shrubbery—shy, knowing its place, while remaining out of sight—but, gradually, it becomes braver, more visible, see?"

"I see a snail slithering along a leaf, yes."

"Don't think snail, Peaches, think woman or women. One of the medieval symbols for women were snails because they remained at home in their shells, as the thinking went. Snails are often seen in medieval manuscripts fighting with men, which is kind of twisted medieval humor implying that housewives were always squabbling with men and must be kept in line."

"Like *The Taming of the Shrew*?"

"Shakespeare is a few centuries later but the sentiment is the same. Look here." I took a deep breath to steady my racing heart. "The snail is a key. I think that some of these snails were actually added to the pages later, not as an afterthought but as a message. The Psalter later tells the story of one particular snail." I scrolled through to the second to last entry where the snail appeared as a worm wielding a sword. "Here, she's broken free from her luxurious shell and now bears a weapon. See how ferocious she looks?"

Peaches leaned over. "Um, I see an armless worm with a sword held before its body. I don't see anything remotely ferocious—it's more like some weird comic strip."

"Trust me: this snail can hold her own against any warrior."

Peaches took me by the shoulders and turned me to face her. "Look at me."

I did as she asked, noting the reflection of the sunrise in her eyes. "You're scaring me. You're connecting deeper and deeper to someone back in the past. I know how this works: you'll slip away. One minute, you'll be Phoebe, and the next, some stranger who lived and died centuries before. What if you can't come back? What if you lose your mind trying to regain yourself in some other century? No timewalking, you said; you had to avoid it for as long as possible, you said; but here you are, timewalking."

"But what else can I do, Peach? If this is the only way we can find the secret of the Templars, I have to go through with it, right?"

"Wrong. We can hop in that Rover right now and head to the airport and home. You can break your connection with whatever or whoever has a grip on you and forget the damn Templars. They're dead and gone but you're not."

"I can't just give up and leave. When have I ever done that? Besides, now we have a priceless book to retrieve and a villain to catch. I'm into it now and there's no turning back. Are you with me, Peach?"

"Don't ask that: of course I'm with you. I'm your bodyguard, aren't I? Only it's bloody hard to protect a body that's going in and out of two centuries."

"My real body will always remain in the here and now, remember. Protect this one." I thumbed at my chest.

"My point is that at the moment we're isolated out here, physically and virtually, so if something goes wrong, there is no backup until Nicolina arrives. And something *will* go wrong. I don't need to be a soothsayer to guarantee that."

She had me there. "What if you keep watching my back in the here and now and let me worry about whatever is happening inside my head? Unless I try walking off the edge of a cliff or something, that is. Whoever she is, she's connecting to me and I know that she was a contemporary of the last Templars. I know this, Peach. How can I not follow through on whatever secrets she's hidden? I have no choice but to continue."

Though Peaches didn't agree with my decision, she threw herself into the task at hand with an almost fevered intensity. She wanted us to locate the treasure and make a speedy exit—preferably that very same day. As if it could ever be that easy.

Meanwhile, I forced my brain into the almost rote and totally methodical process of searching the grounds, not allowing my attention to wander for an instant. It was enough that I suspected that the key to unlocking the Templar secret remained somewhere nearby, and possibly in the home of the Order's last Grand Master. That alone would be enough to lead us forward—I hoped.

But as the day wore on under increasingly cloudy skies, it became more difficult to stay focused. We appeared to be getting nowhere. Though Peaches could form a compelling blueprint of the Templar master's abode back in the 1300s, nothing jumped out on our X-ray screens that indicated a hidden stash of treasure remained on the property. It could be that the invaders had confiscated anything worth taking hundreds of years before, yet I had a niggling sense that wasn't the case.

By late afternoon, we had crisscrossed the ruins five times, carefully studying the depressions at each pass.

"Maybe we need to just take those shovels and start digging where the staircase used to exist? Whoever hid whatever it is that we're looking for must have buried it down there," I said, taking a rest on the crumbling walls.

Peaches collapsed beside me. "Yes, that makes sense. There doesn't seem to be anything under the walls themselves, at least nothing that the detector app can locate. Are you feeling any non-you sensations?"

"Non-me?" I laughed. "Not at the moment but I am trying to avoid any sneak attacks." I gazed down at my phone, habit making me look for texts and messages before remembering that we had no cell signal. Anxiety hit briefly but I stifled it in an instant. I couldn't risk missing Evan or worrying about the people I cared for—all those things that are often easily squashed by a quick text or email. As tempting as it was to switch to the agency satellite service, that would be equivalent to announcing our location to everyone on the network, including Vish, and putting us right back on the grid.

"Our batteries are almost drained," Peaches said. "Let's go back down to the Rover and give them a boost before settling in for the night. All are chargers are dead, too."

We had agreed to stick together, which meant that we both tromped down the hill to sit in the vehicle while we boosted our chargers and phones. The sun that had appeared at dawn had long since been shrouded in masses of thick roiling clouds that delivered the darkness earlier than usual. It looked like rain was coming but neither of us remarked on that possibility.

"I really don't like this place," Peaches said as we sat in the dark. Even with the engine going and the running lights on, Foinikas emanated a cold, otherworldly atmosphere.

"Ghost towns always feel like this; though, admittedly, this one is spookier than most. That's probably because it's not only deserted but isolated," I said, periodically munching on the chips we brought along for a distraction. Never underestimate the power of junk food.

"These things are taking ages to charge," Peaches remarked as she checked our phone batteries. "I forgot that cars don't boost these things as quickly as electrical sockets. Anyway, I have to use the facilities," she said.

That would be the facilities we didn't have. "Can you wait until we have more juice in our phones?"

She gazed at me in the dashboard light. "Three cups of tea and four bottles of water—what do you think?"

"Okay, okay. The perimeter alert should have enough charge to cover us when you go." I pulled the phone from the dash socket and jumped out.

We had decided against buying a port-a-potty. One of us would go in the great outdoors while the other would stand watch from a few meters' distance.

This had worked so far, but neither of us had yet to try that approach away from our uphill base camp. We always used the same discreet pile of boulders beyond the main enclosure.

"I'll keep perimeter alert on," I said as we left the comfort of the vehicle and headed outside. By now it was completely dark, and a chill wind blew across the reservoir.

"I'll just go to other side of that wall," Peaches said as she stood and started toward the edge the fort.

"Stay in sight," I called.

"Can't do anything if my body thinks it's being watched," she called back, disappearing behind a tumble of stones.

"I'm not watching," I called.

"Why not? What kind of a guard are you, anyway?" she called back.

"Then I'll come closer."

"What are you, a perv?"

I laughed while fervently hoping she'd make it quick. I held the perimeter alert up and scanned around us 360 degrees, seeing Peaches's heat signature clearly within the scanner diameter. As long as she stayed inside that viewfinder, I knew she was safe.

But then I thought I saw a flash of light near our camp. I gazed up the hill toward our camp. Something was moving up there, something human with a flashlight.

"Peach!" I whispered. "Trouble on the hill!"

No answer, though I could see her outline on the screen. "Peach, I'm coming to you. We've got trouble, do you hear me?"

But before I could move another step, I felt myself sinking to my knees, a buzzing sensation hitting me between the shoulder blades, turning me numb. In seconds, I knew nothing.

Chapter Fifteen

It was like trying to wake up from sleep when one is hovering just below consciousness. I attempted to force myself to the surface over and over again, almost breaking through before sinking back down into a dark fog. Something was very wrong but I couldn't remember what or why. I only knew that I had to wake and face the danger head-on.

While my head panicked, my body remained inert and unresponsive. Whatever I was lying on or in moved and shifted, bounced and rattled beneath me as if we were traveling over water followed by crossing a mountain by truck or maybe even a wagon. My head lolled from side to side but I was powerless to stop it, and then I ceased being aware of anything at all.

It seemed as if days had passed before my eyes finally opened, but maybe it had only been hours. I was in a dark room, where a sliver of light from a partially opened door washed across irregular stone walls. Sitting up, I found myself on a hard little bed shoved against a wall with a blanket tossed over me, hands bound, feet not.

Kicking the covers off, I stood up. Something burned between my shoulder blades but I was too preoccupied to care.

Still in my leggings and pullover, I could see my jacket draped over a chair with my sneakers tossed beneath. Except for the bed and that chair, the small room—no bigger than a large closet—was unfurnished, and so damp and cold that I couldn't stop shivering. Rain was pounding against a narrow window, and I could hear voices coming from somewhere. I briefly checked the window but it was so dark and stormy that I couldn't see a thing.

Where I was was not as important as who I was at that moment. The fact that I recognized my own skin was shockingly liberating, though simultaneously terrifying, since I had no idea what had happened to Peaches, or what had happened, period. Obviously, I—we?—had been captured and taken to wherever the hell this place was. Were we even still in Cyprus?

My captors seemed unconcerned that I might escape since I padded to the door in my stockinged feet, stepping into a hall unchallenged. After all, weaponless and with my hands bound in front of me, what threat did I pose? And really, I just wanted to meet my captors and discover what was going on before I attempted anything brave or foolish. To that end, I took off down the corridor, following the sound of voices.

The hall was all rough stone with a tall arched ceiling and periodic slit windows, some of which had been boarded up. Furniture was minimal, dilapidated, and definitely antique, everything lit by a few lamps that could have come from a junk shop. Patches of mold slimed the walls and, at one point, I could see a rivulet of water oozing through a crack in the ceiling straight down the walls.

At a junction between two hallways, a lone framed picture hung—the only visible decoration I'd seen so far. Though it appeared to be a print rather than an actual painting, it was no less striking. A man wearing a black robe on which a red cross had been emblazoned stood gazing out at the viewer, the eyes above his gray beard bleak but resolute. Shit—where was this place that hung a picture of a Templar master?

I quickened my pace, still following the sound of voices. Rounding a corner, I stepped into what appeared to be a large baronial hall with swords and armor hung high on the walls, far up into the shadows, and a fire blazing in one of the enormous fireplaces at either end of the room. As I crossed the flagstones, heading toward the four figures seated around the hearth, two stood up and stepped toward me—a man and a woman.

I recognized Dex at once but I was more interested in the woman. "Vish," I said. "We meet again. What have you done with Peaches?" So many questions warring to be asked simultaneously.

"She is alive, if that is what you're asking. We left her in Foinikas."

She was tall, slim, with dark, gray-streaked shoulder-length hair, and I estimated maybe around forty years old. Dressed in a black turtleneck and pants, her expression seemed relaxed, almost welcoming, until closer observation revealed the hard edge thinly veiled below the surface.

"Left her how?"

"Forget her, Phoebe McCabe. We have much to talk about, you and I." She spoke in a surprisingly rich-toned voice, in an accent that I couldn't place at first —a little British, a little bit eastern European, maybe? "Why do you call me Vish? What is this Vish?"

"That's what I was calling you and it still fits. It's short for 'vicious.'"

She snorted. "My name is Katrina. Why 'vicious'?"

"I'm assuming that you are the same woman who shot Clive Hogarth and then kicked him when he was on the ground. That's why 'vicious.'"

"Perhaps if you knew him as I did, you would have done the same."

"I seriously doubt it. Why did you kill him?"

"I did not kill him," she said with some asperity. "He died of natural causes. He had already outstayed his welcome on this earth with his frail, wicked heart."

"But your actions led to his death. He was an old man," I protested.

"An old, evil, selfish man."

As much as I wanted to probe that statement further, I was so tired, thirsty, and hungry that I couldn't think straight. "Do you have anything to drink? And maybe eat?" I gazed around at the huge space with the crates and boxes stacked in one shadowy corner, the sleeping bags and cooler chests strewn among the gear. "Are you camping out?"

Katerina nodded to the two men seated by the fire, one of whom jumped up and removed a plastic bottle of water from a box. He unscrewed the top for me, giving me a chance to check him out—in his early twenties, olive-skinned, hair shorn bald, dressed in black, too. I grasped the bottle and almost drank it dry in a couple of long gulps. When I was finished, he retrieved the empty bottle and dropped a plastic-wrapped sandwich into my hands.

"Better?" Katrina asked.

"What's with the all-black?" I asked. "Color is all the rage this fall."

She flashed smile but said nothing. "Care to sit down?"

I eyed where she had indicated—a battered leather sofa where the one remaining occupant—another youngish man wearing black—suddenly bounded up to sit on a crate nearby. Walking around to his vacated spot, I sat, relishing the feel of warmth penetrating my bones. My shoulder blades seemed to burn. "Where am I?" I asked, unwrapping the sandwich—a pita bread something or other. The first bite told me chicken.

"You are in Kolossi Castle, once a stronghold of the Knights Templar, and perhaps someday to become a tourist attraction. It has been closed for renovation since 2020 so we have commandeered it as our center of operations. It is far removed from any town or settlement. Nobody knows that we are here."

"Okay," I began slowly, gazing around and chewing, "so you have an ancient castle as your office. That's gutsy, if nothing else." That didn't explain why there were what looked to be real swords in their scabbards leaning against one wall, or the pile of clothes I saw heaped on an ancient trunk. Did they perform some kind of medieval fair here?

"You will not escape this place, Phoebe, if that is what you hope. The castle sits on top of a rocky cliff with nothing but ocean on one side and mountains on the other."

That explained why they weren't worrying about me bolting. "What do you want from me?"

"Ah," my hostess said, curling her legs up beneath her as if snuggling in for a long chat with a friend. "Do you know what happened to you?"

"I'm guessing that you ambushed me using the stun feature on the agency smartphone that you stole. You must have used a strong charge because I've been out of it for hours. You need to be careful with those things, Vish. They're not toys, you know. Did you hear that, Dex, or is that even your name?"

I glanced over my shoulder at the man still standing there with his hands in his pockets. This guy looked like Dex but yet not Dex—still a fashion statement in his tight black jeans and equally black T-shirt, only this version came with an almost feral glint in his eye. And this Dex wore an earring.

A slow smile spread across the face that I once thought boyishly handsome. "Did you appreciate experiencing a jolt yourself, Phoebe? Hurts, doesn't it?"

I turned away. Had he been zapped once and, if so, by whom? But I couldn't focus on that right then because Vish/Katrina was speaking.

"You know why I brought you here, Phoebe. Let us not play games. At first, I only thought to stop you from decoding the Psalter but soon I learned that you had skills that made decoding unnecessary. You have a gift."

So she knew about my art-sniffer reputation. "And you discovered this how?"

She held up Rupert's phone, the screen totally black. "Before the battery drained, I read many of Rupert's messages to his son and to you—most interesting. Since then, I have been unable to recharge the battery to either this phone or the other two. You will show me how."

A brief, searing image of Peaches stunned and helpless cut like a knife across my heart. Was she lying unconscious in the storm somewhere? "And why would I do that?" I asked, eyeing the phone. They had been rendered inoperable, not drained of their juice—I could tell that much. That could only mean that they had been deactivated by the only person who knew how. I stifled the joy jolting through me in case it registered on my face.

Vish proceeded to remove two more phones from her pocket, I presumed to be mine and Peaches's. "Because if you do not, I will make things very bad for you. Your continued comfort depends upon your cooperation."

I almost laughed out loud. "My continued comfort? I was kidnapped and dragged to this bastion of yours and you expect me to cooperate?" Maybe that was a foolish thing to say under the circumstances, but I was so filled with hope at that moment that it made me more brave than wise.

Something ruthless flashed behind her eyes. "You have no choice, Phoebe, let me make that clear. You will do as I say or I will kill you. You have no friends, no phone, and are completely at my mercy. If you want to live and your friend to remain alive, too, you will first unlock the phones. After that, you will tell me where the Templar treasure is hidden."

"I can't unlock the phones. They've been deactivated remotely, which is agency policy as soon as one falls into the wrong hands."

She tossed my phone aside and glared in my direction. "That is unfortunate for you and your friend, who is very uncomfortable at the moment."

They had Peaches? She wasn't prone somewhere in the cold and the rain? That was good news in one respect, horrible in another, as it meant that they might try to use her as collateral to force me to do their bidding. And I had no doubt that Vish wouldn't hesitate to kill us both in the end, whether I helped them or not. This villain was not interested in keeping me alive to do odd treasure-seeking jobs, either. She was after only one thing and would do whatever was necessary to get it.

"I don't know where the treasure is," I said truthfully. "We were using the ground-penetrating app without success. If you checked my phone before it went dark, you must have seen that the app screen registered no significant findings." Since the batteries were not the problem, she probably hadn't had time to investigate the apps before the phone blanked out, anyway.

"Then you have not used your full gifts," she said, her melodic voice tense. "Are you afraid, Phoebe? Do you believe that this timewalking gift of yours may leave you stranded in another century?"

Damn, she knew about that.

Unfolding herself from the couch, she stood up, a chill smile failing to warm her long face. "Pity, because you will take that risk while I remain at your side. I will question you while you are in the mind of another, something which

I find thrilling to contemplate. Imagine interviewing someone long dead? It is the historian's dream."

"Are you a historian?" I asked quickly, wanting to keep her talking. "Who are you exactly and how do you fit into all this?"

She hesitated.

"If you want me to help you, then you'd better disclose everything you know. My 'gift,' as you called it, relies on me having a deep understanding of the people and places that I am to experience. Who are you really and what do you already know?"

She nodded as if accepting my rationale. "I am a historian, yes. You might refer to me as a Templar scholar, since it has been an obsession of mine for years, but I have been primarily fixed on the Templar women."

"What Templar women? There weren't any women." I knew better but I wanted to see her reaction.

"There are always women, you know this. Our sex has been 50 percent of the population and, during times of war and unrest, the number has been proportionally higher. There are women in Templar history, too, but they were not heralded, as was the way of the times. One in particular may have altered the course of the Templars' fate through her ingenuity and perseverance. Who was she and what did she hide? You will find the answers for me."

"What do you know of her?"

"I have learned that she was the Shablool. In Psalm 58.8, it says: 'Let them be as a snail which melts away as it goes along...'"

"What does that even mean?" I thought I knew but I wanted to hear her version.

"That has been much contested. The ancient texts suggest that *shabûl* in Hebrew refers to wax that melts away, hence referring to the slime the snail exudes as it trails along. Though patriarchy has determined a negative view, when considered in a new light, the snail is seen to be a hidden, discreet, and persistent element that should not be underestimated."

"Also a voracious pest."

"Or a delicious treat—depending on how you consider it. She may appear humble to some but works her magic while hidden away in the background and leaves a subtle trail that only the wise will follow."

"And you believe that this Shablool—am I pronouncing that correctly?— was somehow involved in the last days of Jacques de Molay's Order?"

"I do, and for years I have attempted to follow her trail, without success; that is, until I learned about something mysterious hidden away in the crypt at the Temple Church. I knew then that I had found what I needed."

"But how did you learn about that?"

"From my father."

I nodded, the pieces falling into place so loudly in my brain I almost heard a snap. "You are Clive Hogarth's daughter."

Chapter Sixteen

"And you shot your own father?" I asked as mildly as possible. I didn't want her becoming defensive, yet I kept wondering, who shoots their own dad?

Vish stood with her arms crossed, staring into the fire. "He was no father to me except in the biological sense. He impregnated my mother, who was fifteen at the time. She swore that his advances had been unwanted but, in those days, 'rape' wasn't a word as commonly used as today. Girls thought that they had led a boy on if they so much as smiled at them."

There was no self-pity in her tone, yet the anger was unmistakable. "The Hogarth family were wealthy landed gentry, so they were able to buy off my mother's parents to keep things quiet. I was adopted by a couple who later moved from Britain to Turkey. Ample funds were provided to finance my education when I reached the necessary age. I went to university in Britain and did well, reading history to achieve my doctorate degree with a specialty in medieval Europe. My father's identity was kept from me."

"You knew who your mother was but not your father?"

"That was another part of the agreement struck between the Hogarths and my adoptive parents, though they were free to disclose my birth mother's identity. Over the years, I remained in touch with my biological mother and we had a cordial relationship until she passed away two years ago. However, my efforts to discover my father were stymied until after her death, at which point I finally discovered his name."

She turned to face me. "Imagine how excited I was to learn that my father was the reverend at the Temple Church, one of the last men on earth to hold the esteemed title of Valiant Master? To a medieval scholar, that was so very exciting."

I had a sense of where this story was heading. "But you approached your father only to find that he wasn't equally thrilled to discover his long-lost daughter?"

"Furious, in fact. How dare I approach him after all this time? Clive Hogarth was the youngest of two sons and did not inherit the family estate, but he was very conscious of his station. He had been denied a title, by his way of thinking. Thus, even though he and his long-suffering wife had divorced decades ago, he strove to appear every inch an upstanding man of God—like hell."

"And the last thing he wanted was for information to get out that he had raped an underaged girl, a union which had produced an illegitimate child?"

"I was his shame."

"Were there other siblings?"

"None. I was his sole issue and he was not unhappy with that situation. He told me he was not meant to be a father or even a husband because he was married to the church. Being assigned as head of the esteemed Temple Church was no small honor for the bastard, and it appeared that he had been angling for the post for a decade or more."

"So, he refused to have anything to do with you?"

"He tried to make me leave but I had information to barter with. If he refused to accept me as a daughter, I demanded that he take me on as his assistant. As a medieval scholar myself with expertise in symbolism and linguistics, I proved that I had much to offer in his quest to locate the Templar treasure."

"He actually admitted to seeking the Templar treasure?"

"That was his true reason for wanting to be Valiant Master, plus it came with obvious perks. He wanted to explore the extensive archives to which only he would hold the key. Eventually, I assisted with decoding a letter we found in those archives, after convincing him that I was a necessary part of his quest, that God had delivered me to his door."

"He bought that—that God had brought you to him?"

"Why not? Clive Hogarth had an exaggerated sense of his own self-importance and believed that, as Valiant Master, he was anointed by God to locate the lost treasure. All his sins would be expunged in the eyes of the Lord if he were to succeed in his noble quest. He believed that he was seeking either the Holy Grail or the Ark of the Covenant and that such a find would make him famous, if not rich. I assured him that, as his only child as well as a scholar, I could help him with his quest. Of course he bought it."

"Nothing like aiming high. What about that letter you decoded?"

"It was in French, dated 1312, and written to Jacques de Molay from somebody—I'm guessing a woman—who signed her name as 'Shabûl,' claiming that the book had been safely delivered to London, per his request. The letter was heavily illustrated with vines, which is peculiar for correspondence at the time, and had a golden snail painted near the signature. Imagine our excitement—the one thing my father and I shared—when we held that letter and understood its meaning? An important book had been delivered to London for Jacques de Molay, who had since been executed, and where else could it be hidden but in the Temple Church? It could only hold the secrets the Order had struggled to preserve, something of great importance."

That was a huge leap, in my opinion, but I knew that treasure had been found on less. "Did you know it was a book?"

"I thought it was a Bible. I knew that it had to be something that would not have been destroyed as heretical."

"And your father?"

"I had enough coded tertiary evidence to convince him, too. In the end, it was I who pointed the way; I who suggested that the book could only be hidden in the crypt; and essentially I who led him right to it. We were to break into the crypt as soon as the time was right. What was my reward? He attempted to buy me off and told me to leave and never show my face again."

There had to be more to it than that but now I would only ever hear one side of the story. "So, he tried to bribe you?"

"To the tune of 20,000 pounds."

"But you refused to accept the terms?"

"I accepted the money but not the terms. I took the money—cash— and left without mentioning that I had no intention of stopping because he said so."

The expression *the apple never falls from the tree* came to mind. "So, your father used you but wouldn't let you share the rest of the journey?"

"He envisioned the glory all for himself and thought he knew my price—idiot. And then the pandemic hit, and London went into an intense and brutal lockdown. I knew he'd take that opportunity to raid the crypt, bastard that he was, but he wouldn't answer my calls. He ghosted me. When the lockdown lifted, Clive Hogarth had disappeared."

"Then how did you discover that he had found something in the crypt?"

"I had the Temple Church watched and put Dex on the job of being my eyes and ears in Sir Rupert's household. A few weeks ago, when Hogarth arrived back in London, I put a tail on both him and your father-in-law, which was easy since Dex worked for Fox. I knew that they were friends. Father Dear had often mentioned Sir Rupert."

"So that's how Dex entered the picture." I checked over my shoulder but he had gone.

"Dex, yes, but with the money Father paid me, we hired others. We followed both your father-in-law and Hogarth to the church that night. I realized then that Father had located the item and had hidden it until he could make his escape with your father-in-law's help. He had to have done this during lockdown when he had the perfect opportunity. That made me furious."

"So, you shot him?"

"I would have happily shot them both, had I the chance, but you interrupted me. It was enough that I shot Father but not with the intent to kill. I just wanted to shake him up a little, cause the conniving bastard some pain, the way he had me."

"But he was an elderly man. A gunshot wound is a pretty brutal way to make a point." I don't know why I said that. It's not like I was talking to a rational, feeling person.

"He deserved it. If not for me, he would never have found the Psalter in the first place, but what did I get for gratitude?"

"But why then kidnap him?"

"Because I needed collateral. My plan was to use him to retrieve the book from Fox, if we were unable to obtain it any other way. We had moles placed among the staff all over Fox's house. It should have been easy to retrieve the book but we misjudged that part when you became involved."

And I could only hope that Peaches and I played a role in making things very difficult. "And then your collateral had a heart attack and died," I remarked. *Your father, a man in his eighties.*

"He was determined to foil me in any way he could, wasn't he? But Dex snatched Fox's phone in time for us to learn all about the amazing Phoebe McCabe and then you and your friend did the groundwork for us. Thank you for that. Now I have the Psalter—and you—so I will win in the end."

No remorse, not even a smidgeon. "May I ask how you snatched the phone?"

She smiled—in a fashion. "Dex knew your father-in-law's habits, including that he would have a long bath most every night, leaving his phone in the bedroom. During the brief time when his personal guards changed watch, he caused a distraction and retrieved the phone."

. . .

"By first making an impression of Rupert's handprints?"

"That was accomplished by lifting his prints from various surfaces. That wax imprint that later was fashioned into a pliable skin-like substance—brilliant, really. We attempted the same for yours before both phones were deactivated."

"And you plan to track down whatever it is that you believe was hidden by the Templars but to what end—wealth, fame?"

She smiled again, at least that's how I'd identify that tightening of the lips. "Wealth, fame, a chance to be the one who finally solves the Templar secrets. There will be monetary rewards, certainly—how could there not be? I will be called upon to give talks, perhaps to go on the speaker's circuit, to write articles, possibly a book."

And what would happen to me, the one who would likely find this secret in the end? I knew the answer without asking: there would be no more me. Both Peaches and I would suffer some tragic accident and disappear. No one would ever know the truth, especially now that our phones were dead. Hopefully Evan had a fix on our location.

I gazed down at the remains of the plastic wrap balled in my hands. I needed to get the hell out of here, wherever here was.

"Enough talk. You now have the background that you claimed is required. Now you will timewalk."

"It doesn't work that way," I said, looking up at her. Backlit in the firelight, she looked almost demonic. I reminded myself that she was a wounded mortal the same as everyone else, only in this case, a wounded mortal with an ax to grind. "I can't just push a button and flip into timewalking mode. Often it doesn't happen at all."

"Then I will provide some incentive." Snapping her fingers, one of the man-minions popped into view. "Fetch me my tablet." In seconds, he was back holding an iPad. "Show her," she commanded.

The man held the tablet toward me, the screen fixed on something I couldn't make out at first but knew it was likely a live feed of Peaches. The bastards must have a satellite signal.

"That won't work," I said, keeping my eyes averted. "If you think that by showing me someone I care about suffering will make me timewalk, you have this all wrong. When and how I timewalk is not in my control, understand? And I can almost guarantee that becoming distraught will push me farther from the past, not closer!"

Squeezing my eyes shut, I attempted to shove away the scrambled images I caught before I'd looked away—Peaches bound in the back seat of the Rover, bleeding and unconscious—but I couldn't keep them at bay. Every passing second burrowed that picture deeper into my mind until I just snapped.

Lurching to my feet, I stumbled to within inches of Vish. "You take care of my friend and ensure her safety, or this lost-art sniffer dog won't lead you to anything!" I was so furious, so frustrated, at that moment that I almost screamed. "I'm not going to do your bidding!"

She lifted her eyebrows at me, a spark of chill amusement in her eyes. "Did you not just say that your timewalking could not be influenced by incentives? If that is the case, what difference will it make if I kill your friend now while you watch?"

Oh, my God, she would, too! I stared up, aghast, thinking that I might have just misplayed my hand. I was on the verge of crying or begging or both.

But suddenly she laughed. "Do not worry, Phoebe. I still have use for her. You will do as I want, regardless. I have read enough of your father-in-law's messages to know what will ensure that your timewalking abilities are activated. We won't even need to return to Foinikas immediately, or at least not until you have successfully identified the location. We will monitor your timewalking experience from here, where we have shelter and a little comfort."

My stomach threatened to expel my pita wrap on the spot. "I need to pee," I said. Mundane, yes, but equally true. Really, I needed to get away from her long enough to clear my thoughts and construct an escape plan. If there was a bathroom in this place, I might learn something more about the castle layout along the way. I held out my hands. "Unbind me, please. There are some things I can't do while shackled."

She gazed steadily down at me. "Maybe I should send one of the boys into the loo to assist you in that department?"

I gazed at her coolly, much of my emotion drained away by then. "Surely that's below their pay grade? Besides, I thought you said that there was no way I could escape from here?"

"There isn't. Untie her hands," she said to iPad guy.

Once I was free, I rubbed my wrists as he shoved me across the room, another one of the goons accompanying him Just before we left the main hall, I glanced back to see Vish gazing after us, smiling slightly. What in that woman's past had made her so hateful and uncaring? It didn't matter, I reminded myself. What mattered was getting Peaches and myself out of this mess alive. If I could preserve the lost treasure, all the better. It didn't appear that Vish planned to keep it for herself so much as capitalize on its discovery.

Without my phone, I had lost my only weapon as well as my communication conduit. Even if Evan had cut off those phones, I hoped that he could still use them—use something—to trace us. I had sent that message to Nicolina, too. She knew we were in Cyprus. Surely they would rescue us soon?

The castle was just as empty and enormous as I expected, but it seemed that my captors had set up camp on the main floor, utilizing only the one level, everything laid out in a huge square with corridors running parallel to the great hall. No castle came with only one floor, of course. There had to be an upstairs, a downstairs, a dungeon, a courtyard—countless places to hide with plenty of avenues of escape.

The toilet turned out to be one of those camping varieties shoved into an abandoned room that smelled heavily of disinfectant. One off my escorts slipped an electric lantern in through the door and told me to make it quick. Along with toilet paper and a roll of paper towels, there was a bucket of cold water for washing and a bottle of hand sanitizer. I did my business while listening to the rain beating against the boarded-up window, trying to stop myself from shivering. The cold wasn't getting to me so much as despair. I had never felt so alone in my life.

I made full use of the water to wash off some of the grime I'd accumulated on my hands, plunging my burning wrists deep into the soapy chill. Minutes later, I was standing inside the room waiting patiently until somebody banged on the door. "Hurry up in there or I'll come in and get you!"

I said nothing, just waited. Soon the door flew open, at which point I threw the bucket of water at one guy and the actual tin pail at the other before sprinting down the corridor. I had no idea which way I was heading—up or down didn't matter, as long as I got away. I needed to find a crack in the bastion in order to escape.

The boys were swearing at my heels by the time I reached the end of the corridor, turned right, and dashed into the darkness beyond. The scent of damp and mold were stronger here, the blackness so intense that I could barely see more than steps ahead. I failed to realize how slimy the floor was and so found myself skidding to my knees, which gave my captors time to catch up.

Nothing broken, though, because as soon as the first guy hauled me back to my feet by the scruff of my neck, I was able to twist around fast enough to knee him hard in the groin. The guy yelped and released me, giving me a chance to kick out at the second bastard, but the first guy soon had me wrestled into a headlock. I was then half-dragged back to the great room where Vish stood beside Dex, her arms crossed.

"We need to tie her back up," iPad guy said. "Bitch knows some moves."

"Do not call her or any woman a 'bitch' in my hearing," Vish said crossly. "Take her over there and keep her under control until we are ready." She was pointing to a table in the shadows that I hadn't noticed before. "Do it! Sit her down and bind her to the chair."

They did as she instructed, shoving me into a chair and using strips of fabric to tie my wrists in front of me and my feet together.

"Now, prepare yourselves," Vish ordered.

I watched as the four men began pulling on long white robes with red crosses on the front, pulled from the pile I'd seen earlier.

"Take the swords and strap them to your waist as I have shown you," she said.

Twisting in my seat, I watched as she dropped a long black habit over her own head, followed by a white mantle and a wimple, using the selfie camera on her iPad as a mirror to make the necessary adjustments. When she turned to face me moments later, she had been transformed. Gone was Katrina/Vish and in her place stood a mother superior from some order I could not identify; it had to be from the Middle Ages, though the habits hadn't changed much over the years.

"I know what you're doing," I said, "but this playacting of yours isn't going to work."

Vish ignored me. "Dex, get the Psalter."

The Psalter? I swallowed hard. Now I understood exactly what she had in mind and had to admit that it was deviously brilliant. I squirmed in my seat wondering how long I could stave off the inevitable. I began by hop-scraping the chair a few inches backward—desperate measures, really. "That won't work. I won't be able to find what you're looking for!" I said.

"If that's true, then both you and your friend will be dead before dawn," said Vish.

I gazed aghast as Dex, now dressed as a Templar knight, placed the Psalter down on the table while two others lifted up my chair and delivered me back into position.

"Untie her hands," Katrina ordered.

One of the men sliced the bindings with his knife.

"Now lay your hands on the Psalter," Dex demanded.

"No!" I said.

In response, the two men roughly grabbed my hands and forced them down upon the book.

"Say your prayers, Phoebe," I heard Vish say. "You are going to need them where you're going."

Chapter Seventeen

A fever must have addled my brain, for I had no other explanation for the strange things that beset me. The nun, the unknown knights, the peculiar castle with its massive hearth that looked familiar but not so —where was I, where was this?

"Allow me to help thee, child," said the woman with an odd manner of speaking, neither local nor French, or of any nature that I did know. My ears heard a foreign tongue and yet I somehow understood the meaning of the words.

I gazed across the table at the strange nun. Wearing the robes and wimple of a mother superior or perhaps a prioress, I could not identify her as being from any convent, monastery, or priory of which I had knowledge. And where was her cross? I knew of no mother superior who did not wear a cross or a rosary, be it ever so humble.

"Pray, who art thou, Mother? From what order doth thee hail and why for art thou here? Why am I? I feel most confused, as if a great fog has descended upon my brain." I spoke the same odd language as my ears heard, almost as if my lips were accustomed to speaking this strange tongue.

The woman spread her hands. "We were attacked, as were thou. We rescued thee and took thee to our castle. Do not be concerned if thou hast no memory of this because it was a quick and brutal act, and it appeared that thy suffered a blow to the head."

I touched my brow, feeling no pain, though my fingers came away with crusted blood. I gazed at the woman. "And the others?"

129

"Who in particular do you mean? We arrived after the massacre but there were no other survivors."

Everything about her seemed amiss, from her speech to the words she used, and the way in which she appeared to pluck answers from the air as if they were birds in flight. Nothing was as I remembered. She must lie, but to what end?

"I do not understand," I said carefully, gazing about trying to see where the light came from—not just from the firelight, it appeared, but from odd lanterns in which no candles burned. "You say that thou hadst rescued me but saw no others?" Where were my sisters?

"They had gone, we know not where, but when we arrived, the fort was deserted but for a few felled bodies. You were found among the rubble."

Fear banged against my heart. Perhaps my order had escaped to a place of refuge but left me behind? "Castle, of which castle do you speak? Who were our attackers? From whence did they come and from whence doest thou hail?" Now I found the words coming forth from my lips near as strange as hers. I knew that I must wrest my panic to the ground before it felled me. This woman lied to some end that had yet to be revealed but I must either awake from this dream or discover the truth.

She continued her tale. "A fleet of ships was spied off the coast, but days past, which we believe hailed from across the seas—Mamluks, perhaps, or invaders from the East. My convent was destroyed many months before, and a small band of knights rescued me with the promise to deliver me to a place of refuge. The knights came across you when word of the destruction of Foinikas reached their ears."

She now said "you" instead of "thou" but that was only the beginning of more such strange mutterings. "Mamluks so far from the East?"

Now it was she who appeared confused.

"Yes, the Mamluks have razed Foinikas to the ground."

I sat back, relieved to find my hands resting on something dear and familiar, for my Psalter, at least, had survived. But how did it come to be that we were reunited? "Foinikas?" I whispered. "I have not been to Foinikas for many decades. And how doth the Mamluks sail so far from their shores?"

The woman hesitated, as if fearing she had made a grave misstep. "You are mistaken—perhaps as a result of the blow to your head—but we are in Cyprus now. What do you remember last?"

"My convent in England." I spoke quickly—too quickly—for I sensed that the woman applied a forked tongue.

"But you have lived in Foinikas?"

"I resided once in the Commandaria della Finchia but that was long ago. Where is this?" I gazed around me, so terribly confused.

"I misspoke. I meant to say the Commandaria della Finchia. My mind, too, is much scrambled by the events that I have endured. Many of my sisters were slaughtered at the small outpost convent I established. Here we will bide until it is safe to sail for France."

France, the name of my home country sounded foreign on her tongue, as if she could not quite form the word with conviction. Perhaps she was testing me, this one, hoping that I would disclose more than she gave in return. I sensed a lack of patience within her, whereas patience was something which I possessed in vast reserves. This was a battle I would win as long as I did not allow my heart to rule. Meanwhile, I must struggle with these peculiar words, though they filled my head and reached my mouth with far more ease than I could have expected.

"My name is Mother Mary Marie of the Sacred Heart, and by what name shall I call you...*thee?*" the woman asked.

I always strove to winnow the kernels of truth from the chaff of deceit and this one made my quest an easy one for she was full of lies. She would not even speak her true name.

"My name is Suzanna de la Cotte," I said, also donning a false mantle, "and I hail from Burgundy."

"And how did you come to live among the Poor Fellow-Soldiers of Christ, my child?"

It rankled that she called me "child" as if she truly was superior to me when I suspected that she ruled over none but the wicked. She was no woman of God, of that I was certain. "I was brought here as a girl to serve in the kitchens after both of my parents were slaughtered at Acre. Pray from whence do you hail?" She hadn't yet disclosed that, though I had asked her thrice.

"I hail from a small priory in the land of the Gauls unknown by most but which was called Camdentown. Have thee had word of it?" she asked.

"I have not."

"I left the safety of my priory to establish an order in Cyprus, but it was sacked months ago. You and I both lack protection and resources, but for these few knights that accompany us here. Please, Suzanna, I beseech thee to tell me how we may further assist thou. Word has it that the Order based in your village held a great secret, one that many would desire to acquire. Should this fall into enemy hands, it might spell further disaster."

Ah, so at last we had arrived at the crux. She sought gold, of course. That should not surprise me and yet it did, for why was I involved, and how? This must be but a dream.

My gaze, which had been fixed on her face, shifted to my hands, clasped on top of the book. The dear Psalter was not as badly damaged as I might have expected, given that it no longer rested in its casket, but how did it come to be here? How did I? Nothing I knew or remembered could make sense of this. Still, a surge of joyful relief coursed through me at the sight of the Psalter, though I immediately attempted to hide it.

But not quickly enough.

"When we found you, you were clutching that Psalter as if your life depended upon it. Why is that?" The woman's eyes quickened with interest, as though she had caught my relief and readied herself to pounce.

I shook my head as memories began to seep into my mind like cold water on a fevered brain. Why did I recall hiding this Psalter in a crypt far away from Cyprus and why did I possess such clear memories of sailing forth back to France with my father and the other members of the Templar Order?

The day we sailed had broken warm and clear across the turquoise sea that embraced the island. I had looked behind me at the retreating shore, thinking of how I would miss those colors, but not the blistering heat that attended them. Likewise, my heart had been filled with dread at the prospect of the long voyage ahead. I longed for home but feared it at the same time, for word had reached us that the new French king was behaving without reason against all who crossed him, even if their only fault was to breathe the air. Rumor had it that the man had gone mad, and yet the fate of the Templars rested in his hands. When we reached French soil and Father heard word that rising forces did question the Templars' continuance, he sent me on to England to protect our secrets.

I remembered all of this and more. No memory of being attacked on this island plagued me but how could I forget such?

"Suzanna, why are you so quiet. Please speak," the woman urged.

But I was lost in my memories. As our voyage progressed, we were to stop at many ports, gathering news as we went, learning of how the Templar fortunes appeared to be tossed upon the waves of changing opinion and fearing that, at any day, the Order would either be dissolved or merged with the Knights Hospitaller. I knew that Father would make one last attempt to rally support around another Crusade, citing the wanton manner in which the heathens did claim the land upon which Christ had once walked. How could good Christians allow this travesty to continue? We had won victory before and surely would do so again.

I could remember the sound of my father's voice, as if he had just spoken those words but moments before. He had been as eloquent as he had been impassioned, despite his advancing years.

And yet, still he would fail. How did I know this? I knew this because I received word of his execution while cloistered at Aldgate Abbey, where I would live until my dying day. The pain of that news still rent my heart as fiercely now as it had when first I heard the news. But here this woman told a different tale, as if I had not lived the true one myself. I knew that I had lived and died in the story I recalled.

A tremor beset my body. I recalled lying ailing in my bed surrounded by my Franciscan sisters, knowing that I had lived a goodly life and would ready myself for a goodly death. I counted nearly eighty-three years when the fever took me that day, eighty-three years of service to our Lord and the Holy Order. The Lord awaited me in Heaven, but if I had truly died, had I gone to hell instead? For, in truth, I believed myself surrounded by devils.

"Suzanna, do you feel unwell? It is no surprise given what you have experienced. It is normal to be confused with such a head injury. Let us fetch you some ale."

I made to stand but a strong hand pushed me back into my chair. Every inch of me shook as if I had fallen headfirst down a deep, dark well.

"Sir Dex, perhaps we might offer our guest a light repast?" the false nun asked.

"It shall be done. I shall check the larder," said the man.

I turned to regard this knight more closely then, noting how the cross on his chest appeared to be painted on and not worked by needle and thread as was the rule. Why the slipshod way in which he belted his sword? No knight would be permitted to wear his weapon so.

I swung back to the woman. My body shook so badly I could hardly speak. "Thou liest! Who art thou, in truth? Thou art no mother superior and this be no knight, for no knight that I have known behaves so!"

Lurching to my feet, I sidestepped the man before he could lay hands on me. Still clutching the Psalter, I regarded closely the hall in which I stood. The manner in which the flickering firelight illuminated objects that I could not identify was intensely unsettling. This could not be real. Was I dead or was this but a dream? Was this the afterlife I had been promised? Would I meet my father here, and others that I had befriended? But no afterlife would come with these demons around me, surely?

The woman was holding up her hands as if to beseech me, her wimple now askew. "You—thou—are unwell," she said, stepping toward me. I noted how strange her shoes were—black with thick soles that did not look like leather.

133

"Pray calm thyself, for you have been hurt and do not think with a clear mind."

"Thou liest!" I cried. Why did I not feel as myself? Even my body did not move as I expected, and I feared that panic would grip me by the throat and leave me too rattled to act. "Speak!" I demanded. "Who art thou in truth? Where is this place and why do I recall living—and dying—differently from what thou claim? Our fort was not attacked while I lived there. We sailed away before the enemy came, which was much later. I—I *died* as a Franciscan nun in England, many miles from home. I must be dead now and my father before me. They executed him like a common thief, whereas he was a noble, loyal knight sworn to his Order." At once, I knew that I had said too much.

Now excitement flared in the woman's eyes. "Who was your father? Tell me!"

"Name yourself truly first!" said I.

I stepped back. At that moment, someone came up behind me and slapped a hand on my shoulder. Clutching the Psalter, I swung around, pulled the sword from his scabbard to brandish it before me. The thing was so rusted it was hardly a sword at all but its weight felt good in my hands, though my arm seemed barely able to hold it up. My fighting skills were as rusty as the blade. "You will step back, or I will bring this down upon your head."

The man snickered. "Come on, lady. Drop the big bad sword before you get hurt."

If I was already dead, what did it matter? I swung the rusted metal hard at the man, hitting his shoulder, and watched him fall to his knees, screaming. "Ah, she broke me bloody shoulder!"

The woman strode toward me holding some small silver metal object in her hand. "Stop before I shoot!"

Shoot? What was shoot? In seconds, I swung the sword at the man named Dex approaching from my left, whacking him broadside in the chest. He fell back on the floor, clutching his breast, gasping. Then I leaped upon the table and stood there on shaking legs, still clutching the sword and holding the Psalter. The two other false knights surrounded me on my perch, one holding a knife, the other the same type of shiny object as the woman—something small, stunted, unable to hurt a thing. "Call off your dogs, false woman," I cried, "or I will beat them down one by one."

The woman tossed off her wimple and laughed, a sweep of lank streaked brown hair shaking free. "You are a swordswoman! Well done you, but that sword you hold has not seen battle for centuries, and neither have you. Come down and let us talk like civilized people."

"No lies. Speak the truth," I cried.

"You have my word, no more lies. We will talk truthfully, beginning now."

I tossed down the sword, its clanging on the tiles echoing across the hall. I craved a better one.

"This object I hold in my hands is far deadlier than any sword. It is called a gun. Watch." She aimed toward an old shield hanging on the wall, and appeared to press down on something like a trigger with one finger, an act that sent a tiny whizzing thing past me to ping into the shield, leaving a perfectly round hole. I stared. "What witchcraft is this?"

"Guns are far deadlier than you can imagine. They can kill many without ever having to lift a sword or throw a spear or shoot an arrow. One need not be strong to wield a gun. I can kill with little effort."

"That is shameful," said I. "There is no honor in killing thus."

"Honor holds no value in this world. Come down from the table and sit with me so we may speak. I promise to tell the truth, no matter how difficult it may be for you to hear."

"It is easier to hear the truth than lies," I told her, jumping down. My body felt young and strong but still foreign. How could I still do these things when the last I remembered I was so stooped over that I could barely walk?

"You may find this truth harder to swallow than you think," said the woman, indicating the chair that I had just left. "We will have something to drink and discuss how things must go."

"You going to let her just go free, boss?" the shoddy knight with the wounded shoulder asked. "I think she broke something. I need a doctor."

"Oh, be quiet, Luke. Dex, if you're still alive over there, bandage him up and stop him from whining. Give him something for the pain, while you're at it. Call up the other two and tell them to join us here. Who knows where this will go?"

Eyeing me warily, the man named Dex picked himself up off the floor. "Kat, I don't think it's smart to let this one go free. Let me bind her hands at least."

I tensed, ready to spring.

"I doubt if she'll let you get that close. She's obviously a warrior, something you'd never understand. Do as I say. Now," she said, turning to me. "My name is Katrina and I do not come from the same century as you and, yes, I have been telling falsehoods, as have you. Let us speak honestly now. Let us speak the truth."

Chapter Eighteen

I f the truth lived on the tongue of a viper, then perhaps I heard it now, for nothing she said made sense,

"You are not in the 1300s but in a time far in the future—2023, in fact."

"That is not possible," I whispered.

"I would not have thought so, either, but the world is full of miracles. Look around you. This castle is one that you probably knew in your time but has since been destroyed by the centuries, countless invaders, and political machinations, as has most everything else you have known. Still, there are many wonders that did not exist in your time."

She lifted a flat metal object that looked like a rectangular pewter plate and turned it toward me so that I could view a painting—no, not a painting, I realized, but something different. The images moved. I could be looking out a window at a ruin, the landscape of which appeared very much like our old fortification, yet different.

It took a moment for me to recognize the Commandaria della Finchia looking as if it had been razed to the ground, or perhaps permitted to crumble away over the centuries. Plants choked rooms where I had trod but years before, the surrounding landscape bleak and deserted. What was stranger still was that the picture was moving, even though it was flat and not a true window. I looked about me but I and everything around me stood still.

"It is magic," I whispered, "and thou truly art a witch."

She smiled, though I saw no mirth there. "If I am a witch and magical, then so is everyone else in this time because we can all perform what you'd consider witchcraft. Dex, show our guest your phone."

The man had just entered the hall carrying two cups that appeared to be fashioned from pale parchment or possibly vellum. "I brought the ale," he said before placing the cups down, one in front of each of us. One hand remained pressed flat against his chest as he winced, casting a suspicious glance in my direction. Soon, he was sliding a hand-sized, rectangular metal object toward me before stepping to the safety of the other side of the table, as if expecting me to pounce. The woman lifted her hand, indicating that he sit beside her.

"Pick it up, please," she told me, pointing to the object.

I did so, turning the strange, hard thing in my hand. It was like no metal I had ever seen or felt—cold yet a peculiar silvery color. I shivered and lowered the thing to the table. Dex reached over and fetched it back.

"With these you can speak to people across vast distances, create a light where there is darkness, and take pictures, which means it will capture an image without using paint or paper. Here's mine. Almost everyone has such a device." She held up a similar object. "Look." Soon she was showing me countless window-like views of people and things, some of which moved, flipping through them using her finger alone. "They are as common as dirt in this age."

Pushing my thumb into my temple, I tried to force reality back into my brain. This could not be real, none of it. I picked up the strange cup, which felt light—too light for either wood or metal—and sipped the contents, hoping it might clear my mind. It was akin to ale but not , as it was weak and tasteless, but I was grateful, for it quenched my thirst. It was then that I noticed the ring on my left hand—gold, fashioned like leaves nested with diamonds, very beautiful. "That is not mine!" I gasped, almost dropping the cup.

"It isn't, and neither is the hand that wears it. Here is the truth," the woman was saying, both she and her escort regarding me as if I was the one who was mad. "Your entire world is gone, as are you in the natural order of things. You are sitting here almost seven hundred years after your death. How is that possible, you ask? Because the body you inhabit belongs to another. This host has the ability to enter another's mind across the centuries by touching an object that resonated with her, which in this case, I believe, is the Psalter you keep so close. You are in her body now."

I gazed from her to the Psalter, dumbfounded. "No," I gasped.

"Yes," she assured me.

"How did you find the Psalter?" I asked.

"We'll talk about that later but first you must understand your situation. Look at yourself here and tell me what you see." She took the larger rectangular object and brushed her fingers across the surface, then turned it to face me. "Hold it," she ordered.

I refused, keeping my hands clasped on my book, it being the only familiar thing in this entire fearsome place.

"It won't hurt you. It is a tool in the way of paper and pen, only far more powerful. It is designed by humans to help us do our chores. If you hold it in front of you now, it will act like a looking glass and you will see your face—or the one which you currently inhabit—as well as everything within its view. Mankind has advanced very far over the last seven hundred years, somewhat to our detriment as much as to our glory."

With trembling fingers, I held the object the way she had instructed, one hand on either side. On the smooth surface—glass?—images shifted according to the direction in which I moved. The central image kept slipping in and out of view until finally I fixed on a woman with thick, curly red hair, pale skin, and a haunted look in her blue eyes. A recent cut on her forehead had left a trickle of dried blood down one side of her head. She appeared haunted yet determined, much the way I felt at that moment. Had I seen her, I would have feared for her life because one such as she could so easily be branded as a witch. Still, I liked her face, and yet I both feared and pitied her.

"Who is she?" I whispered.

"At the moment, she is you, but before you awoke in her body, she was named Phoebe McCabe, a treasure hunter and seeker of other people's belongings. In this age, she is very dangerous and my sworn enemy. She would call what is happening to you 'timewalking,' though I doubt that even she expected her abilities to have progressed to this extent. I understood that she could step into the past but now it appears that she can bring the past into the present."

Another chill racked my body. All those years I had spent deep within myself—writing, painting, drawing, studying, learning—and never once could I have imagined such a marvel as this. I was alive again, like Jesus Christ returned from the dead, but not in that manner for nothing about this abomination felt holy or divine. "Where is God?" I whispered.

Katrina shrugged. "Let us not talk about religion. That subject is as fractious now as it was in your day, and people still slaughter each other in the name of God."

I knew the truth in those words for I had witnessed so many battles, so much death, though this was one subject in which I could never have engaged in discourse with any living soul. To speak ill of relgion as well as any pope or priest, king or queen, would be either heretical or treasonous, and thus we all had good reason to fear such accusations. But my faith in God had never wavered, only my faith in man. This woman feared nothing, it seemed.

Taking a deep breath to steady my heart, I said: "So I am in borrowed form?"

"You are."

"I wish to walk around to explore this century." I did not believe anything she said but was hard-pressed to explain what I experienced.

Katrina stood. "By all means walk, but you cannot leave this room. We are in hiding in this castle as we have reason to believe that Phoebe's friends will attempt to rescue her, and you would not want that."

Why would I not want that? I wondered. Did Katrina think that I would desire to prolong this unnatural situation, which was a travesty to both God and man? Did she think this strange world of hers was somehow so tempting that I would desire to remain here to live and die yet again?

I got to my feet and, tucking the Psalter under my arm, took a step across the flagstones, followed by another and another. This body felt good, not racked with the constant pain I recalled bearing even in my younger years. Then, my bones and rotting teeth had ached constantly. My joints had often been swollen and sore to the touch, though the healers would attempt to ease the aches with poultices and strong ale. Now I stood tall, this body I inhabited fit, though not fighting fit, something to which I had aspired in my youth.

To be alive and feeling well sent intense joy coursing through me, though it brought forth an equal measure of guilt. This body was not mine, this life only borrowed, and yet here I was, standing in another's shoes—actually, stockinged feet. I stuck my leg out, studying the tight breeches I wore, rubbing the fabric of the knitted smock between my fingers. "Is this what women wear in this time?"

Katrina laughed. "People dress in countless ways in this century—all different, however they please. Women don't cover their heads, as in your day, either, and we live as freely as any man."

I stared in wonder. To live freely, to choose one's own path in life, not at the mercy of men—what great wonder is this? Perhaps this was heaven, after all? Maybe this was my reward for long years in the service of God, to be reborn anew to live in a new form, healthy and unshackled?

I turned to face the woman and the two men, now watching me steadily, the men wearing sour faces. "When does this Phoebe McCabe reclaim her body?"

"Perhaps never," Katrina said. "Timewalking is uncharted territory so please let me know what you are experiencing. It's interesting to find that you can speak in modern English when obviously your own language would be quite different. It must be something to do with her physical brain—it, at least, is a product of this century and so must be wired to speak the modern tongue."

I shook my head, baffled. "Wired?"

"It means that the neurons in your brain are accustomed to speaking in a certain way. Never mind—there's no time to sort all that out now. Let's move on. Since you have an opportunity to live again, why not stay? There may be a way in which you can keep Phoebe away and assume her body, as well as her life, as your own. I'm thinking that the longer she stays away, the harder it will be for her to return. Have you felt another tugging at your mind?"

Katrina used unfamiliar words composed in awkward sentences, but it was true that I still grasped the gist and found myself speaking in a similar fashion. It was as if these strange words appeared fully formed inside my mouth. "I do not know what another 'tugging on my mind' feels like but, should I sense such, I will say so. Where is this Phoebe now?"

"I don't know. Perhaps she is asleep or simply unconscious inside of that head you're using."

"Unconscious?"

"It means to be unaware, in some deep mental state of nothingness," Dex said.

"You believe that this Phoebe may be in purgatory?" I asked.

"I don't think in religious terms but, if that works for you, then fine," Katrina replied.

Her way of thinking baffled me. She spoke of belief as if it were not the very air we breathe but something separate from our souls—"religion"—but there was more amiss with her than that. "But this is her life, not mine. I have lived mine."

"You have been brought back for a reason. It must be God's will."

How odd that she embraced the Lord one minute and cast Him aside when it suited her. Yet, if it was God's will that I be here, to what purpose? This Katrina would not be the one to tell me such, but God Himself, if I could but hear Him. "Let us continue on the path and see how matters will unfold."

"Excellent!" This time the woman's smile seemed genuine. "Then let us sit down and become better acquainted. Let's become friends, in fact. You will need a friend in this new life, and we have more in common than you think."

I found that difficult to believe, but in the light of everything else too strange to fathom, that was probably the mildest. Yet, to have her as a friend? Throughout my life, the best that I could hope for were kindly companions bound together by a common goal—such as the sisters at the convent, and

Brother Michael. This woman and I would never be friends but remain two people caught in a dance of deceit.

I stepped toward the table. At that moment, three other men dressed in strange shirts and tunics—neither short nor long—entered the room. Eyeing me warily, one addressed Katrina: "Just heard from the guys at Foinikas. The black woman has come to and is causing grief. They've got her bound up in the back of the van but want to know what to do with her next. They think that they might be being watched. They saw lights up on the hill last night."

Katrina picked up the palm-sized metal object and stared at its surface. "Keep an eye on our guest. I'll be back in a minute." She strolled away, seeming to speak into the air. I watched, baffled. How long would it take to adjust to this new world, and what was a "minute," anyway? Would I know one when I saw such a thing?

"Why isn't she restrained?" one of the new men asked the Dex fellow.

"The boss says to let her remain free. You might say that she's not herself," and he laughed. "She thinks she's somebody in the fourteenth century."

The two men gazed at me, one of them smirking. "Does she now? What gives her a daft idea like that?"

"Just leave it, Sam, and do as you're told." Dex stepped toward me, bowed, and held out his hand. "May I escort you back to the table, m'lady?"

I slapped away his hand and strode past him toward the table. I had known ladies but briefly once, but knew enough now to see it as a useless and silly way in which to live. My mother, bless her soul, must have had aspirations when she bedded my father, but it was never to be. My father's brief dalliance was only that, as he refused to be shackled to the world into which he had been born. The life of a squire or a lord was not his calling, as to be a wife had not been mine.

I took my seat, keeping my attention fixed on the seven men now in attendance. None appeared to be hardened soldiers. I saw no sign of battle in the sinews of their arms and legs, only flaccid muscle too used to wielding tools of air to build brawn sufficiently. My guess is that they could be easily bested.

"Pray tell me, what steed do you ride?" I asked Dex, remembering how I had loved to tend the animals in my free moments at the convent, as well as to ride about the island while residing among the Templars. In Cyprus, I could even ride as a woman, though I chose not to dress as one. Much as Phoebe, I preferred to keep my legs unfettered.

Dex seemed to hesitate while the others stood by, snorting in derision. One had fetched a bottle of something from a case and now stood swilling it with gusto. Wiping his mouth on his sleeve, he laughed. "Eight cylinder dual exhaust is my steed of choice, m'lady." He bowed low but not in deference. He'd be an easy one to best for he was but a thin, weak man who chose to hide behind his words. Yet, I noted that he wore a knife strapped to his belt. Now, knives I had been taught to use as well as any sword, though it had been long ago. How much could I still recall?

I turned my gaze to Dex. "I would like to see these steeds, for I do miss them."

Dex smiled, not unkindly. "I'm afraid that horses have gone the way of swords, m'lady. We use sleek metal wagons for travel now—very fast. Everything is bloody fast these days. Perhaps Katrina will agree to take you for a ride in one of those soon—once we learn where the treasure is, that is."

Two of the men stepped forward, the rest joining the others lounging on the cases and crates against the walls. "She knows where the loot is?" one asked, the lean one with the big mouth, the one with the knife.

"That's what the boss thinks," Dex told him.

"But she's not talking?" asked another.

"Why not beat it out of her? I'd gladly have a go, if nobody else has the stomach for it," Big Mouth said.

"This is not your business, Sam," Dex said fiercely. "Take your beer, grab a sandwich, and shut the fuck up."

Big Mouth stepped back with a sneer on his broad face. Maybe thirty years of age, he no doubt knew how to scrap but not to truly fight. I had been trained in the fighting yards of the Templars on this very isle—if, in truth, that was where we stood. It had been acknowledged that all able bodies who could wield a sword must learn to do so.

We had always expected an attack and remained at the ready. Surely some things are so deeply learned that they can never be forgotten?

Katrina strode back across the hall. Flicking her hand, she told the men to wait somewhere else. We had things to discuss, she said, and only Dex could remain. The men gathered up their things and strode from the room, complaining all the way, while Dex joined us at the table.

"They are not well-disciplined, these men of yours," I said.

"I know it," Katrina acknowledged, "but they are hired guns that I employ for a purpose. The men these days are not nearly as disciplined as those you are used to but are the best I could gather. I had hoped to hire a military team but that was not possible on such short notice. Dex is the only reliable man here." A brief spark of something passed between them. Were they lovers? I felt a brief twist of envy for I had never had a lover, though in my girlish dreams I had often imagined such.

"Now," she said, focusing on me, "tell me what I need to know. We are running out of time."

I raised my eyebrows. Running out of time? I had run out of time many centuries hence, it seemed. "What is it you desire?"

"Begin with your name, your true name."

That much I had resolved to say. "I am Suzanna de Molay, born in France in the year of our Lord 1259, to a peasant mother and a young knight who foolishly permitted himself a moment of lustful pleasure."

Her excitement was unmistakable. She almost couldn't speak under its force. I could see the interest quickening in Dex's eyes also. "Jacques de Molay, the last Grand Master, was your father? But how did you come to be brought here?"

"Though my father did not—would not, in truth—marry my mother. His remorse was so profound that he vowed that his child would fall under his protection, an oath to which he adhered all his days. I was sent to a convent at a young age, instructed how to read and write, in which I grew proficient, and one day in the year 1269, a troop of Templar brothers arrived at the convent in Burgundy and took me with them to the East."

"You, as a girl, were brought into a community of fighting monks?" Dex asked.

"It was not unusual for children to be taken to work in convents and monasteries, but rarely were females so employed by monks, let alone Templars, it is true. In this case, word had reached the Order that, even though I was young, I had not only achieved great skills with my letters, but also as an illuminator.. My father was rising among the Templars and he was instrumental in bringing me along. This I did not know until many years hence."

"Was your father Grand Master at the time?" Dex asked.

"No, not until much later. When we set sail for the East, Thomas Bérard was Grand Master. I fell under the tutelage of Brother Michael, the Order's chief scribe and chronicler, whose task it was to keep an account of the Templar's history for posterity. He was a good man and a kind one, teaching me everything he knew. I lived my days in a scriptorium and, more often than not, in the saddle, traveling with the knights. Eventually, we settled in Cyprus, where the Templars attempted to strengthen our defenses and to muster support for a new Crusade."

Katrina's eyes were wide with wonder. "A woman living among the Templar knights?"

I sensed a hint of something illicit in her tone and quickly quashed it. "Never did I announce my sex openly. I bound my breasts and dressed as a boy, and though many knights knew the truth, none chose to challenge me. I fought as well as many knights in the practice yards, and if any knew of my true nature, none spoke of such."

"How is that possible?" Katrina asked.

"I lived apart, in a cell next to Brother Michael, or in the stables, if one could be found. I kept my head down, my mouth closed, and poured my thoughts and skills into the chronicles, as was my goal."

"Into that Psalter," Katrina whispered, eyeing the book. "You were the one who wrote the final entries."

"I was the one who fashioned the illustrations and applied the paint and gold. Brother Michael was the scribe, I the painter." How I wanted to hide the small volume from view at that moment, as if Katrina's gaze would but sully it but, of course, it was already too late. Still, it felt as though every glance people cast in that direction was an insult somehow.

I met her gaze steadily. "It is—it *was*—my life's work. I strove to ensure that the truth of the Order was consigned to history in the paintings that I fashioned, for we feared that others might attempt to tell another tale."

"Fake news from another time," Dex remarked.

"I beg your pardon?" I said.

"Never mind. Do you know what actually happened to the Order in the end?" he asked.

"I do," I said softly. "My father sensed what was afoot. It was while living in Cyprus that he chose to inform me of my parentage. Before then, I had no idea, thinking myself only another orphan among countless others. I had lived and worked all my days, grateful to be well-fed, with a roof over my head, clothes on my back, and good and noble endeavor in which to engage."

Katrina nodded as if she grasped such concepts.

"My father, by then the Grand Master, wanted me to know who and what I was," I continued. "He made me vow to guard the Psalter at all costs, thinking that as a woman I might better sink into the background unchallenged. He feared that the Knights Templar might someday disappear, though he had no idea of the full truth of that prediction or of its calamitous nature. In October 1306, I left Cyprus in the company of my father and other members of the Order in a convoy of three ships. Two would sail to France with my father, later another to England with me on board that would later sail to parts unknown. My father and I would never meet again."

"You are the Shablool," Katrina whispered, a note of reverence touching her words.

I took a deep breath. "How do you know this?" Nobody knew this except those long dead.

"I have studied you, searched for you for years, both as a scholar and as another woman. You are the one who remained hidden, the one who told the Templars' story, and held its secrets safe. I followed your hidden trail, which led me here. We have much in common, you and I."

"And who are you and what is your parentage?"

"I am Katrina Hogarth of Camden Town. I, too, am not bound to any man but in the manner of my choosing. I'm neither a wife nor a mother but a scholar, as are you."

"And why are you here?" I asked.

"To find what has been hidden by the Poor Fellow-Soldiers of Christ on this very island. Almost seven centuries have passed and the Order no longer exists, except in the honorary sense. There is no need to continue to keep what has been buried secret a single moment longer, when to unearth the truth may give life and purpose to others."

"Such as you?"

"Me and others. You are the Shablool, the secret keeper. We are meant to be allies, you and I, for we are both Templar's daughters and the keepers of secrets. You are honor bound to share yours with me and I mine with you, as if we were sisters."

Chapter Nineteen

I sensed no honor in this one. "How can you be the daughter of a Templar when you say that the Order has been gone for hundreds of years?" I demanded, my borrowed heart thundering in my ears.

"I said gone but, in the honorary sense, it still exists. My late father's title was Valiant Master, as he held the position of reverend of the Temple Church in London until recently."

I shook my head, attempting to make sense of this, and reached for the ale, grateful to take another long draw. "Reverend, not priest?"

Katrina snapped her fingers, which sent Dex away to fetch more ale. "England officially became Anglican—which is rather like a blend of Catholicism and Protestantism—during the sixteenth century under the reign of King Henry VIII. Long story there. Catholicism still exists in England and people are permitted to follow whatever religion they choose, including Muslim and Hindu, without persecution. My father was Anglican."

"And your father was a Knight Templar?"

"Not in the way that you know. It was an honorary title only, but it placed him in a position to research the Order's history and, together, we set off on a quest."

"What became of him?"

"He died of heart failure."

Dex had returned to pour more liquid in my cup. I held the vessel steady for him with both hands.

She shot him. He only died hours later of heart failure after she kidnapped him!

That came to me as half thought, half memory, for I clearly saw Katrina standing over an old man prone on the floor, holding one of those metal objects she had shown to me. I nearly gasped but held steady.

"A quest? In search of what?" I asked, lowering the cup with trembling fingers and placing one hand back on the Psalter.

"We know that the Templars had become a wealthy and powerful Order, one that had accumulated vast amounts of gold and property. Though much of it was confiscated by Pope Clement and King Philip IV, and much given over to the Knights Hospitaller, there has long been the belief that some was hidden elsewhere."

"As I suspected, you are hunting for gold," I said. Snake.

"Gold, jewels, precious artifacts, perhaps the Holy Grail or the Ark of the Covenant." She was almost breathless with excitement, her eyes sparkling with a hunger that must still lure men even to this day. Mankind had not advanced so very far, methinks.

"Why do you think that I can help you with such a quest?" I asked.

"Because you know where such a treasure is buried. As the Shablool, it was your role to chronicle all significant events in the Templar history, as well as to guard that story. If you set sail with your father from these shores in 1306, he must have entrusted you to bring the Psalter to England in order to hide it, along with all the secrets coded in that volume, which you did, in the Temple Church. Nothing is hidden with such care without good reason."

I swallowed, thinking back to the day when I laid the iron box in the tomb of one of the last remaining Templar knights in Britain, following my father's decree. I had entered in a funeral procession of Sir Geoffrey Bracket, donning a nun's robes, and thus had been granted full access to the crypt. "How did you find the Psalter?" I whispered.

Katrina smiled. "Because I am a Templar's daughter, too, and God led me right to it."

Her boldfaced lie hit me like an ache in the chest. She was using the name of the Lord to ply me for her uses now? Yet, I had not survived all these long years without some wisdom of my own. I smiled. "As God has led me to you."

"Exactly! You see, we are bound together, you and I?—two sisters across the centuries. How exciting this is! You will earn your reward in this lifetime, Suzanna, and together we will become very rich and famous. No one will ever know your true story, of course, but as Phoebe McCabe you can live and work by my side. She already has a level of fame due to her strange powers, but your knowledge of the Middle Ages will come in handy as we take this around the world." She leaned toward me, almost panting with enthusiasm. "You will live a life that you could never have dreamed of. This is your heaven, Suzanna!"

But it made me ill to think so. I longed for the comfort of the familiar—the desk where I would work each day with parchment and ink, the brilliant colors flowing from brush or pen. If not life, then afterlife, and neither in this form did I desire. This snake thought she offered me heaven on earth? "How did God lead you to the Psalter?"

She was smiling broadly now, thinking that she had me in her grip. "My father had been a Templar historian in England and I worked with him to discover the trail. I found a letter hidden deep in the archives, a letter written by you to your father. It never reached him, from what we could tell, but ended up in the Templar library where I discovered it. Written in code, as it was, many had not put the effort into deciphering it, but I knew enough to put together the basic information. You are clever at creating puzzles and ciphers, but I am equally good at decoding them."

So, Father never knew in the end that I had fulfilled his wishes. He died at the stake all those brutal years ago thinking himself a failure, with all those he had served during his life becoming monsters, guilty of the worst kind of betrayal. I still recalled the day when Mother Superior brought me word. All of us, at every religious house across the land, believed what happened to the Templars a travesty. Emotion gripped me by my throat but I refused to cry. "And how did you learn that I was the Shablool?"

"Partially through your illustrations and partially through Phoebe McCabe, who actually read the Psalter before I did. My father had hidden it in the Temple Church and her father-in-law helped him to remove it from the premises undetected. I overheard her conversations through this." She held up the palm-sized object. "Phoebe has some skill in these matters and deduced the meaning of the snail first but the book was mine to claim, not hers. I am the Templar's daughter, not her."

And yet she shot her father, the Templar who was not a Templar. "The Psalter was stolen?" I asked.

"How can one steal something that no one knows exists?" Katrina countered.

"And what did Phoebe plan to do with the book?"

"Perhaps give it to a museum or an archive—who knows? Forget Phoebe. She's gone. You and I are all that matters now, and maybe Dex." She lightly touched him on the hand and offered him a fleeting smile. He sat with his palms face down on the table, watching me carefully. He seemed irritated.

"We have no time to talk further, Suzanna," he spoke at last. "Tell us where the treasure is buried so we can retrieve it and leave this island. Trouble is closing in." He showed Katrina his phone object, where it seemed as though words had appeared on its surface.

"Damn," she said under her breath. "How many?"

"Maybe three trucks heading this way but there could be more," he replied.

"Get the helicopter ready." She turned to me. "It's time to tell me where the treasure is buried, Suzanna. We still need to escape this island unchallenged if we are to launch our new life."

I took a deep breath. "Why would you believe there is treasure?"

Anger flashed across her eyes, her true nature revealed in an instant. "Don't waste my time. You have no need to hide anything anymore."

"Why do you believe there is treasure here? What is it that has led you to believe such?" I persisted.

She whipped the book out from beneath my hands before I could stop her and I watched in panic as she flipped open the pages—brittle, each leaf as dear to me as my own flesh, though lost to me now, my whole life carefully transcribed in every line and flourish. I knew that book from cover to cover, line by line. The scribes that preceded me had chronicled every Psalm with the illustrations that told the Order's story, to which I had added the last chapters. All that had become my story, too, as I had lived my life to craft the art that flowed with the words. My contributions, though near the end of the book, were no less important for being last, even though I had not the chance to paint the final flourish.

"There." She turned the book toward me, her finger tapping on the illustration of the snail with the golden shell. "That's the symbol for hidden riches, riches that the location of which the Shablool was entrusted to keep, while the snail without the shell on the last page indicates that the riches were left behind." She slapped her palm down upon the table. "Now speak! We have run out of time!"

"You are mistaken. There was no treasure buried in Cyprus that I know of, and surely the invaders left nothing of value behind when they stormed the fortress? The Mamluks were not only fearsome fighters but would have left no stone unturned in search of valuables. The Templars were not so foolish as to leave riches behind when attack might be imminent."

"Then where is it?" she demanded, voice raised now.

"I do not know. The location of Templar wealth was not a subject that was disclosed to me, a mere scribe and a woman, too. Why would I be entrusted with such things?" I hoped my words rang true for I fought to grant them conviction.

"I don't believe you," Katrina said with such ferocity that it seemed as though she bit down upon her very words. For a moment, I thought that she might strike me. "It's too late for lies! You either tell me where it is buried or both you and your host body will be thrown over the cliffs to die a horrible death. Is that what you want? And I will not hesitate to torture you to make you tell me the truth first, do you get that?" Her fist rattled the table.

I winced, pulling back. For just one fleeting second, I sensed a thought passing through my mind. *Resist her. We have allies.*

"Boss, we've got to leave now." The other men had run into the room. "Our scouts have seen an army truck on the road heading this way," one said.

"Tell the pilot to be at the appointed spot. We will meet there within the hour. Get the trucks and the boat ready." She stood up, turning to me. "I had so much faith in you, expecting you to jump at what I offered—to live another life. What fool refuses that? But make no mistake: you will tell me where the treasure is buried or watch more people die."

"What about the book?" Dex asked.

"Bind it to her chest. The moment she takes her hands off that thing, she could return to being Phoebe McCabe. We need her to tell us where the treasure is first."

Though I readied for the struggle, I was no match for eight men approaching me from behind. They bound my hands before me and strapped the Psalter to my person with brute force. Strange boot-like things were shoved upon my feet, a hooded jacket flung over my shoulders, and I was shoved across the hall and down the stairs with little care.

"Don't break any bones, you dolts," Katrina cried. "She's the golden goose who will deliver our nest egg."

Thus began a vast, fearsome, nightmare voyage. How does one explain a metal, horseless wagon that seemed to roll down a road faster than the speed of twenty beasts, or the sight of candles that were not formed of flames, flitting past? So fearsome did I find all this, that I squeezed my eyes shut as the wagon rolled forth, thinking that I might be ill from the sheer force of such speed.

A man sat on either side of me while I sat wedged in the middle. Once in a while, I'd glance to see one man check his phone thing and seemed to read numbers there before quickly closing my eyes again.

. . .

How much sand remained in the hourglass I knew not, but soon it seemed that the metal wagon drew to a stop and I was bundled out to stand shivering by a vast body of water. Across the water's broad back, I saw lights sparkling that could not be stars for they were so low in the sky, and yet there appeared to be too many to count. Had I been tasked to draw such, I would not know where to begin.

"That's a town," Dex said beside me, but before I could ask for more detail, I was shoved toward a dock where rocked a vessel that appeared like the long-boats of yore but much smaller, and without paddle or oars. Again, pinioned between two men, I sat in an enclosed space while the vessel flew across the water, riding the bucking waves as if they were of no consequence.

When at last the boat came to a halt, I could barely stand, so weak were my knees. I recovered quickly once upon dry land but that was not to last. Soon, I was led to another strange craft formed of metal, with what appeared to be huge blades fixed to its roof. I stared, aghast. They attempted to force me through a door but I dug in my heels.

"It's a helicopter," one of the men snarled. "It'll take you high in the sky— now get your ass in there before I kick it in."

There was nothing I could do to prevent them from lifting me up and tossing me into the back as though I were naught but a trussed sow. I bucked and kicked and struggled to no avail. Once inside the darkened chamber, Katrina ordered that cup things be fastened over my ears. I was strapped to the seat and, while I squirmed and struggled, the illuminated chamber suddenly went dark but for pricks of colored light. Katrina sat in front beside what I assumed to be the captain.

"Where do we go?" I cried.

"Shut your gob," said Sam to my left. And then a powerful beating began overhead, as if thunder was pounding down on the roof, all just moments before the entire craft lurched upward like an awkward bird taking flight.

"No!" I gasped, attempting to sink down in my seat. Though no coward, these things that I did see were so foreign to my eyes and ears that I could not find a place for them to settle. Phoebe must know of these matters for this was her world not mine.

"Welcome to the twenty-first century," one of the older men said.

If I were to recount such an event in any chronicle, I would be hard-pressed to know what to draw or how to capture the feeling of both fear and exhilaration that beset me. From far above the earth's surface, sailing through the air like an angel—if ever an angel could be so rough and devoid of grace—this strange craft flew, more like a hummingbird monster than any gull or other feathered creature. When I chanced to glance out the window, I was startled to see the stars fly by, seeming close enough to touch, while a silvered moon rode away off to one side.

When the craft dipped as if to drop to the earth, I squeezed shut my eyes and prayed as fervently as I knew how. I asked the Lord to allow me to better understand the wonder of this world that seemed no more real than a fevered dream. Above all, I prayed for wisdom and strength, and to know what best to do with my secret and the Psalter that held it safe.

With a jolt and wobbly shake, the metal bird set down. The thunder continued to whip the air as I was unstrapped from the seat and pushed out the door. With no free hands to steady myself, I stumbled, falling full on my face. One of the men hoisted me up by my hood, and I was shoved into yet another metal carrier.

All of this time, Katrina said very little, at least not to her companions. She spoke into the air, as if to some invisible person, while holding the phone object, seeming to give instructions to multiple people. When the next metal wagon began to move at breakneck speed, I had become accustomed to these oddities and thought perhaps that the world was filled with invisible people who would do one's bidding. This Katrina seemed not to be a queen and yet she behaved as such, commanding people at every turn. I thought it best not to attempt to make sense of this but to fix, instead, on keeping my head. Above all things, I would not release the Templar secrets to these devils.

When at last the wagon came to a stop and I was shoved out the door, dawn had just broken over the horizon. I briefly stood gazing at the sweet glow of the sun, firing the sky with colors so brilliant that I could almost imagine painting them, dipping my brushes into hues and sweeping rich carnelian red, golds, and ochres across the parchment. My fingers ached to hold a brush while knowing that I would never do so again, but at least God's colors flowed freely.

"Move!" One of the men shoved me hard, so hard that it angered me enough to wish to kick out at the cur, but I stayed myself: wits were needed now, not temper.

"We will need to climb up there," Dex told Katrina, pointing to a high rocky knoll. "That hill looks down upon Foinikas, but if we drive, they'll see our headlights, maybe hear us, too."

"Do we have scouts posted up there?" she asked.

"We're down to one—George. He just texted to say that the bastards have rescued Williams and scattered the two useless asses we had guarding her. Now there's four agents down there, including Evan Barrows."

"Evan Barrows, the Interpol guy—Phoebe's husband?" Karina asked, a tinge of alarm in her voice.

"I'm afraid so."

"Damn! Change of plans: we'll take her to the house we commandeered. It's time to negotiate with Barrows and his crew. We have our bargaining chip right here. You'll be our emissary."

"Me?" Dex's face was alight with fear.

"Yes, you. Who better to speak to that lot since they'll recognize you? Wave a white flag or whatever. They won't hurt you, especially when you assure them that you'll deliver them to our treasured catch, Phoebe McCabe. Tell them that only Barrows is to accompany you back to meet with me—nobody else. No superphones or weapons of any kind or I'll put a bullet in her skull while they watch."

"Would you?" Dex asked.

"Damn right I would," she said.

Chapter Twenty

I was pushed back inside the metal wagon and the thing again roared into the dark. Three of the men and Katrina attended me this time, leaving Dex behind. The men on either side of me appeared agitated, more so since their queen seemed reluctant to fully answer their questions.

"What will we do if one of those bastards tries to trick us?" one man demanded.

"What happened to Fred and the rest?" another asked.

"That Barrows—I've heard about him. He's a dangerous bastard, they say. Dex sure as hell fears him," said Sam with the big mouth.

"Why do you idiots only fear the men? Anyway, they won't try anything, you bonehead," Katrina replied from up front. "Think: we have the treasured Phoebe McCabe in our possession, and I'll be keeping a gun on her the whole time. The moment he makes a move, I won't hesitate to shoot her, though that would be such a waste."

"So, what's the game plan, boss?" one man asked.

"Do as I say, that's always the game plan. We'll force the agency trolls to give us safe passage back to the ruin and make Miss Lost in Time here lead us to the goods, or else."

"Or else what?"

"Leave that to me."

I had learned a great lesson about Katrina: she was ruthless when crossed but seemingly dealt with a measure of honesty if one appeared to do her bidding.

Nothing more was said until we halted beside a large abode, the likes of which I had never seen. It was neither castle nor fort, but a kind of manor house made of lime-washed stone, with everything low and enclosed behind a tall wall.

Katrina began speaking into the air again as we climbed from the carriage. Before we reached the iron gate, it opened of its own accord as if by magic, and we walked across a courtyard wherein lay a square pool of water that appeared lit from within. Surrounding the water, I saw chairs made of some strange fabric and pots of blooming plants. Cypress trees surrounding the property as if they were a row of tall sentries.

Big Mouth was shoving me along, seeming to take perverse pleasure in my discomfort each time I stumbled but I paid no mind, for I was awestruck by the sights that beset my eyes. No ruined manor this; as the door opened and I was pushed inside, I could only gape at the chamber in which I stood.

It was very large and broad with low padded benches that I thought to be covered in white leather. At one end, I spied a fireplace that did not seem to burn wood or hold true flames yet flickered all the same. Two lanterns, neither of which appeared to hold a wick of any kind yet shone forth brightly into the room, sat on transparent glass tables. Against a far wall, a large, glossy carving of something I could not identify rose on a pedestal—perhaps a rearing horse or a curling wave, I could not tell. On the walls, strange paintings hung, as if someone had thrown paint on the surface and permitted it to dry thus. Who would do this?

"So," Katrina said. "Our reluctant host is a modern art collector, I see. Must have megabucks. Where is the family now?"

"Tied up downstairs in the wine cellar—a man and a woman and two kids. Their security is shit. Other than an electronic lock and an alarm system, there's nada. We had the place infiltrated in seconds. He's got a boat, two cars, and a motorcycle. We confiscated all their devices and cut the landline to the alarm company."

"Where's a table?"

"Around the corner," the man said, pointing. I had never seen either of these two men before, but it seemed as though they could not take their eyes from me. One was tall and well-built, the other much shorter. The tall one had long hair piled into a knot on top of his head. Could he be Viking? But I did not see how such could be possible even in this strange world.

"Does she really think that she comes from the fourteenth century?" the knot man asked.

"She really does, Roy," Katrina said, gazing around. "Tie her up at the table and fetch her something to eat and drink. We need her alert for what's coming next."

"Wine, maybe?" Big Mouth asked hopefully as he steered me across a sheepskin rug, around the corner to a glass table, and shoved me down into a strange cup-like seat. It felt near indecent, the way in which it embraced my bottom.

"Not wine, you idiot. We all need to keep our wits about us," the queen said.

"There's cold pizza but we could heat it up in the microwave. The family was just making some in the oven out back when we joined the party," Roy told her.

"Pizza will do," Katrina said. She was soon back to speaking into the air, asking Dex how things progressed with the parley. I could not stop myself from checking behind us to see if perhaps Dex stood nearby but he was nowhere in sight. Holding her phone up to her ear, she stood by the strange table, looking down at me.

"Does he agree?" she asked. Then she touched something on the phone and suddenly I could hear Dex speak.

"He does. I told him this meeting was to negotiate the terms of his wife's release and that he was to come alone, without weapons, trackers, or one his damn phones."

"Is he there now?"

"Standing right beside me. "He's asking for proof of life."

"Not surprising. Put him on." Katrina held the phone thing before me. A man's face appeared inside the phone, deeply shadowed as if standing inside a dark place.

"Hello, Mr. Barrows. I'm Katrina Hogarth, and here you see your wife, though she's not feeling herself these days." The men standing around snickered. "We are holding her hostage until you agree to my terms. As you can see, she's quite alive so far. If you want her to stay that way, you'll accompany Dex to our location to talk. Leave your friends and all weapons behind. Nobody can make any move on my people. The moment I suspect you're trying to pull something, she's dead." And the phone went dark.

My emotions were astir. Phoebe had a mate? Why did that trouble me so?

Bread with cheese melted atop was delivered before me, and though I struggled to eat while bound, my captors refused to release my hands. Meanwhile, I felt the Psalter pressed against my heart, glad for its presence yet unsettled by it also. This was all so very unnatural.

Before I had finished, they brought to me a drink—a sweet, dark, fizzy liquid served in a glass bottle. At that moment, Katrina's phone emitted a musical sound.

She whipped it from her pocket. "Dex? Right. See you in five."

"Mica, Roy—get outside with your pistols drawn. Barrows and Dex will be here in five minutes. Sam, keep you knife near her throat. I'll keep the pistol on her simultaneously." She pulled up a chair and sat down, facing the door, one foot tapping under the table, the gun in one hand. I felt a sharp blade press into the skin at my neck.

She studied me. "Before he arrives, Suzanna, consider the lives of those who will be lost should you not cooperate—Barrows, who you will soon meet, plus Phoebe's agency friends, who my men have surrounded as we speak. If you agree to lead us to the treasure, you have my word that this will all end."

I remained silent, still unsure of the nature of the bargain but knew enough not to believe a word she spoke. She had no choice but to kill us all. How could she not but do so? I did not trust her, of course, but the question that plagued me still was did I trust the others in this "agency"?

The door flew open and Sam and Dex entered, their guns aimed at the tall man in the middle. The sight of him sent a jolt through me, the like of which I had never experienced. It was as if the body that housed me knew and hungered for this man in ways that I had long ago forgotten and perhaps had never truly known, but for in my imaginings.

He was comely and clean-shaven, with a strong muscled body that truly appeared as if it could fight in any battle. His features were fine, as fine as I had imagined William Marshal to be in my girlish mind, when I dreamed that such a knight might step into my life and offer me his heart. In truth, there was nobility about his jaw and eyes, as if he stood on the side of truth and valor like any great knight.

"Phoebe!" the man said in a deep, baritone voice. "Did they hurt you?" He tried to rush to my side but the men restrained him.

"Sit, Barrows," Katrina said, indicating a seat at the circular table. "She's not yours to claim, not until we have some matters settled."

Barrows slowly sat, his eyes never leaving my face. There was anger there, fear, something like longing, and, I thought, love, though I had rarely witnessed such emotion between a man and a woman. Briefly, I had known a village couple from whom the Order purchased produce, and they would look at one another with such warmth and devotion and...desire. This man loved Phoebe McCabe and I counted her truly blessed to have claimed the heart of such a fine, adoring man.

"Phoebe, speak to me, my love," he said, his eyes fixed on my face.

I blinked, consumed by emotion, wishing I knew him as he did her. "Forgive me, sir, for we have not yet been acquainted," I said. "I am Suzanna de Molay, and I awoke captive inside your wife's body."

It was if someone struck him, so shocked was his expression. His gaze swerved to Katrina. "How did this happen?"

Katrina smiled. "I know that you are late to the party, Barrows, but surely your colleagues filled you in on recent events? We forced Phoebe to hold the Psalter that your father helped my father steal from the Temple Church. Once she touched its cover, her timewalking skills apparently leaped into gear and she became Suzanna de Molay, daughter of Jacques de Molay, the last Templar master. She also happens to have illustrated the Psalter."

Those striking green-brown eyes widened briefly before his face settled into tight lines and angles. He was deeply angry. Timewalking was no shock to him. "You attacked my father's house, kidnapped my wife—and your own father, I understand—and now want what, exactly?"

"I want the Templar treasure, which belongs to me by right. A decree was penned by Jacques de Molay himself stating that, in the event that the Order befell 'tragic and absolute dissolution,' the Templar secrets, as well as all its private belongings, would be entrusted to the Shablool, loosely translated as the snail. Another meaning was 'daughter' or 'of the blood.' Suzanna, as both the last Templar master's daughter and the Shablool, was the secret keeper to whom her father entrusted the knowledge of this treasure. According to medieval law, following the line of the blood, she inherits the treasure since it was her father's will. On the other hand, since she is technically dead, the next in line is me."

Barrows scoffed. "I have never heard a more convoluted rationale for theft and murder. Am I to understand that you consider yourself a living Templar's daughter? Never mind that no medieval law would state that the wealth of an entire religious order would be within the rights of a Grand Master to assign to his own offspring—that is if he was even permitted to have offspring, which we both know he was not."

Katrina wiggled the gun at him, seemingly without a care. "Both Suzanna and I are illegitimate, as are you, as I understand, but she and I still carry the blood, don't we? It doesn't matter, since you might say that I am taking the law into my own hands, as my father did before me."

"Is that the father you murdered?" Barrows inquired.

"I shot him, I admit, but he didn't die of those wounds. Enough time wasted! This is the deal: we'll take Suzanna back to Foinikas where she will locate the treasure. If she does so, we'll release her. Everyone else will go free, but first you have to guarantee us safe passage. Tell your friends to lay down their arms and not stand in our way. Once the treasure is unearthed, we will board a helicopter that will deliver us to safety. We have friends waiting for us farther east."

"The Middle East?"

She smiled. "Let's just say we are heading into a country not friendly with NATO or her allies, one that is willing to offer us protection. If any attempt is made on our craft, it may start a war. You wouldn't want that, would you?"

"Why should I believe you?" Barrows asked. "How do I know you that won't kill us all, anyway?"

"What choice do you have? If you don't go along with my plan, I'll shoot your lovely wife right here and now. I have no compunction. The only one I really care about is Suzanna de Molay, who's already long dead, and not nearly as cooperative as I'd have hoped."

Barrows sat back, his palms flat on the table with his gaze fixed on me. "Do you know where the treasure is, Mistress de Molay?"

"She says not but I don't believe her," Katrina said.

"I was asking Suzanna," he replied.

I licked my lips, tasting salt, but I did not respond.

"She knows but she's not saying, no doubt following some touching code of honor to an order long gone and a father long dead."

"What if she's telling the truth and she doesn't know of the treasure's whereabouts?" Barrows inquired.

"Then you all die. Let's hope for your sake that she does know. Do you agree with the terms?"

"As you say, I have no choice," he said, and yet his eyes spoke a different tale. "How do I inform my team not to resist when we arrive in Foinikas?"

Katrina held up her phone. "I shall call one of my men who will then pass the device to you. You will tell your staff to make no attempt on any of my men."

"They are not my 'staff,'" he remarked.

Katrina raised her shoulders and allowed them to drop. "What do I care what name you use?" She turned to Dex. "Call George."

Dex did as he was bid. Barrows barked a brief command to a woman whose face I could not see. The woman agreed and it was done.

"Let's go." Katrina made to stand.

"Wait," I said.

Everyone turned to me. I took a deep breath and picked with care through the new words that appeared at the ready within my head. "I do know where the treasure is hidden and will lead you there as you request, but I have conditions of my own to put forth." I near trembled when I uttered those words but held fast.

Katrina raised an eyebrow but lowered herself back into her seat. "Go on."

"I have resolved to live and to continue to explore all that is bright and novel in this new world. After much thought and prayer, I see that it must be God's will that I do so, or why would he return me thus? However, I believe I cannot continue amid bloodshed. Should I lead you to the treasure, Katrina, you must vow that no one will fire a gun or kill any of those on the other side." I turned to Barrows. "You must promise me likewise, sir. Surely in this life, after all the bloodshed I have witnessed, I can beseech you both not to shed one more drop in my name."

Something calculating flicked across Katrina's eyes but it appeared mixed with pure glee. "I promise that if you do not attempt to trick me, I will do as you request. In fact, there should be no need for this to be anything but a cooperative endeavor if you and I leave together with the treasure."

Barrows drilled me with his sharp gray-green eyes. "Do you mean to say that I will lose my wife, mistress? Am I to stand by and watch her leave me?"

"Is that not better than to stand by and watch her die, good sir? For I do not know how long this miracle will last and when I may be taken from this body and your wife returned. Surely it is better to live in hope than to have all hope doused? This way you will not see a gun turned on this body, for if you do not agree to allow me to go with Katrina, she will kill us both." I turned to Katrina. "Do you deny this?"

The woman did not flinch. "I would keep my promise only if you both keep yours but I suspect that he will try trickery, in which case I will respond in kind, of course."

"Of course," I said, turning to the man. "You must permit us safe passage in order to keep your wife's body alive and in my care." I turned to Katrina. "And you must untie my hands for I cannot find the treasure so bound."

"And how do I know that you won't try to escape or hurt my men?" she asked.

"Am I not a woman of God? My honor is something which I uphold. Surely you have learned that much about the Shablool?"

A small smile tugged at her lips. "Yes, I believe I have." She looked up at Dex. "Untie her hands."

"Is that wise?" he ventured.

"Do it!" To Dex she said, "Get the cars ready. We're all leaving now."

"What about the family locked in the cellar?" asked Roy.

"Leave them. I'm sure the agency crew will have them released once we're gone."

And with that, she stood up, watching as Dex sliced my bindings.

"I have need of the Psalter in my hands as I must gaze upon its pages if I am to locate the treasure," I told her. "The Psalter will grant me courage."

Katrina nodded as if she had no care what became of the Psalter once she had what she desired. I clutched the Psalter close, Barrows watching my every move, as if to see if the woman he loved resided in me still.

Alas, she did not.

Chapter Twenty-One

A s I was led from the house into another metal carriage, I could not help but crave life. The sun poured warm, burnished gold upon the world, fresh after rainfall, with everything sparkling in the puddles and glistening in the grass. I had been so cloistered in my later years that to walk freely now in a young, strong body was a tonic to my soul. For so long I had lived between walls, locked deep inside books and prayers, that I had near forgotten the pure grace of being alive. How can one but feel full of light when one stands within the cathedral of the sky?

The way was not long but no less filled with wonder. I gazed through the window at the world whizzing past, as eager as a child discovering everything anew for the first time, for, in truth, I was just such a child in many ways. So many strange sights, such as people riding astride small, wheeled devices that travelled with incredible speed. I would surely topple off such a beast and break my neck, yet I longed to try. We passed many of the enclosed steel carriages such as the one in which we rode, but each appeared different in color and shape.

"Why the need of so many varieties of fast wagons?" I asked, sounding like a girl even to my own ears.

"People prefer to have many choices in this century, my lady," Barrows said, staring straight ahead.

I sat in the back seat with Dex on one side and Barrows on the other, my mind fixed on the scenery rather than the unsettling sense of his thighs pressed close to mine. Dex, in the meantime, kept a gun pointed at Barrows; it appeared not to disturb his target in the least. I sensed that the closeness of my body disturbed him far more.

We traveled for many leagues along a dirt track, not unlike those upon which I had traveled long ago. Here, the terrain had the same wild roughness that I recalled, and some sights had not much changed from when this was my home. We stopped on a high bluff where Barrows, Dex, Katrina, Sam, and I again transferred into the big metal bird. The others were to travel in other wagons. This time I did not hesitate but leaped into the cabin to gaze from the window as we took flight.

As the earth shrunk to the size of a toy, I thought how wondrous it would be to explore all that this new world had to offer, to ride on the back of these metal beasts that hurled people vast distances in so little time, and to more deeply understand how matters since my own lifetime. It was as if I awaited a grand feast of extraordinary experiences with an overwhelming craving to taste it all. When the bird set down upon land again, I was eager to begin.

"Pray, sir," I asked Barrows as I trod beside him down the hill. A mass of scraggly bushes hid the view ahead but I still spied the spread of a vast lake that I was certain had not been there before. "Are there wars still?"

"I am afraid so, mistress—a great many. Wars between countries, wars between religious beliefs, wars amid individuals. Any place where people live, it seems, there are wars."

"And in Jerusalem?" I asked.

"Now caught in a brutal war between the Palestinians and a country called Israel, both of whom claim religious and historical rights to the land upon which the Temple Mount stands."

"And Christianity?"

"Jerusalem remains a place of Christian pilgrimage, but no Christian nation or territory lays claim to it."

I could not grasp these revelations as it seemed as though the world had tipped upside down over the centuries. As we then began descending the hill and I caught my first glimpse of Foinikas, all other thoughts escaped me. Though I had expected dereliction, I had not anticipated what effect the sight of the ruin would have on me. Truly, the first glimpse was as a blow to the chest.

All around stood the broken bones of what had once been a mighty fortress, the very heart of the Templar Order in Cyprus, and briefly my home. For a moment, I imagined my father striding up the hill to the small chapel and the force of the memory near knocked me off my feet. I stumbled, caught myself, and trudged onward.

Below, seven men—no, I realized: four men and three women— awaited.

They stood on opposites sides of what had once been the main route into the village, women on one side, men on the other, each watching one another with great wariness.

Katrina waved and all eyes turned toward us. As we strode closer, I saw that the women were all dressed as men in breeches and short tunics, with one tall, dark-skinned woman stepping forward at the sight of me.

"Phoebe!" she cried, joy lighting her face. "You're alive! I thought these bloody bastards had done you in!" She broke into a run.

Sam—Big Mouth—walking behind me, fired his gun, the shot biting into the earth at her feet, exploding bits of dirt in all directions and stopping the tall woman in her tracks. She stood, hands in the air, staring at him with a furious look. "What the hell?"

"Stand back, Peaches," Barrows called. "This isn't Phoebe but a timewalker, Suzanna de Molay. And you, you bloody idiot," he said, turning to Big Mouth, "put down that damned gun!"

"Shit!" the dark woman said.

"Shut your face, asshole," Big Mouth said to Barrows, hand gripping the gun. "I don't take orders from you."

"Enough!" Karina barked, her command accompanied by a chopping gesture. "You take orders from me. Put the gun down."

"With these bastards around? Are you kidding, boss?" he protested. "They're a bunch of dangerous bastards!"

"Do as she says, Sam," Dex ordered while Barrows stood as if ready to pounce. I could snatch Sam's knife and have this matter turned around shortly but the timing was not right. There were six men plus others spread about the hill on Katrina's side against five on Barrows's, should I count myself among the latter.

Sam put away his gun while the others farther down the hill—each standing as though ready to spring—held steady. We continued downward, the Peaches woman's attention seeming fixed on my person, as if desiring to ask me questions and to demand the answers. I had seen others of her tribe before in parts east and had always marveled at their stance and grace. This one appeared strong and self-assured and very much a warrior. I would not wish to cross her.

Who were these people that Phoebe had called friends? All appeared hardened and ready for battle and yet feminine at the same time. As we neared the group, I could better study the other two women—one lean and beautiful with thick, dark hair gathered into an easy tail at the nape of her neck, while the other stood short and fierce as if ready to scrap at any provocation.

"You!" said the smaller woman, making as if to step toward me. "If you are not Phoebe, you must let her go!"

The tall, beautiful one placed a hand on her friend's shoulder as if to hold her back and spoke in a language I did not understand. The smaller woman immediately stopped but seemed eager to lunge.

"Boys, listen carefully," Katrina said as we drew closer, the boys being a raggedy group of mismatched soldiers ill-fit for battle. "We have entered into an agreement with Barrows and the agency: if Suzanna de Molay here leads us to the Templar treasure, we will not harm the others. Suzanna will be leaving with us following the dig—or I presume there will be a dig—and Barrows here will not obstruct our plans as long as we do not harm Suzanna slash Phoebe. We will not make a move on any agency member unless provoked, understand?"

The other men standing near either nodded or muttered but appeared to agree, yet I could not help but think that they were all untrustworthy, each working for himself. The three women appeared equally dissatisfied with the arrangement but said nothing, though watched the enemy—and me—as if on high alert.

"Barrows, tell your friends to put their weapons there, and that goes for phones, guns—every damn thing they're carrying. And power them off, too!" Katrina pointed to a rock with a flat surface. "Do it!"

Each person did as they were bid, placing phones and guns upon the rock and backing away, Barrows the last to comply.

"If you're afraid that we'll call for backup, it's too late, Hogarth," he said, pointing toward that strange lake where many vessels appeared to lie in wait.

Katrina shielded her eyes at the three boats on the lake. "Who are the—the army, navy, what? Are you bloody kidding me?" She pointed a gun in my direction and said to Barrows: "Tell them that if they make a move by either air, sea, or land, your lady love is dead."

Barrows's features had turned fierce and hard, though no less handsome. "They know that. No one will make a move on you as long as she remains unharmed, but obviously I'll need to give them instructions if they are to provide you safe passage."

Now turning to gun on me, she said: "Take your phone and tell them not to make a move. Make sure they understand the consequences if they do something stupid. As it now stands, you have all been disarmed. She will come with me to the helicopter once the treasure has been retrieved and from there to a ship offshore. If anyone makes so much as a move toward harming me, they will harm her, too."

Barrows retrieved his phone and spoke into the air, giving directions to whatever invisible soldiers must be standing nearby. As he did so, every man pointed his gun at either me or at Barrows.

"Now place the phone back on the rock," Katrina ordered.

He did so.

"One more thing," Dex said. "Before we leave, we want you to reactivate Phoebe's and your father's phones, both of which are in my jacket." He patted his leather pocket.

Barrows tightened his lips into a grim smile. "Do you really want to do that, Dex? You of all people know that once they are activated, I can command them from a distance."

Dex frowned. "Think I don't know that, Barrows? But we'll have your precious Phoebe here so I doubt you'll do anything stupid, and these phones are additional collateral for our allies waiting offshore."

Katrina issued a chill smile. "I almost forgot about that—thanks, darling. Consider it nonnegotiable, Barrows. You'll do as he suggests but first things first."

I looked away to see if I could spot the shapes of the buildings I had once known but saw nothing but their bones biting hard into the muted earth. The place where my father had once stridden as master of the land had deteriorated to dust and rubble, much as my own body must have, wherever it lay. Would even the convent cemetery where my bones lay still exist or had it, too, been ravaged by the ruthless march of time?

Yonder sat a pile of stones—all that remained of the chapel where we had once worshipped. I could almost hear the bells ringing. Behind where we now stood, the few crumbling walls marked the remains of the once-mighty fortress.

"Suzanna."

I turned to gaze at she-wolf Katrina.

"Remember that your continued existence—and Phoebe's and her friends' here—depends on whether we find the treasure. Don't break your word."

"I never break my word," said I.

"Good." She nodded. "Sam here will be your private guard if I am otherwise engaged. He's a bit trigger-happy so don't give him any provocation. Now, we'll head up to the manor."

I glanced toward Sam, thinking him an odd choice. Yet, there was nothing to be done for I was instructed to move, as were Barrows and the three women. We were to trudge up the hill toward the manor, under the guard of these men with their guns and knives. At no time did anyone ask me where the treasure lay and at no time would I willingly tell them.

"Are you not Phoebe?" the woman with the long dark hair asked me.

"No, I am Suzanna de Molay, and who are you, my lady?" For she did seem much like a lady despite her strange dress.

"I am Nicolina," she told me. "Both my friend and I hail from Rome."

"Rome?" I exclaimed, pausing. "I have oft wanted to travel to Rome to meet the pope. Is there a pope still?"

"Yes," Nicolina said with a smile, "but he is not as all-powerful as you may have known."

Sam dug the gun into my back and ordered me to move faster.

"Stop bullying her, you slime ball," the tall, dark woman said, walking on my other side.

Sam only grinned and drove the nose of the gun deeper into my back.

The tall woman sneered. "Do that again and I'll break your face before you have a chance to pull that trigger."

Sam appeared ready to respond but Dex caught his eye. "Knock it off, Sam."

The tall, dark woman continued walking beside me as if oblivious to the gun pointed at her back. "I am Peaches, and the woman beside Nicolina is Seraphina. Let Phoebe go, if you can," she continued. "Phoebe has always had compassion and empathy for all those who came before, but now it's time for someone from the past to pay it back. Give her up. You've lived your life. Let her live hers."

I had nothing to say in return for, in truth, I did not fully understand her words. "Pay it back"—what was the meaning there? "Pray be full of care, for these people will kill you," I warned. She only scowled and looked away.

When we reached the top of the knoll, the sun was hanging high in the sky, starkly illuminating the bitter truth about the ravages of time. I could not regard the shapes before me without remembering the way they had once been —proud and mighty as if nothing could tear them asunder. And yet, the mighty had fallen.

"Wait here," Katrina told everyone, holding up a hand. "Dex, Suzanna, come with me."

Katrina and Dex led me into the enclosure of what had once been the court-yard of my old home. I gazed about, my heart close to breaking. "Well?" she asked.

"Up on the topmost floor is where I would work, day in and day out, painting the illustrations in this Psalter. The sun would pour through the case-ments to illuminate my drawings, but those last days I was beset with great haste, for I knew we would soon set sail and thus painted late into the night by candlelight alone." I gripped the book tightly in my hands. How old and battered seemed its cover in the light of the cruel sky overhead.

"Very interesting, but we haven't time for reminiscing," Katrina said, standing nearby. "Where is the treasure?"

I turned to her. "The Templars were not fools. Why would they hide their riches here, in the very seat of the Grand Master's house?"

Katrina looked furious. For a moment, I thought she might strike me. "Why? Because this is where Phoebe was looking, that's why. There must be something here."

"A small pouch of my personal possessions only. I had placed them under the floorboards, for my father thought it unwise to bring them should they identify me as the Shablool."

"Then where are they now?" she demanded.

"How can I say after so many years?" I pointed to the air above. "They were once up there, that is all I know."

"Is that it? Is that the only thing of value that you know of?" She near screamed at me.

"My father instructed his trusted knights to bury the treasury—all that was not to be transported across the sea, that is—on the hillside leading to the valley. Know that these were clever men, wise in the ways of building and hiding, and such a place would not be easy to locate."

She took a step toward me. "But you told me that you knew where it was!" She near bit the words from the air.

"I have the guide in my hands and I will lead you, as is my vow," I said, gazing up at her and lifting the Psalter. Her temper was close to the surface and I feared that she would snap if I did not appease her. "The Psalter shows the way by following the path of the snail through the foliage, beginning with the chapel and following the hillside down toward the valley. I drew the hidden map as my father decreed and thus it is as I transcribed."

She attempted to take the book from my hands but I kept it at arm's length. "Only I will understand the illustrations that will lead you thus."

"Then lead me, and no tricks." She pointed beyond the ruined courtyard.

Chapter Twenty-Two

I trudged back to join the others, continuing past them without a word, Sam following at my heels with his gun pointed at my head. I strode directly to where the chapel had once stood, locating where the door had been secluded amid the shrubbery. Turning, I counted the paces according to the number of dots I had been instructed to paint into the underlay of my trailing vines—fifty-two steps in a man's stride. My steps were not as long as a man's so I gauged accordingly. Never had I expected to use this map myself, for that had not been its purpose, and yet I held no misgivings in leading these people thus.

My painting led me to the bluff, beyond which the lake glistened in the sun, three boats awaiting offshore. Much had changed since last I stood there but I knew the way as if my map had been engraved into my very heart. The broadest features had not changed overmuch despite the lake that had swallowed the valley below.

I took a turn but stepped away from the edge and marched twenty paces according to the spots on my lady snail's shell. Once reaching the final spot, I paused and turned back to the edge where I could gaze down at the water lapping at the foot of the cliff. "Beyond is a cave in the cliffs, with a hidden opening marked by two large boulders."

Katrina peered over the precipice. "But that's in the cliff," she said.

"Are you playing us for fools?" Sam said, wagging his gun at me. I ignored the cur.

JANE THORNLEY

"Did you think it was going to be easy?" Barrows asked, his fierce gaze fixed on Katrina.

Katrina ignored them both and turned to the rest of her men. "Bring the ropes, explosives, shovels—everything. Where is that explosives expert? she asked Dex.

"Desmond, the guy in the baseball hat," he replied. "He understands the basics. That's the best we could do."

Katrina cast him a quick glance. "Desmond, we're going to blow up the opening of a cave below. Do you have the correct equipment?"

The man in the strange blue peaked cap stepped forward. "Yes, ma'am."

"Move it, then," she commanded, sending them all scurrying away but for Dex and Sam, who guarded the prisoners. "Where'd we find him?" she asked Dex as soon as they had scrambled off.

"Same place as the others—online. We didn't have much time to check references, remember?" Dex replied with a jerk of his head. "He probably knows more about explosives than the bunch of them put together."

The "he" that Dex indicated was Barrows, now sitting in the grass with the three women, all of them watching us, no doubt calculating the enemy's every move. Dex never removed his gun from their direction for good reason.

"How far down that cliff does the treasure lie?" Katrina asked, fixing me with her dark eyes.

I held up the Psalter, pointing to the next to last page. There, I had fashioned two rocks beneath a large leaf, marked by the growth of three red flowering plants that it pleased me much to see still aglow like rubies in the sun. "The entrance to the cave is there but the builder knights would not have made the way in easy."

"Maybe, but they didn't have our technology, either." Katrina peered at the pages before gazing again over the cliff. "So maybe a ten-yard drop at most. Those boulders should be easy enough to find as they look somewhat pointed at their tops. We'll get in." She shoved me aside and, as I stumbled backward, Sam steadied me with his hand, clutching my elbow as if I were an errant child. I attempted to shake him loose but he held fast.

"Kat, are you sure it's wise to blow up anything on a cliffside? The whole thing could come tumbling down," Dex said.

"What else can we do?" she asked him sharply. "We're running out of time!"

The men soon returned with bags of tools, ropes, and trunks marked with bright yellow symbols. Two carried a large contraption that even I recognized as a winch.

"Quickly now," Katrina told her men. "If we can blast away those rocks and

170

get in, there will be a bonus for all of you. You're looking for two large, pointed boulders wedged closely together." She paused to glance toward the water. "We have maybe an hour at the most before my helicopter lifts off and your boat leaves. Don't mess around. Make it fast!"

The men nodded and began to discuss how to proceed, while two men each donned a strange harness, which I assumed would lift them over the edge. Soon, they were hard at work while Dex indicated that the three women and Barrows were to remain sitting in the grass. The air seemed thick with tension as Phoebe's friends thus awaited, and Sam held me in his grip while Katrina continued to speak into the air.

"Have you spotted them? Put your phone on live image so I can see," I heard her say. The two men were over the side now and it seemed that one was speaking to her because she indicated 'more rope' to the man operating the winch.

"Are these the rocks?" Katrina asked me, holding up her phone with a blurry image of deep shadowy stones. I peered closer.

"I know not. I have never seen them but only drew what I was told," I said. "They were described to me thus."

Katrina swore and spoke to the phone again. "Those must be the ones. Blow them up."

One of the men suspended over the cliff edge yelled down. "Detonate the explosives!"

Though I did not understand the meaning of "explosives," I could measure the effect of the word upon Barrows and the women, see the concern in the eyes of everyone.

The first blast shook the earth beneath our feet. When Katrina called out for a second, we braced ourselves for the explosion which hit like the great quaking I had known in times past and which sent everyone waving their arms for balance. It was the moment for which I had been waiting. I swiftly pulled the knife from Sam's sheath and pushed him into Dex. At a glance, I saw Phoebe's friends leap into action, tackling the other men standing by, the tall, dark woman lunging for Katrina while Barrows made for me.

A gun went off like a crack in the air as I bolted across the top of the trembling cliffs.

*　*　*

The sun was warm as I scrambled over the rocks, the Psalter clutched in one hand. Once I had walked these cliffs daily. Though the stones had seemed sharper then, footsteps still wore a faint path along the edge of the bluff. Little had we known that by far the greatest threat to the Order came from far across the seas, rather than close at hand. Treachery awaited everywhere, then as now.

With the sky above and the water far below, it seemed a good place to die. My father would have wanted it such because there was much honor in this death, and though I had thought to stand and fight with the others, I knew this to be the finer way.

As I made along the path, the ground trembled twice more beneath my feet, forcing me to grip a rock to steady myself. I looked behind me to see Barrows in pursuit. Ahead lay a sharp, jutting precipice that did bite into the air with near the same vigor as I recalled from days past. I must reach that before he caught up with me.

From somewhere below and behind me, I heard the chaos rather than saw it with my own eyes—the cracking of guns, the cries of men, and one most horrible scream. It was not the first time that I had heard such. But after all of the battles I had witnessed, the constant cries of agony that men did inflict upon their fellows, I had no stomach for more. Not for me another lifetime lived amid such carnage. Why could not mankind find peace after so much blood-shed and struggle? Had nothing been achieved after so many centuries? It seemed that we were thus destined to repeat the same folly over and over again, as if we had learned nothing of God's intent.

Barrows did gain upon me now. I must make haste.

I blinked toward the path ahead, surprised to find that tears filled my eyes. I did not expect to feel such emotion, but since I would soon commit myself to yet another death, I should not have been surprised. This time I would leave this world with a heavy heart. Thus, I commanded these strong legs to bear me up to stand on the very crest of the cliff, my eyes fixed on the water, my soul filled with resolve.

He was upon me now. "Suzanna, wait!"

I turned.

Barrows stood at the top of the bluff, his hands spread as if to beseech me. "Please don't do this."

"I must," I said, gripping the Psalter more closely, "for I see no other way home."

"There are other ways, there are always choices. I beg you, come away from the edge and permit my wife to return to my arms. If anything should happen to her, I don't know how I could go on."

His words startled me. "But you left her side. You were not near at hand when she was taken."

172

Something shifted across his comely face—surprise, calculation, hope? "I was not," he agreed, his hands dropping to his sides. "Phoebe and I are both committed to our work, it being what drew us together in the first place. We are driven to preserve all that is good and beautiful for others to enjoy, instead of permitting them to fall into the hands of the greedy few. This treasure, if it exists, should be placed somewhere for all to appreciate and its story told so that future generations will better understand the history of the Templars and all humankind. Phoebe, too, shares this passion to preserve. She's a true warrior."

Phoebe a warrior? I measured my words with care. "I did not tell the full truth concerning where the Templar treasure lies," I told him.

"I did not think you had." He took another step toward me and I, in turn, inched closer to the edge.

"But neither did I break my word," I said fiercely. "I told Katrina that the illustrations lead to the treasury and that much be true," I continued. "In truth, only a small cache of gold was left in the cliffs below. My father withdrew most of the gold before we set sail, for he believed he would have need of it in France. Another cache—by far the most holy of relics taken from Jerusalem—was to be deposited elsewhere. The third ship, the one that delivered me to England, then set sail across the ocean to secure the most treasured items of the Templar riches."

The man appeared breathless at this recounting, but I pressed on.

"The ship sailed with instructions to deposit that treasure in a place of great protection, one that had been determined years before when another Templar ship created a storehouse in this hitherto unknown land. The details of this location are all here." I lifted the Psalter in the air and held it aloft. "With this, you will be able to locate the treasure and achieve great wealth and acclaim, but only if I am alive to read the code. You cannot have both Phoebe and the treasure. Which would you choose?"

"Phoebe, without hesitation." He smiled then and it was as if the sun did full burst from the clouds, and I thought to myself how blessed was Phoebe. "But please take no insult, Suzanna, for it means only that I value the life of my wife over all else, and you, after all, have already lived. The treasure means nothing to me personally. I always believed that I became the richest of men the day I married my wife, no matter how foolish that sounds."

Now it was I who smiled. "I admire your devotion, dear sir, and how you ofttimes speak like a bard."

A metal bird beat its blades above our heads at that moment. Barrows shielded his eyes with his hand to see the insignia. "It's one of ours. We'd better hurry. Come away from the edge, Suzanna."

"One request before I consign your wife to your arms."

"Name it," he said with eagerness.

"I wish to experience a single kiss before I die. Pray bestow such a token upon my lips."

"Gladly." He opened his arms. "Come to me."

"You come to me, fair sir," I said.

He gazed toward the cliff edge where I now balanced. He thought I might attempt to tug him over the edge? But if that was his thought, it did not stop him from striding toward me, his arms wide for our embrace. When he encircled me in his strength and warmth, I believed that surely this must be as heaven on earth, and when his lips touched mine, my heart full exploded with all manner of color and light. Love, I knew, was the truest of all riches.

When the blades of another metal carriage beat in the sky above, I pulled away, breathless, my borrowed heart almost as loud in my ears as the thunder above.

"I never meant to jump, Barrows," I said. "Never would I take any life but my own."

With one strong thrust, I flung the Psalter over the edge, briefly seeing the pages flap in the wind like a wounded bird as the book tumbled toward the water. "With the Psalter gone, your love may return to your arms, but as long as the Psalter exists, so I fear must I. Thus I consign myself to the Absolute once again."

Chapter Twenty-Three

I knew that I must go home, yet it was as if I was trapped in some kind of dream, or perhaps caught inside a badly edited movie in which I played a dual role. Suzanna had gone and though part of me recognized that fact, it was as if I could feel her still as her memories mingled with mine, fogging my thoughts. My voice could not speak the words my brain formed, and my legs only moved when someone led me. What my eyes saw didn't register—people talking at me, embracing me, demanding that I come back. The world flew past as I was delivered to other places, all of the images spinning in a dizzying blur.

I thought that I might be home but where was that, anyway? The rooms in which I sat didn't contain my furniture or any of the objects that I had collected over the years, which left me floating. Then, gradually, I began to find meaning in what my senses were picking up.

At first, I began recognizing voices.

"Should we call a physician, dear boy?" a man said. "I know of an excellent chap who has a practice in Chelsea and who specializes in afflictions of the mind."

I felt myself seated in a big, pleasant room that I almost remembered, but then it was as if understanding began pouring in and around my fragmented thoughts, clarifying everything all at once.

"And tell him what, Dad—that my wife was recently possessed by a woman who died in the 1300s?" I watched the tall man striding about the room and felt my heart beat faster. Oh, yes, I knew my love.

"He'll think she's flipped," said the dark woman in the purple suit—Peaches? "But we have to do something. It's been two days now."

She swung around to crouch before me, taking me by the shoulders to give me a little shake. "Phoebe, are you in there? Come back, will you? We're in a bit of a pickle without you, see. Your guilt-ridden father-in-law, your heartbroken and desperate husband, and your dear friends like me are all here to welcome you home. So, what's taking you so damn long?"

"I would hesitate to say I was guilt-ridden exactly, Penelope, though I do admit to bearing a tremendous sense of responsibility for the abominable circumstances that unfolded on my watch," Rupert said from nearby.

I blinked, staring. Yes, Peaches, and Evan—Evan!—and Rupert. And was that Nicolina and Seraphina I saw on the other side of the room, talking into phones? An overwhelming sense of joy washed through me.

Peaches jumped up and began to pace the floor beside my husband, Rupert looking on nearby with an abject expression.

"Did they catch you with your pants down?" I asked Peaches. Everyone froze.

"They damn well did!" Peaches exclaimed, swinging around to face me. "Bastards stunned me while I was doing my business and, boy, did I kick butt when I had the chance!"

As I got to my feet, Evan strode toward me. When I fell into his arms, all the chatter surrounding me sank into the background for quite another reason. Coming home for me was captured in that single embrace. Where was home but with the people you love?

"You kissed another woman," I said, laughing as I pulled away moments later, "but said that you wouldn't trade me for all the Templar gold."

"I did," he agreed, smiling broadly. "I wouldn't trade you for all the riches in the world, and that's the truth."

"Suzanna enjoyed that kiss," I teased. "It was almost enough to change her mind about leaving but, in the end, she knew that remaining in my body was wrong on all counts."

"She was an honorable woman," he acknowledged.

"But thanks to you, she did experience a few carnal thoughts." At that moment, I was stifling a few carnal thoughts of my own.

"Okay, you two. Time out." Peaches stood beside us. "Business first, then pleasure. I'm so glad that you're back, Phoeb, because spoon-feeding you was getting old."

She elbowed Evan aside and crushed me into one of her full-frontal hugs.

"I hope I ate everything put in front of me," I said.

"Don't you remember?" she asked.

"Vaguely. Everything is kind of spun together in my head, along with wisps of memories for events that I have never lived," I said while untangling myself from Peaches's squeeze.

Nicolina came up to me to bestow a brief, perfumed embrace while Seraphina waved at me from across the room. "We are so happy to see you, Phoebe. At last, I think, we may return to normal."

"Thank you, Nicolina. It's so good to be back but I don't know how normal things will ever be for me."

"Did you remain conscious while this woman lived inside of you?" she asked.

"Off and on. When she removed her hands from the Psalter, I could briefly communicate with her and sometimes even impose a thought without that contact, but it took a great effort and I soon sank back down again. Still, I recall every memory that she recalled while inside my head and that's the hard part. I still feel a bit befuddled, so bear with me."

"Always." Nicolina beamed one of her beautiful smiles as I turned to speak to the one person who had yet to greet me.

Rupert had stepped forward. He appeared simultaneously stricken and joyful as he stood next to Evan with his hands clasped. "Dearest Phoebe," he began as I approached him, "I do hope that you will forgive my behavior in the recent debacle. Indeed, I am uncertain what came over me, except possibly the desire to stir the adrenaline once again, though ultimately I have no excuse for the problems that ensued as a result of my appalling digressions. You have my heartfelt apologies. Please know that you are very dear to me and I would never knowingly cause you harm or put your life in danger."

I had so many questions, so many things I wanted to say and needed to ask him, but this wasn't the time. "Of course I forgive you, Rupert. Let us talk later."

"Oh, most assuredly," he said with relief as he dabbed his eyes with a hanky. "Now, do excuse me for I must check on dinner." And with that he hastily scuttled from the room.

"I've been hard on him," Evan told me after he'd gone. "Dad crossed the line this time and it will take everything I have to keep him from prosecution. Katrina will stand trial for her crimes, as will Dex, and most of the others we rounded up, but it will take considerable maneuvering to leave my father out of it."

"But it all began with Clive Hogarth," I pointed out.

"Yes, but it was through Rupe's efforts that the Psalter even left the Temple

Church in the first place, right?" Peaches said. "Who else but the Agency of the Ancient Lost and Found has the technology to disarm the security cameras and break into the Temple Church?"

I rubbed my forehead. "Yes, but Clive initially stole the Psalter from the crypts on his own volition using the usual devious routes. Hopefully, that counts for something."

"It would definitely have been helpful had Hogarth been around to answer for his crimes," Evan said. "As it is, Katrina will stand trial and will no doubt accuse both you and my father."

"The agency smartphones will be key evidence," Nicolina stated.

Evan sighed. "Yes, providing that their existence can be proven. If ever those phones are brought to the court as evidence, I'll ensure that they'll appear just like any other smartphone and very benign, as a result. As for Katrina's and Dex's testimonies, they will hardly be credible, given that they'll claim that Suzanna de Molay, a Templar's daughter and a woman who has been dead for centuries, was forced into Phoebe's body to provide a map to lost treasure."

"Sounds bonkers, all right," Peaches agreed.

"No one will buy that," I said, rubbing my temples. I hardly bought it myself and yet I knew it to be true. "She was an amazing person, by the way. Throwing that Psalter over the cliff was excruciating for her and yet that moment of letting go—including letting go of life itself as she was experiencing it inside of me—was incredibly liberating for her. She actually gave me back my existence with an open heart. I will count knowing Suzanna as a deeply humbling experience."

"How well did you know her?" Evan asked, one arm encircling my shoulders as we headed toward the dining room.

"Well enough," I said, "but it's challenging to disentangle her thoughts from my own, even now. Up until a few minutes ago, it still felt as though I was living a movie of someone else's life, with periodic interference from another film. Then suddenly something clicked and I became fully myself again."

"How did that even happen?" Peaches asked from behind us. We had just reached the central foyer.

"I have no idea. It's as if the sound of your voices finally registered. It just took time, I guess," I told her.

"But it's taking longer and longer for you to return, Phoebe," Nicolina pointed out. "This is not good and perhaps it is best to avoid these timewalking episodes where possible."

"I do try to, at least initially," I said, turning to meet her eyes. But I couldn't stop myself once I heard a voice from the past and my agency friends knew it.

"Either way, we were afraid that you might not return," Evan whispered, holding me close.

"It was almost as if you'd had a stroke or something," Peaches added. "I could tell you what to do, which was fun while it lasted—just kidding. If I said to get dressed, you'd do it as if you weren't all there, which was unbelievably weird. We led you around like a child."

"I would have been at your side in an instant had the true London weather report reached me," Evan said, assuming his sternest demeanor. "Instead, I was assured that blue skies prevailed."

"I didn't want to distract you," I said in my defense.

A flash of anger darkened his gaze. "Distract me anytime you or anyone I care about is in danger or does something inadvisable—" he paused "—or unforgivable or illegal, in the case of my father," he added.

"We'll catch you two at dinner. Sloane's having a proper feast prepared. Until then, we'll just be in one of the lounges and leave you guys alone," Peaches said, leading Nicolina and Seraphina down the hall toward one of the back salons.

I nodded, waiting until they were out of sight before returning my attention to Evan. "I should have told you the truth, but once I was in it, I hoped that we could handle it on our own without involving you or Interpol," I told him. "I admit that maybe there was the teeniest part of me that wanted to do this thing on my own, without calling in my big strong husband and his cavalry."

He stood before me, hands on my shoulders. "More on that later, but first I have something to tell you, Phoebe, and I need to tell you this before you hear it from anyone else."

"I don't like the sound of that." I swallowed hard. "Is Toby all right, Max —everybody?"

"Toby is fine, as far as I know, but Max has disappeared. What sent me away so suddenly was notification that Noel had been released from prison and had swiftly vanished into the proverbial woodwork. We had a tail on him from the moment he left Rome, yet he disappeared, but not before he sent a message to his father, Max, which we intercepted. Max must have gone after him."

"Noel?" My thieving ex-boyfriend? A familiar shock coursed through me. Noel and I had once been lovers, though he would claim that we had been more like partners—he the thief, me his personal lost-art sniffer dog—and to add to the complications, Max was my godfather. "I thought he was gone from my life for good."

"He's served his time in the Italian prison system, apparently—don't ask me why or how the sentence became so short—and was subsequently released.

Phoebe, we have no reason to think that he's up to anything illegal at this point. We were just keeping an eye on him, but when Max disappeared, matters took on a new course. Don't worry, we'll find him. The two matters may not be related—"

"Of course they're related!" I interrupted. "Max has taken after Noel, and if Noel does anything to hurt him—"

"Listen, my love." Evan, his hands still on my shoulders, attempted to steady me with his eyes. "You need to stay out of this. Finding Max and Noel is my responsibility. Promise me that you'll stay as far away from this case as possible."

I gazed deeply into his eyes but didn't say a word.

Dear Phoebe readers, join Phoebe and The Agency of the Ancient Lost & Found in book nine, *The Hunt for Kangaroo Dreaming*. Guess where we're heading this time? Please preorder by clicking on the title link.

About the Author

JANE THORNLEY is an author of historical mystery thrillers with a humorous twist, mysteries, tales of time travel and just a touch of the unexplained embedded into everything. She has been writing for as long as she can remember and when not traveling and writing, lives a very dull life—at least on the outside. Her inner world is something else.

With multiple novels published and more on the way, she keeps up a lively dialogue with her characters and invites you to eavesdrop by reading all of her works.

To follow Jane and share her books' interesting background details, special offers, and more, please join her newsletter using the link below. All newsletter signees will receive an option to download *Rogue Wave*, book 1 in the Crime by Design Series.

NEWSLETTER SIGN-UP

Also featuring Phoebe McCabe:

SERIES: NONE OF THE ABOVE MYSTERY

None of the Above Series Book 1: Downside Up

None of the Above Series Book 2: DownPlay

SERIES: TIME SHADOWS

Consider me Gone Book 1

The Spirit in the Fold 2 (companion to The Florentine's Secret)

SERIES: THE COSMATI CHRONICLES, a Historical Fantasy

The Cosmati Prophecy, Book 1

The Cosmati Connection, Book 2

Made in the USA
Middletown, DE
18 June 2025